Stiffs
and
Swine

Books by Ellery Adams

The Secret, Book & Scone Society

The Secret, Book & Scone Society

The Book Retreat Mysteries

Murder in the Mystery Suite
Murder in the Paperback Parlor
Murder in the Secret Garden
Murder in the Locked Library

The Charmed Pie Shoppe Mysteries

Pies and Prejudice
Peach Pies and Alibis
Pecan Pies and Homicides
Lemon Pies and Little White Lies
Breach of Crust

Antiques & Collectibles Mysteries

A Killer Collection
A Fatal Appraisal
A Deadly Dealer
A Treacherous Trader
A Devious Lot
A Killer Keepsake

More Books by Ellery Adams

Supper Club Mysteries

Carbs & Cadavers
Fit to Die
Chili con Corpses
Stiffs and Swine
The Battered Body
Black Beans & Vice
Pasta Mortem

Hope Street Church Mysteries

The Path of the Crooked
The Way of the Wicked
The Graves of the Guilty
The Root of All Evil
Fate of the Fallen

The Books by the Bay Mysteries

A Killer Plot
A Deadly Cliché
The Last Word
Written in Stone
Poisoned Prose
Lethal Letters
Writing All Wrongs
Killer Characters

Stiffs and Swine

ELLERY ADAMS

BEYOND THE PAGE PUBLISHING

Stiffs and Swine
Ellery Adams
Copyright © 2008, 2014 by J. B. Stanley

Beyond the Page Books
are published by
Beyond the Page Publishing
www.beyondthepagepub.com

ISBN: 978-1-958384-68-8

The only time to eat diet food is while you're waiting for the steak to cook.
—Julia Child

Chapter One

Tuna Casserole

James Henry, head librarian of the Shenandoah County Library, counted out five quarters to deposit in the powerful vacuum at the self-service car wash. He was hoping to rid his aged white Bronco of the sand that had accumulated on the floor mats during his vacation to Virginia Beach. There'd been a thunderstorm on the last afternoon of his trip, and the sand that had worked its way into the mats' grids now had the consistency of grits.

As he grumbled over the exorbitant cost of two minutes' worth of vacuuming time, James removed the snakelike hose from the tin base, slid the quarters in the slot, and waited for the vacuum to roar to life. When it remained silent, he jammed his index finger on the return change button. He was not rewarded for his effort. Frowning, he assaulted the button, jabbing at it viciously, but the machine refused to relinquish a single quarter.

Now, irritated and sweaty, he draped the vacuum hose in a sloppy coil back on its steel hook and approached the dollar-bill changer. His wallet, which was stuffed with slips of paper bearing the names of books he wanted to read, contained a ten and two singles. The first single had a fleabite on its top left-hand corner that was approximately three millimeters in size, but the machine spat it out like a child rejecting a forkful of brussels sprouts.

The second single must have passed through the hands of an origami artist. It looked like it have been folded horizontally and vertically, twisted into a pretzel, and balled into a tight wad before James received it as change from a gas station outside of Norfolk. In addition to its battered paper, the bill had been decorated with a woman's name in bubbly letters, a drawing of cartoon lips, and a series of x's and o's. The bill changer refused the dollar the moment James placed its top edge inside the machine. He tried again. The machine ejected the bill so rapidly that it fluttered to the ground.

"Look here!" James pointed a threatening finger at the machine and made one last attempt to straighten out the dollar's kinks against the lip of the bill changer. Taking a deep breath, he whispered, "Just take it. Take the damn dollar." He pushed the bill in. The machine pushed it out. In. Out. In. Out.

"Damn it!" James hit the bill changer with the palm of his hand and stuffed the dollar back inside his wallet.

"You don't look very relaxed for a man who just got back from a week at the beach," an amused voice said from inside a sheriff's department cruiser. "Will I have to run you in for property damage?"

James smiled, delighted to see the lovely face of his friend, Lucy Hanover. As usual, her beautiful skin radiated good health, and her cornflower-blue eyes sparkled with humor. Her caramel hair was pulled into a tight French twist. The sophisticated hairstyle allowed James to gape over how thin Lucy's face had become since the beginning of the summer.

"Have you lost more weight?" he asked.

She nodded. "I'm doing a protein diet right now. It's really helped me get toned, and I'm not as hungry as I used to be. Maybe the rest of the supper club should give it a try." She examined herself in the rearview mirror. "I think gorging on all that Mexican food over the winter might not have been the best idea for a dieting group. Between the enchiladas and the donuts at the station all spring, this summer has been all about my being more disciplined."

"Those enchiladas tasted good going down," James said as he studied her uniform—beige pants and a chocolate-brown shirt bearing an embroidered shield. He took a step closer to the cruiser and peered in the window at the gun belt strapped around Lucy's waist.

"Wow." He looked her over, unaware that his blatant ogling of her body could very well be perceived as too forward or even downright rude. Luckily for James, Lucy knew that he was focusing on her uniform, not on what was underneath the uniform.

"It's been ages since we were all together," she said. She turned off the car engine and relaxed in her seat. "I'm excited about getting back to our regular dinner meetings tomorrow night."

"Me too," James replied. "I can't believe how busy we've all been. I guess our little group just needed a change of pace and a change of scenery for a spell. Every one of us has been out of town— just on different weekends."

"Speaking of getting out of Dodge, how *was* the beach?" Lucy's tone was purely conversational, but the sharp glint in her eyes warned James that a full interrogation was imminent. When he hesitated, she quickly added, "Did Murphy go with you?"

Here it was: the moment James had dreaded for over five months. He was finally going to have to tell Lucy that Murphy Alistair, editor and reporter of the *Shenandoah Star Ledger*, was officially his girlfriend. The supper club members knew that James and Murphy had been dating, but James had never made it known that they were serious enough to take a vacation together.

In truth, James had had a wonderful spring with Murphy. They went to the movies, local plays, music shows, and a slew of events all over the valley because Murphy needed material for her articles.

When they weren't hiding away in a mountain inn or browsing antique shops or farmers' markets, they were at work. They rarely spoke on the phone during the day, but after James left the library, he often went straight to Murphy's. In her neat and tasteful apartment, they shared delicious meals. Afterward, they made love with the windows open. Soft music swirled through her bedroom, and the stars perched so low in the summer sky that James felt as though they might be blown away by the oscillating fan on the sill.

The only odd thing about their time together was that Murphy preferred for James to sleep in his own bed. She was working on a book, she explained, and did her best writing late at night. When he asked what the book was about, she told him it was a work of fiction and that she'd tell him all about it once it was finished. James knew that many people had aspirations to write a book but lacked the discipline to make their dreams a reality, so he didn't take Murphy's claim about being a novelist too seriously. Still, he respected her desire to give it a try, which meant he'd return home before midnight. He felt like a guilty teenager as he crept up the squeaky stairs to his bedroom.

All in all, James and Murphy had shared five blissful months together. And to James, the best part was that they never argued.

That is, until Murphy arrived at the beach to spend the Fourth of July weekend with him.

James had been alone for the first four days of his vacation week. Because of the multitude of responsibilities required to operate a daily newspaper, Murphy could take only a few days off. Though

James happily anticipated her appearance on Friday, he was utterly content at the beach without any company. He slept late, took leisurely strolls, and let the days slip by as he read book after book and drank copious amounts of iced coffee.

Though he hadn't been aware of it until he left Quincy's Gap behind, James had been in desperate need of some downtime. After all, he and his supper club friends had become embroiled in yet another murder case over the winter, and his relationship with Lucy Hanover had not taken the romantic turn he'd hoped it would. Instead, Lucy had fallen head over heels for a hunky aspiring sheriff's deputy and dropped James like a rock. And even though Lucy later regretted her decision to chase after the dashing deputy, James rejected her appeals to give their relationship another try. It was too late anyway, because James was already involved with Murphy.

In addition to hunting down a murderer and coping with romantic upheaval, James's home had undergone a major kitchen and bathroom makeover. The house and yard had been a mess, and Jackson Henry, James's father, had hired an assistant. Together, the pair of handymen began sawing and hammering well before six o'clock every morning.

Exhausted by the improvements, even though he hadn't done any of the work himself, James was almost grateful that Jackson had reverted to his hermitlike lifestyle to focus on producing new paintings to be sold by a famed DC gallery. Jackson locked himself in his shed for hours each day, surfacing only for meals or to receive visits from Milla, the owner of Fix 'n Freeze, a company that provided cooking classes and handled small catering jobs.

Milla had become such a regular fixture in the Henry home that James often wondered if she would close her business in New Market and conduct her classes from their cozy kitchen instead. James wasn't complaining, but after an entire spring of Milla's fantastic cooking, he'd packed on at least ten of the twenty-plus pounds he'd lost the year before.

Luckily for him, Murphy didn't seem to mind the expansion of soft flesh that had appeared around James's middle, and he was grateful that she didn't complain about his preference to make love with the lights off. Recently, however, it seemed to be the only thing she didn't complain about. During their three days together at the beach, Murphy had been bossy and sulky. She'd also displayed an irrational jealousy whenever a pretty girl passed them on the beach.

"Are you done staring at that girl?" Murphy had barked when an attractive young woman wearing a pink bikini and matching pink headband sashayed past them during the first afternoon of Murphy's arrival.

"I was just looking at her tattoo," James had responded honestly. "She seems too preppy to have the lyrics of one of those gangster rap songs tattooed across her shoulder blade."

Murphy had scowled. "You checked her out long enough to see whether the tattoo artist had spelled everything correctly, that's for sure!"

"Isn't people-watching part of the beach experience?" James had said, trying to placate his girlfriend. In truth, he didn't pay much attention to the other beachgoers. His eyes were usually fixed on a book page.

Ignoring him, Murphy had marched down to the water and, garnering plenty of stares for her own trim body and sun-streaked hair, dove into the Atlantic and swam away from the shore with such confident strokes that it looked like she had no intention of returning.

After their tiff at the beach, Murphy had nagged James for allowing his hotel room to become untidy and fussed over his thermostat settings. Once he'd straightened the room and moved the temperature gauge to her satisfaction, which meant he could barely feel any air-conditioning, she insisted on sitting on the balcony and planning every second of their next two days.

"Can't we just relax and live spur-of-the moment?" James didn't like to follow a schedule when he was on vacation. "If we run around and check off everything you have listed, we'll be exhausted by the time we're done."

"Well, I want to visit the lighthouse and rent jet skis." Murphy had tossed some brochures on the table. "And I haven't been to the battleship *Wisconsin* in years. I'm going to write a couple of travel articles on the Norfolk area while I'm here. I've been so busy editing my manu—" She'd abruptly halted and pointed at him. "You're a guy. You should like military history."

James had bristled. Though he liked all kinds of history, he'd rather read about it on the beach than traipse around a battleship beneath the blazing August sun alongside hundreds of other perspiring tourists. Eventually, Murphy wore him down and he agreed to spend Saturday and Sunday as she saw fit, but he didn't enjoy himself, and there'd been nothing romantic about their time together.

"Guess we're not quite ready to buy a house with a picket fence and have a bunch of kids," Murphy had joked at the end of their weekend.

James saw no humor in their situation. They'd bickered and snapped at each other too many times for such a short interval, and he spent the entire drive home wondering whether he and Murphy were as compatible as he'd once believed. She'd become jealous, controlling, and insecure, but he had no idea why.

When James asked about her atypical behavior, Murphy had brushed him off and claimed that he was exaggerating the situation. However, since their return to Quincy's Gap, her demeanor had remained tetchy at best. James was worried that she was keeping something from him, but Murphy insisted that he was overreacting and being paranoid. Still, they hadn't spent the night together since their botched holiday weekend, and that spoke volumes. James couldn't understand why Murphy suddenly needed her space when they'd had so many lovely months hanging out on a daily basis.

"Yoo-hoo!" Lucy waved her hand at James, forcing him back to the present. "Planet Earth calling. You ready to land your rocket and answer my question?"

James started. "Yes. Murphy came for the last few days." He avoided Lucy's penetrating gaze. "However, things didn't turn out as I'd hoped they would."

Lucy tried to conceal her delight, but failed. "That's too bad," she said without a trace of sincerity. "Things rarely end up how we expect them to."

They both fell silent, and while James searched for an excuse to continue abusing the change machine, Lucy suddenly seemed to remember something. She gave a little squeak and began digging through a pile of papers, empty plastic soda bottles, and other assorted trash until she pulled out an envelope. After examining the return address, she brushed a scattering of crumbs from the business-sized envelope and held it out for James to see. "Have you received a letter from the Hudsonville Chamber of Commerce?"

"I haven't gone through my mail yet. Why, should I be expecting one?"

"Yep, but since you haven't read it, I want to watch your face while you do. Here." She handed him the letter. "Apparently we're celebrities now. Well, at least in Hudsonville."

"Hudsonville?" James asked. "Where's that?"

"South. Off of I-81. Close to the North Carolina border. I hear it hosts the region's biggest barbecue festival." Lucy smiled mischievously. "But don't let me spoil the surprise. Read on."

James briefly examined the town seal, which depicted an apprehensive Native American man handing a suckling pig to a complacent pilgrim. Pine trees grew in abundance on a hillside behind the two figures and the text *Incorporated 1885* was written in block letters above the tallest tree. The letter read:

Dear Ms. Hanover,

First and foremost, congratulations on your new career with the Shenandoah County Sheriff's Department. I am confident that the citizens of Quincy's Gap will benefit from your experience in apprehending criminals.

The officers of the Hudsonville Chamber of Commerce have followed the endeavors of you and your friends in our local newspaper, the Hudsonville Herald. *We are very impressed by the fact that your group has assisted in the capture of several dangerous felons. For the most part, the media has credited members of law enforcement for these arrests, but we have friends in Quincy's Gap and know the whole story, as do most of the fine citizens of our county. The* Herald *has run a very popular series of articles on your supper club.*

In short, you and your friends are celebrities in Hudsonville, and we would be honored if your group would consider spending the week with us as we celebrate our forty-seventh annual Hudsonville Hog Festival. We'd like you to serve as guest judges. Your judging duties would entail choosing this year's Queen Sow as well as awarding the cash prize and trophy to the winner of the Blueberry Pie-Eating Contest.

Of course, the town of Hudsonville will gladly pay for your lodgings at our famous five-star bed-and-breakfast, and our area sponsors will provide you with plenty of free meals and merchandise during your stay.

The festival begins in two weeks and, while we apologize for the short notice, we truly hope that you will join us for this fun, family-oriented, and finger-licking-good festival.

If you have any questions, feel free to call me.

The letter was signed by a Mr. R. C. Richter. Several titles, including President of the Hudsonville Chamber of Commerce, as well as four different telephone numbers, were listed below his name.

"Is this for real?" James folded the letter and slid it back into the envelope.

Lucy nodded. "Sure is. Word is, their *original* celebrity judge canceled at the last minute, so they're scrambling to find a replacement."

"They must be desperate if all they can come up with is the Flab Five!" James laughed. "You know, we're going to need a different name, considering how incredibly unflabby you are."

Lucy shrugged, dismissing the comment. "Come on, James. We're celebrities, too. I think Murphy's coverage of our activities has given us exposure in papers well beyond the *Star* and the *Hudsonville Herald*. We're big news in these parts. The deputies on our bowling team tease me about our being household names all the time."

"Are you on the team? I thought *Deputy* Keith Donovan was adamant about keeping it an all-male endeavor." James grimaced as he spoke Keith's name. He and Donovan hadn't gotten along since high school.

"I'm not *on* the team." Lucy frowned. "I just go to support them. That jerk Donovan hands out all the duty assignments, and he gives me desk jobs whenever he can while he and Glenn handle all the larceny and A&B cases. The most exciting thing I've done all summer was transfer someone from jail to the courthouse."

"A&B?" James asked.

"Assault and battery." Lucy's radio crackled. A dispatcher spoke a stream of unintelligible code, causing Lucy to sit up in her seat and reach for the keys. "Gotta go, James. We have a case of possession of a firearm by a convicted felon. See you at Gillian's tomorrow night."

• • •

Gillian, owner of the Yuppie Puppy dog salon as well as Pet Palaces—custom-made homes for pampered pooches, felines, and birds—had prepared a creamy tuna casserole loaded with cheese, green peas, and fried onions for the supper club meeting.

Lindy Perez, high school art teacher at Blue Ridge High, had brought a tossed salad, while mail carrier Bennett Marshall had purchased a peach pie from the local bakery, the Sweet Tooth. Lucy arrived with a basket of fresh blackberries in case her friends preferred a low-calorie dessert, and James had followed one of Milla's easier recipes and had thrown together a cucumber, tomato, and dill salad.

"Did everyone get the same letter from Hudsonville?" Lindy asked, helping herself to greens.

Gillian poured glasses of chilled mint tea for her friends. "I cannot imagine being surrounded by all that *meat* for four days! It would be inconceivable for me to be trapped there, channeling the distress and agony of the pigs, chickens, and cows who've given up their lives for such an inhumane contest."

"Woman, this is barbecue!" Bennett threw his hands into the air. "What do you think cavemen did back in the day? They didn't plant organic soybeans or hunt for tofu. This festival is about food the way it's meant to be." Bennett's dark eyes gleamed. "Racks of beef ribs wrapped in foil, cooking over a slow-burning fire—yessir! Peel back the foil and brush on a thick layer of spicy sauce and then rip the butter-soft meat off the bone with your teeth. Hmmm. That's the way man was meant to eat!"

James took a bite of the tuna casserole, which had the consistency of lumpy pudding, and silently agreed with Bennett.

"We don't have to judge the food, Gillian, so you don't have to eat any meat. And just think: whichever pig we choose as the queen of the Hudsonville Hog Festival gets to live out the rest of her days at a local farm. The schoolkids take field trips to go see all the winning sows living high on the . . ." He didn't finish his ridiculous sentence. "Anyway, I thought the fact that she'd be spared would make you happy."

"How do you know all this, James?" Lucy asked.

"I visited the Hog Fest website." James reached for the salt and pepper and sprinkled a generous amount of both over the remains of his casserole. "It sounds like it would be fun to serve as a guest judge. Besides, we've seen one another so little lately that it would be a good way to reconnect." He jerked his finger at Lucy. "And since Lucy has turned into Deputy Skinny, we could use our time together to come up with a new name for our supper club."

Bennett stopped pushing food around on his plate. "I'm in, so that makes two of us. Lindy, do you think you can tear yourself away from that handsome principal of yours to embark on a little trip with your friends?"

Lindy blushed. "Luis and I haven't been together *that* much, though he's taken me out for enough late-night dinners that I've had to move up to the next dress size." Frowning, she crossed her arms across her chest. "Besides, y'all have been just as busy as I have. We've gotten together only once since Lucy became a deputy. I've missed this, so count me in!" She turned to Lucy. "How about you? Will Sheriff Huckabee let you off for a few days?"

Lucy helped herself to some blackberries. "He should. The big bowling tournament is the week before Hog Fest, and I have to pull double shifts so that a bunch of the *men* can practice. They'll owe me vacation time."

Gillian tugged at a strand of orange hair, which had been recently streaked with strands of bright blonde. "Am I the only one who feels that this event won't be a valuable bonding experience?"

James put a hand on his friend's shoulder. "The festival's not just about barbecue. I read that dog agility trials are one of the main attractions. It might be the perfect place to distribute your Pet Palace brochures. If these folks can spend ten thousand bucks on a grill, they can ante up for a custom doghouse for their fancy RVs. You should have seen the photos of some of those campers on the Hog Fest website."

Though Gillian was best known in Quincy's Gap for behaving and dressing like a middle-aged hippie, she was also a shrewd and successful businesswoman. She considered James's suggestion and, after a lengthy pause, she smiled at him. "I could expand our line to include doggie travel homes, so I'll go, but I'm bringing incense and healing candles for my hotel room. I don't want the aura of murdered animals to pollute my living space in Hudsonville."

"Then you'd better get your own room," Lindy said wryly. "No offense, Gillian, but I am not fond of patchouli."

"All right, my friends and fellow pig pickers," Bennett said happily, raising his glass of iced tea in a toast. "I'm ready for cold beer, a plate piled with pulled pork, and a whole mess of hush puppies!"

"We're going to have to start another diet as soon as we get back," Lindy said with a sigh. Without missing a beat, she cut a generous slice of pie and transferred it to her plate. "But until then, *carpe diem!*"

Chapter Two

Banana Bread

At the library the next day, James was busy attending to the weekend's hold requests. After reviewing the requests sent in via email as well as those written on index cards, he printed each patron's name in block letters on a sheet of paper, wrapped the paper around the requested book, and slid a rubber band over the book to hold the paper in place. The books were then arranged alphabetically using the patrons' surname behind the circulation desk.

James liked to start off every week with this task. He liked the orderliness of it, but he also enjoyed having the books ready and waiting for his patrons to collect. Week after week, there seemed to be more and more requests. With every new request or new library card printed and laminated, James's heart swelled with pride.

Even now, as he gazed at the mothers reading aloud to their young children in the Reading Corner, he thought of how the number of library patrons had grown since he'd reluctantly accepted the position of head librarian a few years ago. Though most of the townsfolk still called him Professor Henry out of respect for his former position as an English professor at William & Mary, James wouldn't trade his current vocation for anything.

After finishing the requests, he spent a moment observing the Fitzgerald twins, Francis and Scott. The twentysomething brothers were conducting a seminar in the library's new Technology Corner — yet another satisfying improvement implemented by James and his devoted staff. The twins, unaware that their boss was watching them with paternal fondness, were completely absorbed in instructing a group of elderly patrons on the workings of the Internet. Suddenly, one of the old women let out a bloodcurdling shriek.

"What's wrong, Mrs. Hastings?" Scott asked, moving quickly to the woman's side.

Speechless, her wrinkled lips agape, the woman pointed a trembling finger at the computer screen.

"I typed in Pussycat Girls!" the woman squawked. "My granddaughter mentioned their music and I wanted to see who they were." She put a hand over her heart and filled her lungs with air. "Lord have mercy, but *these* girls are stark naked!"

Both of the male patrons flanking Mrs. Hastings craned their necks to catch a glimpse of the gyrating bodies of the two young women who'd appeared on the screen. The name of the website, which bore a similar title to that of the pop band, was illuminated in electric pink letters and surrounded by pornographic images and videos.

"Sorry, Mrs. Hastings." Scott's cheeks were ablaze in embarrassment. He hurriedly brought up the library's home page. "I believe the musical group is called the Pussycat *Dolls*. Why don't you try your search again?"

"Hey!" one of the old men protested as the sexy women disappeared. "I didn't get a chance to look." He cast an imploring glance at Mrs. Hastings. "What'd you type the first time, Doris?"

Mrs. Hastings smiled and said, "I put in p-u-s—"

"Okay, folks!" Scott raised his voice above his customary whisper and ran a hand through his unruly hair. "Let's move on. Francis and I will show you how to find news and weather reports."

"Oh, good. Weather!" The woman seated across from Mrs. Hastings applauded. "I hear we're gonna have record-breakin' heat for the next few weeks."

"In that case, I'm not goin' outside," a male patron replied. "I'm going to buy a computer and search for those cute *dolls* Doris found a minute ago."

Once the brothers had successfully redirected their small class and the patrons were industriously checking the forecast or watching weather disaster videos, Francis pulled his brother aside. He pushed his thick glasses up the bridge of his nose and said, "Someone's been messing with our filters again."

"I think it's those high school kids who hang around on Fridays. Things are always out of whack with the computers after they leave."

Francis frowned. "And they never check out any books. Mrs. Waxman says they just mess up all the magazines and make a bunch of noise. I've been feeling guilty about leaving her to deal with them without backup. I know she's a battle-axe and can hold her own, but she shouldn't have to play maid to a bunch of rude kids."

"You're right. And battle-axe or not, she's not getting any younger. Guess we should tell Professor Henry what's been going on," Scott said. "He'll know what to do."

As the twins wrapped up their seminar, Wendell Singer entered the library. The retired school-bus driver was the library's sole book mobile operator. He was a whiz with engines and had kept the aged bookmobile, named Lena Horne after the jazz sensation, running at minimal cost. Lena was greatly prized by many patrons throughout Shenandoah County, as she and Wendell delivered library materials to day-care centers and hospitals, nursing homes, correctional facilities, and to rural patrons who couldn't leave their farms during harvest times. Lena also provided services for the handicapped and housebound. Unfortunately, the stress of traveling up and down the steep mountain roads had taken its toll on the fifteen-year-old bookmobile. Wendell had repeatedly warned James that it wouldn't be long before Lena would make her final run. She was already operating on what Wendell referred to as "duct tape and a prayer."

When James saw Wendell's solemn face that Monday morning, he feared that Lena's end had arrived. He was right.

"What happened, Wendell?"

The older man removed his Stihl baseball hat and scratched the bald spot in the middle of his head. "She's done broke down again, Professor." He crushed the cap in his hands. "I don't think anyone's gonna bring her back this time. She's finally crossed over to the other side, sir."

James placed a comforting hand on Wendell's shoulder. "You don't need to call me sir. Come on back. Let's sit for a minute." He led Wendell into the break room. "Let me get you a cup of coffee and a slice of banana bread. Mrs. Hastings baked it for us just this morning."

After he'd served Wendell a piece of the moist bread, James peered out the window in search of the bookmobile.

"You won't find her out there," Wendell said in between bites. "She's sittin' like a dead duck at one of those tourist view spots on Skyline Drive. Transmission's shot, and I think her timin' belt's given up the ghost, too. She's gonna have to be towed outta there, sir. No way she can move usin' her own steam."

James sat down across from Wendell and sighed. "It's that bad?"

Wendell nodded. With a trembling voice he said, "She's got nothin' left to give. We've done taken it all."

Afraid that Wendell might start crying, James offered the older man another cup of coffee, but he shook his head. And though James hated to let Wendell down, he had to be honest with him.

"We don't have the budget for a new bookmobile," he said. "I sure wish we did, but that Technology Corner emptied our coffers. I'm not sure what we'll do without Lena."

Wendell stood and carried his cup to the sink and donned his cap. "It'll take more than winnin' the Halloween float contest to buy a brand-new bookmobile. I'll have Lena towed to my place. I've already got two old buses there, so she'll have company." He gave James an imploring look. "You've got to come up with a plan, Professor. I gotta have a job and there's a whole mess of folks that'll have to go without books until we have a new set of wheels."

"We can't have that," James said solemnly. "After all, a life without books is an unfulfilled one at best."

"Eh?" Wendell cocked his head.

James told him to forget it and walked him to the door. "I'll find a temporary vehicle for you until I figure out a more permanent solution. You need your job, and people need their library materials. I'll work something out."

"This is why I didn't ever wanna be the boss of nothin'," Wendell said. "Too many headaches. I'll drive any vehicle you want, Professor. Shoot, I'll put books in an ice cream truck if I have to. Good luck, sir."

"Thanks." James returned to his chair behind the circulation desk and began to mull over how to come up with the necessary funds to replace Lena. Having already researched the cost, he knew that a new bookmobile would require a minimum of one hundred fifty thousand dollars. James planned on holding another lucrative Spring Fling to benefit the library come May, but the patrons depending on the bookmobile couldn't wait nine months for service to resume.

Where on earth am I going to get that much money? he thought while staring at the image of Lena on the library's homepage. *Why did you have to leave us now, Lena?*

"Professor?" Scott broke into James's grim musings. "Francis and I are concerned about what's happening here on Friday evenings."

"It's the high school kids," Francis chimed in. "I think we might need to stay later so we can help Mrs. Waxman keep an eye on them."

James paused to consider the unusualness of having a bevy of high school students in the library on a Friday evening during summer vacation. "Mrs. Waxman mentioned the notable increase of teenagers hanging out here. Why? Is it the computers?"

"That's what we thought at first," Scott said. "They do fill up all the seats in the Tech Corner, but mostly, they just sit around reading magazines."

"I think they're up to no good," Francis said hesitantly. "One of the kids, Harris, has always been into fantasy novels. But now, whenever I try to talk to him about the newest Steven Erikson or Jim Butcher books, he acts like he doesn't care. It's totally weird."

"Some people grow out of certain genres, bro," Scott said.

"Not this kid," Francis argued. "You look inside any of his school notebooks and you'll see dozens of drawings of wizards, trolls, and fairies. For some reason, Harris hides his interest in books when he comes here on Fridays. I see his artwork only when he visits during the week and is studying by himself."

"Some things about high school never change," James muttered. "Is Harris trying to impress one of the other kids?"

Scott and Francis exchanged knowing looks.

"My guess would be a rising senior named Martin Trotman," Scott said. "They all gather around him when he comes in, but we don't know why. Honestly, we never stuck around to find out. But we will now!" he added fervently.

Francis nodded. "Scott's right. We've heard enough about this crew from Mrs. Waxman to know that there's no way Martin is coming to the library for books. According to her, he curses like a character from an HBO drama and has more piercings than the whole High Hills Harley Gang put together."

"And half the brain cells," Scott chortled.

"Why don't you two take this Friday off?" James suggested. "I'm going to miss the following Thursday and Friday to be a guest judge at the Hudsonville Hog Festival, so I'll work with Mrs. Waxman this time and see what these kids are up to. Have you changed the computer passwords recently?"

"Just a few days ago," Scott said. "If they can break through our firewalls, they're smarter than we thought."

"Harris is the only one with enough computer savvy to do that," Francis said. "He and I have talked shop more than once."

James looked up and saw a line forming at the reference desk. "We'll get to the bottom of all this, gentlemen. Francis, why don't you help those patrons while Scott handles shelving? I need to make some phone calls to my fellow Virginian librarians."

"Is there a conference coming up?" Scott asked.

"No." James rubbed his temples. "I'm hoping one of them knows of a big, fat grant just sitting around waiting to be claimed. Lena's run her last trip, men, and I need to find a way to get us a new bookmobile."

• • •

After work, James forced himself to visit the YMCA. He spent forty minutes on the elliptical, breathing hard and trying to read the latest Jeffrey Deaver thriller.

"You know, you'd burn twenty percent more calories if you'd lose the book," Bennett said as he stepped onto the machine next to James's.

"No, I'd burn one hundred percent less, because I wouldn't be here," James said breathlessly. "Everyone thinks librarians sit around and read all day, but this is one of the few chances I have to catch up on my To Be Read pile."

Bennett brandished a copy of *The Big Book of American Trivia* and set it on top of his elliptical with a thump. He then used a potato chip bag clip to keep the pages from closing and programmed the machine. Smoothing his toothbrush mustache, he climbed onto the elliptical and began pumping his arms and legs. "I hear you, man. If I want to be a contestant on *Jeopardy!* I have to read every free second of the day. Maybe I'll get lucky and there'll be a barbecue category when I get to the tryouts in Philly in August." His face grew stormy. "If only I was ready when the contestant search was in DC last March. I couldn't pass that damned online test, so I knew there was no sense in going and making a fool out of myself. Shoot, *Alex* might've been there."

"Don't be too hard on yourself," James panted. "You said it was nearly impossible to pass the written test, right?"

Bennett nodded. "Most folks fail. You need to pass the test and then play a mock game. I've been practicing every night for years, so I'm not worried about that bit. I've passed the online test a mess of times this summer too, so I feel like I'm close to my goal."

"Well, I've seen you push buttons on your TV remote like you were an actual contestant. You have a lightning-fast trigger finger," James told his friend. "I know you're going to make it on the show, Bennett. Maybe you can win enough money to buy our library a new bookmobile."

Bennett rolled his eyes. "I'm sure you'll dream up a crazy scheme to get your hands on some greenbacks. You've done it before." He snorted. "Shoot, just get your girlfriend to put an ad in her paper saying that the new bookmobile will be named after the person who gives the most dough."

James considered Bennett's idea "That's not half bad. I will ask Murphy to run an ad on behalf of the library."

"Things still going strong with you two?" Bennett asked, and James wondered whether his friends approved of his relationship with the feisty reporter. Even though Murphy had helped the Flab Five solve a murder case last winter, James suspected that his friends were leery of trusting her. After all, she'd published several stories containing intimate, and sometimes embarrassing, details about their weight battles. And while none of the supper club members minded seeing their names in print, they didn't enjoy seeing their current weight or body mass index listed in black and white.

James pumped his arms and legs rapidly for a few moments and then answered Bennett's question. "Murphy and I are doing fine, thanks."

"Is she coming to Hog Fest?"

"No, she'll be covering a wine festival, some equestrian event, and a yodeling contest while we're gone. No time for pork," he joked.

He suddenly realized that he was relieved to have some time alone with his friends. Guilt turned his feet leaden, and he had trouble moving the elliptical forward. He pressed the red Stop button, waited for the machine's momentum to ease to a crawl, and stepped down. "Maybe I'll take her out for barbecue this week since she's going to miss all the fun."

"A woman who'll tear meat right off the rib bone and is willing to get sauce all over her face is a keeper. Go on home so I can finish this chapter on seventies sitcoms, will you?" Bennett made a playful shooing motion.

"I'm always eager to leave the gym," James said. He wished Bennett a productive workout, gathered his things, and left.

Driving home, James prayed that today was one of the days Milla had come to call on his father. If he lucked out, his father's sweetheart would be filling their kitchen with tantalizing aromas as pots boiled on the stovetop and dishes bubbled in the oven.

When James saw her minivan parked alongside his father's old pickup truck, he smiled in anticipation.

"Hello, James!" Milla trilled as he walked in the back door. The aroma of sautéing garlic immediately assaulted him—a favorable sign that Milla was preparing something scrumptious for dinner. The diminutive woman, who was in her mid-sixties but had the energy of a young girl, pushed back a cluster of pale curls from her forehead and grinned at James.

"You look hungry," she said while removing a bottle of white wine from the fridge.

James kissed her cheek in greeting and peered under the lid of a large skillet on the stove's back burner. "How's Pop?" he asked, his stomach gurgling at the sight of food.

Milla frowned. "He's neck-deep in paint. I swear, he'll be sleeping in that shed pretty soon."

James sat at the kitchen table and ripped off a heel of homemade bread. Without bothering to butter it, he popped the warm bread in his mouth and watched Milla move about the kitchen. It seemed like she'd always been there, cooking for the Henry men, but it was James's mother who'd once filled the room with warmth and good cheer. James knew that his mother would be pleased that such a kind-spirited person now cared for the two people she'd loved most.

As if sensing his thoughts, Milla turned from the stove and said, "Is this okay with you, James? My taking over this kitchen?"

"It's more than okay," he said, pouring glasses of wine for them both. "You're a blessing, Milla. To me and to Pop."

Milla blushed. "Thank you, dear." She sipped her wine, her cheeks pink from her culinary exertions. "I do love coming here, but it's getting harder and harder to commute to Quincy's Gap, take care of my Fix 'n Freeze clients, and make sure Prince Charles is getting enough attention."

James paused for a moment before remembering that Prince Charles was Milla's Corgi. "Pop still doesn't want to drive to New Market? Even if it means seeing you?"

"Lord, James. I've barely convinced him to run into town for groceries. That's the only progress I've made. He says he has to paint. Says that he's got plans and these paintings are the key to those plans. He wants them to sell out. It's really important to him."

"I haven't seen any of his recent work," James said.

Milla jumped up. "The veal needs to simmer a bit, so come out and look at the piece he finished yesterday. It's so incredible; you won't believe your eyes."

James hesitated. "He's not fond of me entering his space when he's not around."

"Pffah!" Milla grabbed his arm. "He's just an old dog with a sharp bark. He's not going to bite anyone, though he sure likes to pretend he would."

Trailing after Milla, James approached his father's shed. Jackson had told him time after time not to bother him while he was working. For the most part, James had respected his father's wishes. Jackson tended to be rather surly as a rule, so James avoided antagonizing him whenever possible. Milla, on the other hand, never walked on eggshells around Jackson Henry.

As Milla called out a hello and rapped on the shed door, James gazed at her in admiration. Her companionship had softened Jackson's sharp edges so much that he'd truly begun to stop exhibiting the reclusive behavior that had gripped him since James's mother had died. James had heard his father laugh more this summer than he had since he'd moved back into his boyhood room following his mother's death. James was glad to hear Jackson's laughter, for it was a rich sound, deep and rumbling like a peal of thunder or a train's echo inside a tunnel. The three of them filled the house with pleasant noises—the way a family should—and James hoped that their present state of harmony would last forever.

Jackson growled upon seeing two people in his shed, but Milla swatted at his shoulder with the potholder she'd forgotten to leave in the kitchen. "Don't glare, Jackson. I forced James to come out here against his will. After you show him that wonderful diner painting, we'll eat."

When Jackson hesitated, Milla put her hands on her narrow hips. "I made veal with shallots and garlic, and it'll be tough as the bottom of your work boots if you don't show the boy that picture this second."

Wordlessly, Jackson gestured to a large canvas hidden beneath a tarp. "Cover it up before you leave, ya hear?"

Jackson ushered Milla out of the shed. "I can't wait to sink my teeth into that delicious veal. I'm starvin'."

"Of course you are! You're turning into a bag of bones," Milla chided. "Lord knows what would happen if I didn't show up at your door every now and then."

"Nothin' good, my dear. Nothin' good," Jackson said and James could hear the smile in his father's voice. He tried to ignore the rumblings of his own belly as he reached forward to remove the tarp. When the painting was revealed, it took James several moments to soak in all the details he saw before him.

Jackson had painted a diner scene, but it was different from what James had expected. Instead of a painting depicting the faces of diner patrons seated at the counter, Jackson had portrayed only their hands and breakfasts. The row of hands gripped forks, knives, and coffee cups, or sprinkled salt or Tabasco sauce on scrambled eggs and hash browns. The hands belonged to workmen. James could guess that much without seeing the flannel shirt cuffs on their wrists, or the enormous breakfasts each man had ordered so that he'd be fueled for a long morning of physical labor.

The hands demanded individual attention. Each one varied in size and shape. Some had dirt-encrusted nails or nicked knuckles, while another's palm was marked with grease stains. The waitress's hands were more slender than the men's, but they bore their own blemishes—lines, burns, and brown age spots acquired from a life of service. One of her hands held a glass coffee carafe, while the other was frozen in the act of placing several paper napkins next to a plate of flapjacks.

James studied the painting and marveled over how Jackson had cleverly manipulated shades of blue and yellow in order to create a feeling of movement in his piece. The two colors, highlighted by touches of black or white, were filled with wonderful contrasts of light and shadow.

Look out, Norman Rockwell, here comes Jackson Henry, James thought. Once again, he was awestruck by his father's innate talent.

"It's fantastic, Pop," James said when he reentered the kitchen. "What diner is that painting based on? When did you have the chance to study those people and their hands?"

Jackson tapped his temple. "It's all right up here, boy. That's an old memory." He buttered a piece of bread on both sides and took a bite. "That diner's long gone now. I heard it's some kind of spa. You can pay a hundred bucks to have someone slop mud on your bare ass cheeks." He chuckled. "I'd toss the paying customers in a pigsty for half the price!"

James admired Milla's beautifully arranged platter of veal cutlets and sat in contented silence as she chattered away. She brought dish after dish to the table, arranging things just so.

As Milla searched in the fridge for some Parmesan cheese, Jackson dumped a heaping spoonful of tortellini on his plate and, finally blinking, said, "All things change, son."

Not knowing what to make of his father's cryptic statement, James simply nodded. He focused on savoring every bite of Milla's dinner. Afterward, he did the washing up, leaving Milla and Jackson to enjoy decaf coffees in the den. He then went upstairs to call Murphy from the privacy of his room. He asked her out on a dinner date. She cheerfully accepted, and James was certain that she was pleased and was still invested in their relationship despite their rocky weekend at the beach. He and Murphy small-talked about their day for a bit and, when their conversation started running dry, James asked Murphy if she would run an ad on behalf of the library to raise funds for the bookmobile.

"I don't think I can, James." Murphy's answer surprised him. "People know we're dating. If I give you the ad pro bono, they'll think you're getting special treatment."

"But it's for the library. It's not for me," he protested.

Murphy sighed. "I know, but it's all about perceptions."

James felt his ire rise. "And who is the *they* you're worried about?"

"Other local governmental agencies, charitable organizations, et cetera. The *Star* has pretty extensive coverage in our county, you know." Murphy's voice grew tense. "Don't get angry. I'm just trying to separate my personal life from my professional life."

"You didn't seem to care about the two intertwining when you wrote that piece on Virginia Beach," James argued.

"Oh, *please*," Murphy said, clearly exasperated. "I didn't mention *us*!"

"That's true," James argued. "I definitely didn't read anything about dragging your partner around until his feet bled, when all he wanted to do was relax!"

Murphy fell silent and James instantly regretted having picked a fight. His intention had been to smooth things over with her, not to dredge up fresh doubts about their relationship.

"I have to go, James. I'm on deadline," Murphy said and hung up.

James flounced onto his bed and covered his eyes with his hands. As the darkness deepened outside his window, he thought about what his father had said at dinner. "All things change."

They sure do, James thought miserably. *And I hate change.*

Chapter Three

Cole Slaw

A few days later, James and Murphy treated each other with stiff politeness for the better part of their dinner date at Blue's Barbecue House. Their conversation centered on work. James agonized over the broken bookmobile and shared his puzzlement over the presence of the teenagers at the library on Friday evenings, while Murphy talked about how pleased she was with the creativity and ambition illustrated by her newest reporter, Lottie Bronte.

"Scott still has a huge crush on her, but he's afraid to ask her on a date," James said. "They seem perfect for each other, too. I mean, how many people are named after authors?" He cut into his barbecued chicken breast. "Did Lottie ever mention that *Battlestar Galactica* birdhouse Scott made for her?"

Murphy smiled for the first time since James had picked her up. "I'll tell you one thing. That birdhouse isn't doing the world's sparrows or finches any good. Lottie says it's a work of art and can't be exposed to the elements. Instead, it holds a place of honor on her desk next to her computer." Murphy's hazel eyes twinkled in amusement "I think she may even take it on the road with her when she's covering stories in other counties."

"That's sweet," said James.

Murphy took a bite of her chicken and grimaced. Lowering her voice, she said, "I've never been a big fan of this place. This sauce is way too sugary, and the meat isn't exactly fall-off-the-bone tender. Maybe you can collect a few recipes while you're in Hudsonville and give them to Blue."

James glanced at the ancient proprietor of the restaurant. Blue was hunched over the counter, his head resting on his fist and his eyes shut tight.

Wiping his hands on a paper napkin, James eyed the greasy pool oozing from beneath his chicken breast. The red-tinged grease had infiltrated his pile of cole slaw, so James shoveled the slaw into his mouth to avoid further contamination.

"The slaw's good," he said. "But I agree about the sauce."

"Should you even be eating this kind of food?" Murphy

gestured at their meals. "I thought you were on a salt restriction."

James pulled more napkins loose from the napkin holder on the table. The contraption's stainless-steel surfaces, which were marred with scores of greasy fingerprints, sprang open like a trap and dozens of napkins fluttered across the table and onto the floor. Several fell on top of James's chicken and were immediately saturated in barbecue sauce.

Murphy sniggered, which annoyed James.

"I just saw Doc Spratt the day before yesterday," he replied defensively. "My blood pressure is back to a normal level. Doc told me to be careful not to eat too much salt, and I'll watch my intake, but I'm not going to pass up all foods containing sodium for the rest of my life." He closed the napkin holder. "Something's going to kill me one of these days. Might as well be food that tastes good. I'm not going to spend my days eating lettuce, turkey breast, and multigrain cereal. I want to *savor* life — not just live to avoid dying."

"That was *deep*." Murphy mocked him with her wide eyes. "Have you been reading books from the self-help section again?"

Despite the fact that James knew Murphy was teasing, he felt a wave of anger wash over him. "We can't *all* have naturally speedy metabolisms or blood pressure so low that it borders on being categorized as the walking dead."

Murphy sighed. "I have to confess, it's tough to be perfect." She then poked James playfully with her fork. The tines left four greasy pinpricks on the back of his hand. "Come on. If your blood pressure can get back to normal, then so can we. I liked us the way we were before our beach trip, James. Yes, we had a lousy weekend. It happens to the best of couples. Sometimes, for all sorts of different reasons, people just get out of sync. Can we forget it and move on?"

The warmth and sincerity in her voice made James feel ashamed of his churlishness. He rubbed at the spots on his hand with a napkin before taking her hand and squeezing it. "Yes, we can move on. That's what this dinner was supposed to be about."

"It's settled, then." Murphy pushed away her plate with her free hand, her eyes shining with what James hoped was happiness. "I wish we could do something fun together this weekend, but I have to go to the historical society's benefit dinner on Friday and the cat show on Saturday. Feel like hanging out with me at either of those fun-filled events?"

James shook his head. "Sorry, but I'm giving the twins a day off on Friday so I can spy on the high school kids. On Saturday, I promised to drive Pop to New Market so he can watch one of Milla's cooking classes. He wants to do a painting of the students making pastry dough." James gulped down the remains of his painfully sweet tea. "This is a big step for him—visiting Milla instead of her coming to our place."

Murphy sat back in her chair. "They're such a cute couple. Do you think they'll get married?"

James had been wondering the same thing. "I think so. It's how folks their age do things. They date for a bit and then, they get married. They don't really dither around. They know time is precious and they follow their hearts."

"That's the way things are *supposed* to be for couples of *all* ages," Murphy grumbled.

Sensing they were entering hazardous conversational waters, James kept the focus on his father and Milla. "If they do decide to wed, I'll be really happy. They're both widowers and they seem really comfortable with each another. Plus, I'd love to have Milla around all the time. She's a lovely person."

Murphy tossed a wad of soiled napkins on the vinyl tablecloth. James sensed that the subject of marriage had soured Murphy's mood, but he didn't feel inclined to ask why. Glancing at Blue, who had a trickle of drool running out the side of his mouth, Murphy said, "You might be happy for them, but it'll be a big change for you."

"Why?" James said, placing money on the table.

Looking at him as though he were a complete simpleton, Murphy said, "Because you'll finally have to grow up and move out of your boyhood room!"

• • •

On Friday, temperatures soared into the nineties, and the humidity pressed down on the Shenandoah Valley like a heavy hand. The library overflowed with patrons, but it was especially full during the hours of eleven and two This was when the temperature peaked and the sun threatened to scorch the hair right off of people's heads.

James was aware that almost half of the patrons reading in upholstered chairs or waiting for an opportunity to use one of the computers for the forty-five-minute maximum had come to the library because it was air-conditioned. The elderly were especially susceptible to the hot weather and they'd arrived in droves, blatantly disregarding the *No Food or Drink* sign posted on the front door. Bearing thermoses of sun tea or lemonade as well as paper bags stuffed with sandwiches, potato chips, and cookies, they gathered in groups at the wooden tables and played bridge or chatted about recent stories in the newspaper.

James didn't have the heart to remonstrate them, even when they scattered crumbs on the carpet or raised their voices above a whisper. Besides, all of the older patrons adored the Fitzgerald twins and plied them with baked goods and hard candies until the boys swore that they had more adoptive grandparents than they could handle. Having taken the twins' place that Friday, James found himself with a treasure trove of fresh oatmeal cookies, cranberry scones, and cheese biscuits.

"Well, I *am* going to be here until nine," he said, happily examining the pile of goodies on his desk.

The oatmeal cookies proved the perfect accompaniment to James's afternoon coffee. As soon as his break was over and he'd finished washing out his *Forget Google, Ask a Librarian* mug and returned to the circulation desk, the high school students began to drift in.

By the time Mrs. Waxman arrived at five thirty, there were at least six teenagers seated at computers or leafing through magazines. By six thirty, the number had doubled, and by seven thirty, it had tripled.

James and Mrs. Waxman took turns hushing the boisterous group and asking them if they needed help finding materials. They all refused, declaring that they were meeting friends or waiting to use one of the computers. One teen even pretended that she was a member of a book club and insisted that she didn't want to check out any books until her group decided on which novel to read next.

When James offered to provide recommendations, she shook her head vehemently. "That's okay. We only read the *It Girl* books." She then turned her back on him and began to type a text message on her cell phone.

Deciding to approach the kids on an individual basis, James strolled up to a young girl in a denim miniskirt that barely covered her rump and asked, "Can I help you find something, miss?"

The girl hastily closed a folder and stuffed it, along with what appeared to be a pen-sized X-Acto knife, into her canvas purse. Smiling nervously, she said, "No, thanks. I'm waiting for a computer to open up."

"And what might you be using our fine new computers for?" James asked, trying to keep his voice from betraying his suspicion. "Are you interested in a particular topic?"

A boy sitting too close to the girl with the short skirt sneered. "Dude, she doesn't have to tell you anything. There's, like, privacy laws. What she does on the computer is her business. You're a public *servant*." His lip curled. "Be careful or you could get sued."

Though James felt like grabbing the surly teenager by the throat, he flashed him a patient grin instead. He wanted to use this opportunity to discover what had driven the motley assembly of kids into the library, and he felt that he had a pretty clear idea of what their goal was, having glimpsed the small knife. Leaning close to the boy, he whispered in a low, ominous tone, "That's right, son. I am a proud servant of the public. Our town is filled with a host of public servants. We have mail carriers, the folks working at the DMV, and the fine men and women of our sheriff's department. I have one friend in particular, a Deputy Hanover, who feels *very* strongly about preventing young people from driving while under the influence."

The boy averted his gaze and did his best to appear bored.

James looked at the girl. "This officer is also devoted to tracking down each and every fake license in the county. She truly wants to keep all of the drivers within our county lines safe, and those possessing fake licenses are often some of the worst drivers, due to their inexperience."

The girl blanched. James had struck a nerve. Silently apologizing to Lucy for taking such liberties in her name, he plowed on. "I believe you could spend six months in jail for carrying one of those licenses." James glanced back at the boy, who continued to act uninterested, but his fidgety hands betrayed his agitation. "A person could face a fine *and* a year's time in jail for making and distributing fake IDs."

At this opportune moment, a hulking young man wearing a thin leather coat entered the library. His hair was dark, long, and greasy, his skin shone with oil, and he was clean-shaven except for a straight line of hair growing down the center of his chin. The hair had been dyed orange. In addition to the odd facial hair, the imposing young man had a row of small silver hoops protruding from his right eyebrow and a barbed-wire tattoo encircling his wrist. His walk had all the swagger of a gun-toting cowboy.

This must be Martin Trotman, James thought, recalling the twins' description of the teenage alpha male. James casually approached Mrs. Waxman and pretended to consult her about a damaged book. While they talked, he asked her to watch Martin without being obvious. Mrs. Waxman patted her bouffant hair as she reported in hushed tones that Martin had usurped the chair of the girl in the miniskirt. The girl then leaned over to whisper into Martin's ear and the young man's smug grin had turned into an angry scowl.

"He's staring this way," Mrs. Waxman murmured. "At the back of your head. He doesn't seem too pleased, either."

"He must be the ringleader. My guess is that these kids have been dealing in fake IDs." James felt quite pleased that he'd solved the mystery so quickly. "I doubt Martin does any of the labor himself. I'd guess the girl in the short skirt is one of his assistants. He's probably in charge of fulfilling orders and collecting money."

Mrs. Waxman considered his theory. "It's possible. But how many of these IDs can one kid need? These teens are here week after week."

James frowned. "I'm not sure. I guess they're using the licenses to buy alcohol or order alcoholic beverages in bars. Not at Wilson's Tavern, however. Sammy would throw them out on their ears and call their parents."

"On the other hand, this could be quite an entrepreneurial group." Mrs. Waxman eyed Martin again. "Perhaps they're selling the IDs to other teens around the valley. There are dozens of kids who'd like to pull one over on the liquor stores or less observant barkeeps."

Rubbing his temples, which had begun to pulse with the beginnings of a headache, James glanced at the door in time to see a scrawny teen with glasses and acne enter the library. The boy furtively slipped a book in the return slot before edging over to where Martin sat. James hustled behind the circulation desk and removed the eight-hundred-page fantasy book the teen had returned.

I believe Harris has arrived, James thought.

Scott had said that Harris liked fantasy novels, but pretended to be disinterested in books whenever the other teens were present. Intrigued, James watched the conflicted young man settle himself at a wooden table by the magazines and pretend to read a copy of *Dog Fancy.*

James kept one eye on Martin and the other on the rest of his patrons, but as the evening wore on, he found that he could only find cause to reprimand the teens for raising their voices or putting their feet up on top of the wooden tables.

Martin seemed restless the entire time he was in the library. He often disappeared into the lobby, and although James immediately trotted into his office and looked out the window whenever the young man ventured out, he never saw Martin in the parking lot.

"Where's he going if not to his car?" James asked the darkening sky.

By the time the library closed at nine, most of the high school kids had dispersed. Martin left first, and then slowly, usually in groups of two or three, the rest followed.

"They were calmer tonight than on previous nights, James," Mrs. Waxman said after the last patron had left. She began to straighten the magazine area with swift, efficient movements. Mrs. Waxman was one of the few townsfolk who didn't call James Professor. After all, he'd once sat in the back of her classroom, praying that her eagle eyes would pass him over whenever he forgot his grammar worksheets, and he still felt like a child in her commanding presence.

James assisted the retired schoolteacher in tidying up the library. Mrs. Waxman was moving more slowly than she had in the past.

She'd recently been diagnosed with rheumatoid arthritis, and he worried that the evenings and one weekend day she worked were too hard on her inflamed hip.

Opening the front door for her, he asked how her medication was working.

"I won't be dancing the polka anytime soon, but it's keeping the aches at bay." She gave James a maternal pat on the back. "Don't worry, I have plenty of life left in me yet, and I'm going to work in this library until I can't walk anymore." She smiled. "I'm at home here."

"Me too," James said. He gazed at the vibrant row of fairy-tale character drawings done by the students in a local second-grade class, which Scott and Francis had posted around the lobby. "Now that those high school kids know we're on to them, we can reclaim our peaceful branch again."

Mrs. Waxman shrugged. "I rather enjoyed being in the midst of a mystery for once."

James walked the older woman to her car. "The best thing about mysteries is solving them," he said brightly and wished Mrs. Waxman a good night.

Chapter Four

Warm Chicken Salad Sandwiches

James and Bennett drove through the town of Hudsonville in search of Fox Hall Lane. The bustling berg was larger than James had imagined. It was also extremely charming. Wooden barrels bursting with red geraniums, yellow strawflowers, and purple salvia lined the sidewalks. The spotless glass windows of the storefronts glinted in the midday sun, and colorful flags depicting a crowned pig sitting in a field of buttercups hung from every streetlamp. Bunches of pink balloons were tied to the park benches, and there wasn't a piece of litter, or a parking space, in sight.

James was fascinated by the variety of the vehicles in the public lot. They ranged from expensive sedans to family-oriented minivans to rusty pickup trucks. Most of the cars had Virginia plates, but there were also many visitors. Some people have driven all the way from Arkansas and Kansas.

Bennett rolled down his passenger window, and the jaunty sounds of a fiddle floated into the Bronco. Shopkeepers wearing pink and black baseball caps had lined tables filled with Hog Fest wares along the sidewalk. Families examined the tables or hurriedly tried to finish their ice cream cones before the summer heat reduced them to sugary puddles.

The energy of the street fair was contagious, and James was eager to check in to their bed-and-breakfast so he and his friends could wander around Hudsonville before the festival's opening ceremony later that afternoon.

"There's your turn." Bennett pointed ahead at a signpost partially obscured by a mammoth oak tree. He examined the sheet containing their driving directions for the tenth time and then gestured at the odometer. "After two-point-seven miles, we'll see the sign for the inn. Turn left, and then proceed point-seven miles to the gravel parking lot." He swiveled in his seat. "The girls are still right behind us. I'm sure glad everyone was able to get a couple days off."

"Did you bring any homework?" James asked, keeping an eye out for the sign.

Bennett nodded. "Yes, I did. I have a book on world culture trivia, a book on bird trivia, and a book on sports trivia." He snorted. "Shoot, my bag was so heavy, you'd think I was a woman getting ready to fly to Paris instead of a bachelor heading out for a weekend of barbecue."

Ignoring Bennett's rather sexist comment, James spotted a wooden plaque reading *The Inn at Fox Hall*. He turned into a narrow lane lined with tulip poplars.

As the house came into view, Bennett whistled. "Man, we have nice digs for a bunch of small-town celebs here to decide who's the fairest piggy of them all."

"It's certainly picturesque," James agreed. The nineteenth-century house was white with black shutters and had a long front porch lined with rocking chairs and potted ferns. "But I hope it's been updated. If we don't have air-conditioning, I'll be checking into the Comfort Inn pronto. I can drown out the sounds of the highway by cranking the fan to its highest setting."

"Hog Fest is pretty huge in these parts, my man. I don't think you could find room in a manger if you wanted to." Bennett examined his printouts again. "According to the inn's website, it was renovated five years ago. All the rooms have A/C, Jacuzzi tubs, and digital cable. And if the A/C doesn't do it for you, there's a big swimming pool out back."

Thinking of how his round belly would look in a swimsuit, James pulled a face. "I'll stick with the Jacuzzi tub, thanks."

James parked his white Bronco in the gravel lot and waited for Lucy to pull her Jeep into the adjacent spot.

"This is *paradise*!" Gillian exclaimed. She'd already leapt out of the car and was twirling around with her arms spread à la Julie Andrews in *The Sound of Music*. "I'm *so* glad I decided to let go of my misgivings and join you, my friends." She pointed at a rustic wooden sign to the right of the parking area. "Look! Nature trails! An indigenous garden walk! The pond and gazebo! You'll *never* get me back in the car."

Bennett glanced at his watch. "There's also a welcome lunch on the back porch. I'm more interested in food than in some mosquito-infested pond. If we hurry, we can just make it."

"I'm ready to eat, too." Lindy dragged an enormous suitcase

onto the flagstone path leading up to the main house. "I wonder if we're staying in the house or in one of those cute cabins."

James glanced at the miniature log cabins in the distance, which were almost entirely obscured by trees. His eyes then returned to Lindy's bag. "We're only here for four days, Lindy. What on earth have you packed? A small child?"

Bennett sniggered as Lindy stuck her tongue out at James. "They invited us because we're minor heroes to them. I consider it my responsibility to look the part."

Lucy grabbed Lindy's suitcase and shoved the handle of her much smaller wheeled bag into Lindy's hand. "I see you have a fresh French manicure, too. You'd better let me carry this or you could chip the polish." Lucy pulled the suitcase effortlessly up the path.

"Wow, you're really strong," Gillian said as Lucy carried the bulging bag up the front steps with ease. "Are you channeling some kind of inner power?"

Smiling indulgently at her friend, Lucy said, "Nothing as complicated as that. I've been eating mostly lean protein and doing strength-training workouts."

"A protein diet?" Bennett immediately perked up. "That means lots of meat, right?"

Opening the front door, Lucy stepped inside the inn's main hall and waited for her friends to join her. "It's not a diet. You don't count calories or carbs or monitor your portions. It's just a particular way of eating. It makes me feel good and I have tons of energy." She patted her nearly flat stomach. "I've also been trying to strengthen my core."

"Forget about your core. Tell me more about the meat part," Bennett persisted, but before Lucy could continue, the proprietress of the inn appeared in the hall and welcomed them with a bright smile.

"You must be my celebrity guests. What an honor," the slim, elegant woman gushed. "I'm Eleanor Fiennes, and I am delighted beyond measure to have you staying with us."

James found Eleanor's warmth a bit forced, and as he gazed at her shiny brown hair and small, darting eyes, he couldn't help comparing the woman to a ferret. Pulling two sets of keys from the top drawer of an antique desk, Eleanor handed one key to James and one to Lindy. "You two gentlemen are in the Hunt Room and the ladies are in the Equestrian Suite."

James studied the weighty brass tag that was stamped with the image of a fox head.

"I hope you don't mind the light being on late into the night." Bennett grinned. "I can't take time off from my studies."

"Um, excuse me." Lindy cleared her throat as she held out her key. "Are all three of us sharing one bathroom?"

Eleanor Fiennes nodded. "That's the best I could do, I'm afraid. Fox Hall's been booked for Hog Fest weekend since last year! I had to push a whole family into one of my older cabins to accommodate you five on such incredibly short notice."

Sensing that she'd offended their hostess, Lindy quickly backpedaled. "We really appreciate that, Mrs. Fiennes, and we're grateful to be staying at your beautiful inn. Thank you so much for your trouble."

Eleanor eyed the suitcase on the floor next to Lucy. "Can you manage your luggage?" When Lucy assured her that she could, the proprietress looked relieved. "Good, good. Your rooms are on the second floor, and lunch is being served as we speak, so get settled and then come on down for some of our famous hot chicken salad sandwiches."

James was quite hungry, and the idea of lunch was more appealing than spending time examining his room. As it turned out, there wasn't much to see. There was a set of twin beds covered by ivory quilts stitched with maroon stars. The walls were a forest green and decorated with three oil paintings depicting fox hunts. James had never been fond of the tradition of a pack of dogs and a group of armed horsemen tracking and cornering a terrified fox. He saw foxes as beautiful and clever animals and wished the practice of shooting them for sport had never been fashionable.

While James hung up his favorite jeans and two pairs of khaki pants, Bennett dumped a pile of books on the nightstand and poked his head into the bathroom.

"It already feels like home," he said, surveying their cozy room.

Finished with their unpacking, the two friends hustled downstairs and out the back door. They found the wooden porch crowded with glass-top tables, white metal chairs, and dozens of guests, all contentedly chewing or drinking tea from perspiring tumblers.

Several children frolicked in the pool, and a young woman in a minuscule black bikini sunned herself on a lounge chair on the emerald lawn bordering the porch.

Eleanor appeared next to James and Bennett. She cast a brief, disapproving stare in the direction of the gorgeous girl and then, through a slightly clenched jaw, gestured at a laden buffet table. "Please help yourself to our lunch buffet, gentlemen. We have a watercress and mint salad with walnuts, delicious warm chicken salad on toasted croissants, fresh berries, and Key lime or lemon tartlets for dessert. Pitchers of tea, ice water, or limeade are on the sideboard. Enjoy your meal."

The two men watched their hostess march off in the direction of the sunbather in the bikini before joining the buffet line.

After James had dished food onto a china plate decorated with running foxes and taken a seat at the only available table, he realized that he'd forgotten to get something to drink. As he headed back to his table with a glass of limeade, he noticed Eleanor berating the young woman in the bikini. The girl stood with deliberate slowness. Draping her yellow-and-white-striped towel over one shoulder, she slid her feet into flip-flops and sauntered past the diners. The conversation on the porch was momentarily quieted as all eyes fixed on the bronzed form of the young woman. Tossing her mane of lustrous dark blonde hair, the girl cast a dazzling smile at one of the male guests. James could see that the young lady was clearly Eleanor's daughter. She was also a great beauty.

The girl had reached the end of the porch by the time Lindy, Bennett, and Lucy joined James at the table. James's three friends looked perplexed.

"Why did everyone suddenly stop talking?" Lindy asked.

Bennett pointed at Eleanor's daughter, who'd stopped to chat with a woman in an apron. "It was probably that lovely vision. I guess everybody's brains just shut down for a moment."

"She certainly looks like a, er, healthy American girl," Lindy said. "Still, I'd hate to see her skin in twenty years. I hope she's wearing some sunscreen."

"She favors her mama, too. Eleanor must've been a real looker in her day," Lucy said. "They've been blessed by good genes and we shouldn't hold that against them. The rest of us have to work just to fit into our uniforms and that's all there is to it."

"Where's Gillian?" James suddenly asked.

Lucy squeezed lemon into a glass of ice water. "She wants to cleanse our room before she comes down to lunch."

"I must have been in the bathroom when she made that announcement." Lindy rolled her eyes. "Please tell me she's not using patchouli. I hate that smell."

Lucy smirked. "I thought I saw a package of Egyptian Kush Musk sticking out of her purse. Who knows? It could smell even worse than patchouli."

Before anyone could respond to Lucy's remark, a heavy man wearing a Hawaiian shirt stepped onto the porch. He cast a complacent glance around until his bloodshot eyes fell on the figure of Eleanor's daughter. Strutting over to the attractive young woman, the man shook his head and made bubbling noises with his lips. As he did so, his pink and fleshy cheeks shook, and his enormous stomach wobbled beneath his shirt's pattern of dancing hula girls. Sweat stained the chest area of his shirt and dripped down his puffy face and neck.

"Lord Almighty, girlie!" he bellowed at the startled young woman. "You're hot enough to fry an egg on! Mercy me! I've seen napkins that are bigger than that bikini." He smiled, displaying a row of yellow teeth. "Allow me to introduce myself. *I* am the world-famous Jimmy Lang, winner of more first-place barbecue trophies than I can count, and the future champion of Hudsonville Hog Fest." He nudged the young lady in the side with his meaty elbow. "You come on down to my pit anytime, sweet girl! You can find out why they *really* call me the Pitmaster. I know I'm a bit on the big side—seems I gained a whole 'nother person this year—but I've got skills other men just don't have. These hands like a nice piece of tender meat, and you're about as tender as they come."

Most of the diners frowned in distaste. Others watched Jimmy with obvious amusement.

Eleanor, who clearly found nothing funny about the situation, made a beeline to her daughter's side. She tried to shoo the girl inside the house and whispered, "Francesca, please," but her daughter ignored her.

Francesca slowly wound the towel around her waist and struck a coquettish pose. "Do barbecue contestants make lots of money?" she asked Jimmy coyly.

"You get right to the marrow of it, don't ya? You're my type of gal!" Jimmy roared with laughter. "We get a nice pile of cash for bein' named the champion, but winnin' the money's nothin' compared to landin' a big-time sponsor. This year's sponsor is Heartland Foods, and they want to expand their line to include barbecue. I win this one, and I'm all but guaranteed my own line of sauces and rubs, along with my very own TV show on the Outdoor Livin' channel." He rubbed his tummy as he visually devoured Francesca. "Lots of money there, darlin', and I'd be more than happy to spend some on you. You could be the gal lucky enough to be with Jimmy Lang, champion pitmaster, and the face of barbecue." He held up his hands as though reading a banner upon which his new title had already been written.

"Um, thank you, Mr. Lang." Eleanor stepped in front of her daughter. "Francesca needs to get ready for tonight's opening ceremonies." She took a firm hold of her daughter's arm. "She's the Hudsonville Festival Princess. She's been chosen to drive the Queen Sow in the victory parade, and her photograph will be in all the area papers."

"Francesca's or the pig's?" Jimmy asked and then guffawed at his own joke.

Eleanor looked irritated. "My daughter's, of course. She's won so many pageants over the last five years that she's a shoo-in for the top five at the state competition." She pushed a lock of Francesca's hair off her cheek. "You might just be talking to the next Miss Virginia, and after that, Miss America."

Now it was Francesca's turn to be annoyed. Breaking away from her mother's grasp, she sneered. "I've told you a million times that I'm going to win scholarship money based on my brains, not my boobs!"

And with that, Francesca stormed into the house.

Jimmy laughed heartily and began to sing, "There she is, Miss America." He strolled around the porch kissing the hands of the ladies seated nearby. They giggled and twittered among themselves in response.

Visibly trying to conceal her displeasure, Eleanor asked Jimmy if there was something she could assist him with. Jimmy announced that he wanted to meet the contest judges and the representative for Heartland Foods.

"Word around the campfire is that they're all staying here at Fox Hall," he said, winking at Eleanor. "I'm just gonna help myself to some free lunch and start my campaign for the championship!"

Rudely turning his back on Eleanor, Jimmy filled his plate with three sandwiches and six tartlets, humming the Miss America theme song all the while.

Except for Lucy, the supper club members exchanged panicked stares as they realized that the only available seat was at their table. James swallowed his Key lime tartlet in two bites and gestured frantically at Lucy to finish her meal.

"It's not good to bolt down your food," she protested, taking a minuscule bite of watercress salad.

However, as soon as Jimmy Lang pulled out the empty chair next to her and asked, "This seat ain't taken, is it?" Lucy began to eat as if it were her last meal.

As she chewed, Lucy scooted her chair close enough to James for him to be able to smell her almond-scented body lotion. Swallowing hurriedly, she said to Jimmy, "We're just about done, so if anyone's planning on joining you . . ."

"Don't rush off on my account." Jimmy shoved half a sandwich into his mouth and continued talking. James noticed that the skin on his face was dry and flaky, and that overall, the man appeared swollen. It was like he was retaining large amounts of water. Wiping sweat from his forehead with the back of his arm, Jimmy raised a thick pair of eyebrows and asked, "Y'all judges?"

"Yes. We're judging the sow contest," Lindy replied importantly, turning her face away as Jimmy began to noisily lick chicken salad from his thick fingers.

"Aha!" He pointed at Bennett. "You're those crime-solvin' folks, ain't ya?" He surveyed the group while pushing an entire tartlet in his mouth. After several chews he declared, "I don't mean any offense, but you don't look like detectives."

Wiping her mouth with her napkin, Lindy stared intently at Jimmy. "Lucy is the only *trained* member of law enforcement, but the rest of us contribute to crime solving by using our natural gifts and abilities. It's important to us that right triumphs over wrong in our community."

Jimmy's mouth hung open, exposing a partially decimated Key lime tartlet. He closed his lips, which were also flaky with dried skin, and looked at James. "What's she talkin' about?"

"She's saying that we help each other," James said.

He noticed that Jimmy's eyes seemed to shift between blue and gray depending on the light. Jimmy had crumbs stuck in the sparse hairs of his salt-and-pepper beard, and as he ran his hand over his shaved head, he left a trail of Key lime filling behind.

"I help folks, too. I'm a tow-truck driver by trade." He wiggled his hairy eyebrows. "But not for long. Whether I land that contract or not, my ship is comin' into port this weekend. When I get back to Waxahachie—that's south of Dallas, Texas, for those of y'all that don't know God's country—I'm gonna tell my boss he can take that rusty truck, those hours from hell, and the whiny customers and shove them all where the sun don't shine."

Lindy placed her napkin on the table and stood up. "I'm going to unpack. Nice meeting you and good luck with your grilling."

Lucy also got to her feet, followed by James and Bennett.

Jimmy slurped his tea and looked at his watch. "Make sure y'all ain't late for the openin' of the party. I'll be givin' out samples of my mouth-waterin' 'cue, so stop on by my trailer, ya hear?"

"'Cue?" James inquired of Bennett when they were out of Jimmy's earshot.

"Slang for barbecue," Bennett explained. "I imagine Jimmy knows every barbecue term known to man. I'm going to make it a point to try his cooking."

"You are?" James was astonished.

"Man with that big a belly and that much swagger knows his food," Bennett said. "And you heard him. He's already won a whole mess of competitions. He must have figured out some tricks by eating all his own mistakes. Look, here comes Gillian. She doesn't know what she missed." He poked James in the ribs. "Maybe you should've cleansed *our* room, James."

Back in their room, the men finished unpacking. Afterward, James flipped through Bennett's trivia books.

"How's your cache of barbecue trivia?" he asked his friend.

"Pretty poor, my man. I hope to store away a hundred facts or so by the time this festival is done." Bennett held up a mini recorder. "I'm going to carry this with me wherever we go so I can think of questions to research later on. What I do know is that barbecue is different around the country and that everybody thinks *theirs* is the best."

"All I've had recently is Blue's, and his was definitely *not* the best."

"Poor Blue." Bennett frowned. "How he's eked out a living on that dry meat is beyond me. And his sauce doesn't fit into *any* of the popular categories. Texas and the western states like a feisty tomato-based sauce, the Kansas City folks favor sweet over spicy, North Carolina likes a vinegar sauce with lots of black pepper, and I believe South Carolina and parts of Georgia make a white vinegar sauce mixed with sweet mustard. Kentucky adds Worcestershire to theirs." He paused. "I read that Florida actually makes a white barbecue sauce using mayo in the tomato base. Doesn't sound too appealing if you ask me, but I'll try it if someone's serving it at the festival."

Once again, James was impressed by the random bits of knowledge stored in his friend's keen brain. "I can't wait to watch you on *Jeopardy!*"

Bennett, who'd gathered his trivia books and sunglasses, hesitated at the door to their room and wiggled his index finger at James. "Don't go jinxing me now. I'm going down by the pool to read. You coming?"

Grabbing a book on the history of barbecue from his duffel bag, James flopped onto the bed. "I was going to check out the town, but I think I'll stay in the room for a bit longer. That Jimmy Lang fellow might not have gone back to his RV yet, and I think we're going to have more than our fill of that guy by the end of this festival."

Bennett grinned. "Our fill? Nice culinary pun, Professor. I hope you get through that book fast so you can educate the rest of us on standard contest categories before we eat a piece of barbecued possum."

James was alarmed. "You're kidding, right?"

"No, man." Bennett shook his head. "They have a category called Anything Butt. And if there are already categories for chicken, pork, and beef, then what meats do you think are left?"

James rifled through his book until he located the table of contents. "I don't know, but I'm going to find out before I end up with a piece of rattlesnake 'cue on the end of my fork!"

Chapter Five

Roast Corn on a Stick

When James and the rest of the supper club members arrived at the Hudsonville town park, they were astonished by how many people had gathered to celebrate the kickoff of Hog Fest. Swarms of men, women, and children waited at the park entrance, talking animatedly and glancing excitedly at their watches.

The park had been divided into quadrants, the largest of which was further partitioned by the main road. Flanking the road, which led to the recreation center on one end and the tent where the barbecue entries would be judged on the other, were the food vendors. These booths offered all types of batter-dipped foods from sweet potatoes to fried okra to fried bananas to fried peanut butter cups. Behind their napkin-stacked counters, multiple vats of oil bubbled away. Perspiring merchants wearing colorful aprons and matching visors rushed to prepare their booths for the imminent arrival of hungry customers.

The Flab Five were allowed to enter the festival grounds early because R. C. Richter, the head judge of Hog Fest and president of the Hudsonville Chamber of Commerce, needed to review the rules of the sow beauty queen contest with them.

Strolling down the park's main road in search of the indoor recreation center, the group gazed wide-eyed at the assortment of merchandise for sale. The fragrant line of food vendors was separated from the dry goods merchants by an area full of picnic tables and garbage cans. James and his friends walked by booths of plush pigs dressed in jean jackets and straw hats, personalized leather key chains, handmade pottery, carved wooden walking sticks, necklaces made from crystallized grains of rice, watercolors of the Blue Ridge Mountains, neon windsocks, Hog Fest T-shirts, and more.

James's vision began to blur by the time they reached the last booth, but his eyes were assailed by a fresh variety of primary colors as they viewed the area where caricaturists, clowns selling pig-shaped balloons, temporary-tattoo artists, and face painters were arranging their supplies or stirring paint as they occasionally checked the time. In less than thirty minutes, the festival would open, and the feeling of anticipation among the vendors was palpable.

Inside the recreation center, a modern glass and steel structure, volunteers bustled about, holding clipboards and walkie-talkies. A slim man in a blue button-down shirt waved at James and his friends as they approached a reception desk stacked with park maps, contest times and locations, and schedules for the entertainment events.

"Welcome! I'm R. C. Richter, president of the Hudsonville Chamber of Commerce and head judge of Hog Fest. Thank you kindly for agreeing to be our celebrity judges this weekend." He smiled at them, though it was clear that he wanted to dispense with the formalities and get down to business. "I trust you're finding the Inn at Fox Hall satisfactory? Eleanor Fiennes works very hard to please her guests."

"It's simply divine!" Gillian gushed. "Why, I saw so many species of birds on the nature walk I took after lunch that I felt like I was in a sanctuary."

As Gillian took a breath to describe Fox Hall in more detail, James put a hand on his friend's shoulder to silence her. He then answered R.C.'s question. "The inn is great, thank you. But I'm sure you're very busy and would like to give us the lay of the land before the festival begins."

R.C. nodded gratefully. "Yes. Please follow me, folks. I have name badges for you. Kindly wear them at all times. They are your tickets to restricted areas around the festival. They'll also get you discounts at the majority of the vendor booths. Of course, any entertainment you'd be interested in attending is free of charge. Just show the ticket takers your name badges and they'll let you in."

"Wow. We're getting the red-carpet treatment. I'd better check out which singers are performing. I love country music." Lindy grabbed several schedules from the reception desk and glanced at them as the group moved down a long hall to a conference room.

R.C. directed them to take a seat in one of the maroon leather chairs. "The Hog Queen Contest will take place after the opening ceremony events. At eight p.m., the contestants will be paraded down a length of purple carpet. The name and weight of each contestant will be announced, and your duty will be to judge each female on her size, personality, grace, and costume." He grinned. "Unlike most beauty contests, the more a contestant weighs, the higher her score. But it's not always the biggest sow that wins. Some of their owners can get quite creative with their costumes."

Lucy took out a small notebook from her bag. "So we have four categories?"

"And each category should be given a score of one to ten?" James asked because he didn't want to make any errors.

R.C. gave an affirmative nod to both questions. "I must also emphasize an important point. The owners, regardless of their appearance *or* behavior, are not to be considered as part of the contestant judging. I'm sorry to say that some owners have tried to bribe judges in the past. I know that you five will remain unmoved by such attempts, but I thought I should warn you all the same."

"Do some of the owners dress up like their pigs?" Bennett joked.

"Indeed they do, Mr. Marshall." R.C. reddened slightly. "Some barely dress at all. Allow me to show you a slide from last year's contest."

When R.C. reached over to hit the light switch, James noticed that the armpits of his shirt were stained with sweat.

I wouldn't want to run this show, James thought.

Once the lights were off, R.C. projected an image from his laptop onto the white screen at the end of the room. It showed an enormous and rather hairy-looking black sow wearing a pink tutu. A pink ribbon had been tied around her ear. The photo had been taken directly in front of the judges' table and the owner, a rather large woman stuffed into a matching tutu, was caught in the middle of an awkward attempt at a plié. The impression she achieved, however, was of a person with a severe case of constipation.

"My, my," Gillian uttered.

"Is this last year's winner?" Lucy's eyes glimmered with amusement.

R.C. turned the lights back on. "I believe this contestant was one of the more memorable entries, but she didn't win. I just wanted you to get a sense of what you'll be seeing tonight. Of course, there's no way for an individual sow's personality to come across on-screen."

"What kind of personality can a pig have?" Bennett mumbled, but R.C. overheard.

"You'd be surprised, Mr. Marshall. Some of these ladies will trot up the carpet like a thoroughbred racehorse. Some will give you flirty snorts or roll their eyes. There are plenty of ways the contestants can stand out from the field."

"I appreciate the respectful manner in which you refer to these contestants," Gillian said, beaming at R.C. "I was afraid that this contest might belittle these lovely and intelligent animals, but I can see that you approach this pageant with a high degree of dignity. I applaud you!" Gillian clapped her hands as R.C. blushed.

Just then, R.C.'s walkie-talkie began to crackle and he excused himself to respond to what sounded like an urgent stream of babble. As the supper club members watched him from his place near the door, they saw the veil of sweat on his forehead began to drip down his temple. He dug a red bandana from his pocket and dabbed at his face. "Are you sure?" he asked the person on the other end before hurriedly adding, "Over."

"I'm sure, boss," came the reply amid a fresh crackle of static.

R.C. replaced the walkie-talkie into the case on his belt. "I need to beg a favor. Four of our judges, who happen to be family members, have contracted pink eye. Due to the fact that they're contagious until their antibiotics take effect twenty-four hours from now, they've withdrawn from judging the Brisket category. Could I ask four of you to step into their shoes?"

Gillian put her hand to her breast. "I simply cannot come face-to-face with that much meat. I'm sorry."

James exchanged glances with the rest of his friends. They issued subtle nods. "The rest of us would be glad to help," he said.

R.C. exhaled in relief. "I do thank you. We'll be reviewing the judging policies for the food contests in the morning." He distributed schedules and a baggie filled with red tickets to the supper club members. "These tickets are for the food vendors around the festival. Each ticket is good for a single item. Should you need more, just show the receptionist your name badge and she'll refill your baggie. We have a small token of our appreciation for each of you as well, which we'll present to you tonight at the Hog Queen contest."

The head judge led them back to the main doors of the recreation center and then marched off to solve a dispute between two barbecue contestants over a parking spot.

"That guy will need a stiff drink by the time the day is done," Bennett said.

"I'm kind of parched myself," Lucy said, shaking her bag of red tickets. "Let's go spend some of these."

"This is so much fun!" Lindy squealed as they approached the food vendors. "I feel like a kid who just got birthday money from her grandparents."

Suddenly, a deep voice boomed over a loudspeaker, welcoming all visitors to the town of Hudsonville and the sixteenth Hudsonville Hog Fest, sponsored by the Hudsonville Chamber of Commerce and Richter's RV Sales & Rentals.

"As soon as the mayor cuts the pink ribbon at the entrance gates," the voice proclaimed, "Hog Fest will officially be under way! Don't forget to visit Richter's RVs for the best motor homes this side of the Appalachians!"

James and his friends ceased paying attention as the announcer listed locations for maps, ticket sales, and restrooms.

"I'm getting a hot sausage with onions and peppers before the mob shows up," Bennett said, pointing at a booth selling Italian sausages and all-beef hot dogs.

"Me too," Lindy agreed. "But without the peppers and onions."

Gillian twisted a strand of orange hair on her finger. "What am I going to eat at this place? I'm either going to starve or survive on a diet of greasy fries."

"Come on." James steered her toward a nearby vendor. "It's not all pig or fried foods. Just smell the aroma of roast corn on the cob." He handed two tickets to a woman wearing a green apron. "Your corn smells delicious."

"Thanks, hon. It's roasted with enough butter to stop your heart."

James smiled at her. "In that case, we'll take two heart attacks on a stick."

The five friends filled their empty bellies with sausage and corn and shared two elephant ears. After they dusted confectioners' sugar from their pants, they decided to check out the area where the barbecue contests would take place.

The judging area consisted of a large white tent erected on the park's soccer field. The two tent openings were cordoned off by thick pink twine. A sign taped to the twine warned that admittance was granted to contest officials only and that any contestants entering without permission would be instantly disqualified.

"This barbecue contest is so serious. I had no idea it was such a big deal!" Lindy exclaimed, and shifted through the schedules in her hand. "Are the prizes listed anywhere?"

James pointed at an orange sheet of paper. "The festival champion gets the biggest prize. That person receives ten thousand dollars, a new commercial trailer cooker—valued at almost nine thousand—and a contract with Heartland Foods. You heard Jimmy at lunch. That contract's worth a ton of money."

"Who's Jimmy?" Gillian poked at a piece of corn caught in her lower teeth with her fingernail. "Did you have lunch with a barbecue aficionado?"

"You could say that." Bennett grunted. "Mostly, we watched as he inhaled enough food for three people."

"That's because half of it ended up on his shirt, the tablecloth, and his beard," Lindy scoffed.

"He's one of the contestants," James told Gillian. "He has, ah, a rather *loud* personality. And he calls himself the Pitmaster."

"According to this schedule, everyone competes in teams." Lindy studied the orange paper. "Jimmy's team is called the Pitmasters, but there are five other teams competing." She grinned. "You guys are going to love these names. The other teams are the Thigh and Mighties, an all-female team called Adam's Ribbers, the Marrow Men, the Tenderizers, and the Finger Lickers. Each team has a leader, or spokesperson, and theirs is the only name listed in the program. The leaders turn in the team's food to the judges."

The group climbed a small hill leading to the cooking area. "It makes sense to cook as part of a team," Bennett said. "That way, you can enter every category and have a better chance at winning. According to this rule sheet, most of these guys will be taking turns staying up all night. Some of these entries, like barbecued brisket, take more than a day to cook."

"Looks like they've already started." Lucy gestured at the campground area spread below them.

The five friends paused, taking in the view of hundreds upon hundreds of RVs parked alongside one another in remarkably straight rows for what seemed like miles. Striped awnings had been unfurled, and lawn chairs and folding tables had been unfolded. Music poured out of boom boxes, while American flags or banners representing favorite sports teams flew from camper roofs. Some of the travelers had even put down outdoor carpet to make their temporary parcels homier.

But one piece of equipment was the centerpiece of each campsite: the grill. There were grills of all shapes and sizes. James spotted tiny camping grills; full-sized backyard grills with propane tanks; egg-shaped cookers; and enormous, cylinder-shaped cookers that required their own trailers and were no doubt used by the professional barbecue teams.

"Those things are so big they have to be towed behind the RVs," Bennett said, looking at one of the professional cookers. "I've seen European cars smaller than these grills. You could hide two grown men inside." He inhaled blissfully. "Ah! Folks are cooking meat, all right."

Gillian frowned at him. "You just ate. How can you possibly be enticed?"

"I can eat more later, woman," Bennett replied pleasantly. "You know, they'll have chicken barbecue here, too. You don't have to eat corn and hush puppies the whole time, unless you're going full-scale vegetarian on us this weekend."

Gillian stared at the grills and curtains of smoke with distaste. "That's my preference."

"Let's check out what the teams look like," Lucy suggested, hoping to distract Gillian. "I'd like to meet the all-female team."

James hesitated. "Are we supposed to fraternize with the contestants?"

Lucy shrugged. "We haven't been given the food-judging guidelines yet. As of now, we're just tourists and I find this all pretty fascinating."

Gillian studied her map. "I would prefer to view the sand-drawing event. It's being held in Area C. The combination of flowing sand and graceful motion is very soothing. Would anyone care to join me?"

Receiving no offers, Gillian told her friends she'd see them at the Hog Fest beauty contest.

"Poor Gillian." Lindy watched their friend stride away in a flowing skirt of lavender with tiny brass bells stitched around the hem. "I hope she'll be able to enjoy herself at this festival."

"She will." Bennett waved off Lindy's concern. "Did you get a load of all those hippie vendors? And what about the trained dog performances? And she loves our hotel. She can take nature walks for the rest of the festival once we're done picking the piggy princess."

As the foursome strolled by RVs the size of commercial buses, they heard the familiar voice of Jimmy Lang. He had his arm slung around a familiar-looking young woman. The supper club members slowed in order to witness their exchange, Jimmy whispered something into the girl's ear, gave her a light swat on the bottom, and laughed as she waved goodbye.

"Wasn't that Eleanor's daughter?" Lindy asked, appalled.

Just then, the side door of a mid-sized RV opened, and a plump woman with blond hair and black roots stepped down onto the trampled grass, eyeing Jimmy warily. "Who you talkin' to, Jimmy?"

"No one, Sugar Lips," Jimmy said hastily. "Your Big Daddy's sure thirsty, though." Once again, Jimmy was sweating profusely. "Can you be a doll and get me a cold one?"

The woman pulled her tank top down over a roll of exposed flesh and said, "Sure, hon."

At that moment, Jimmy looked up and saw the supper club members staring at him.

"Why, if it ain't the beauty judges!" His flaky lips peeled back in a smile, revealing his yellow teeth. "I'm glad you popped by. I've got some ribs that are just 'bout ready to eat. Gotta wait 'til the bark's just right."

"The bark?" Bennett asked, his eyes sparkling with curiosity.

"Yessir. That's the crust of rub that forms on the outside of the meat when it's been cooking loooong and slooooow. It's so good, you'd think you'd died and gone to heaven." Jimmy swung around as the woman reappeared with his beer. "Thanks, darlin'. Y'all, this is my gal, Hailey."

James and his friends shook hands with Jimmy's girlfriend. James figured Jimmy was about fifty years old, and Hailey was easily ten years Jimmy's junior. A tattoo of a dove flew across the round swell of her left breast, and James couldn't help but stare at the revealed flesh. Noting his gaze, Hailey pulled down the tank top, revealing a fuchsia lace bra and the rest of the dove's body.

"Isn't she purty?" She grinned at James. "I did some time in juvey. Had a drug problem until I found Jesus. Now, I'm clean and free as a dove, which is why I got this tattoo. Those were the only good things that came out of all my days as a user. This tattoo and my Jimmy Bear. 'Course, he's clean now, too."

"That's right, baby." Jimmy looked less than pleased by Hailey's confession. Wiping his puffy face with a dishcloth, he said, "Why don't you fetch these fine folks some brewskis? They's judgin' the pig contest in a bit and are gonna need a bit of a buzz." He took a pull of his beer and frowned. "Just doesn't taste like it used to."

"That's okay, thanks," Lucy quickly said to Hailey. "We're really full."

James made a show of looking at his watch. "And we'd better head over to the contest area."

As he and his friends began to turn away, a woman dragging several small dogs behind her passed by Jimmy's cooking area. She stopped abruptly when she saw Jimmy and Hailey. Her eyes narrowed and her lips curled in anger and disgust. To James's surprise, the trim and petite woman marched over and spat on the closed lid of Jimmy's cooker.

"I hope your meat rots on the bone!" she hissed. "I hope your sauce tastes like mashed maggots! I hope that you lose every single contest you enter for the rest of your life!" She spat on the cooker again as Jimmy stood in amused silence, his meaty arms crossed over his formidable gut. The smile playing around the corners of his mouth only incensed the woman further.

"You redneck bastard! I hope you drown in beer and barbecue sauce and bad luck! I hope you get *exactly* what you deserve in this life!" She looked at Hailey. "You're with a *bad* man. He's going to bring you down. Mark my words."

She tugged on the leash and stormed off.

Hailey issued Jimmy a bewildered look, but Jimmy simply

saluted the departing woman with his beer. Then, he shouted, "Everybody hates a winner!"

His tone was downright jolly. "Yessir. That's me! There's losers all over this here festival, but I ain't one of 'em!" His shouts attracted the attention of the competing teams, who broke off conversations in order to listen to the bellows of the Pitmasters' leader.

"That's right!" Jimmy called out to them. "You can count on nothin' but second place, suckers! I've got the secret to perfect 'cue and you ain't got it! I'm the winner! I'm the champion! I'm the future face of Heartland's barbecue line. Y'all can go on and pack up now. Save yourselves the trouble. Jimmy's here, and Jimmy's as good as won! Y'all hearin' me?" He guffawed. "Y'alls' entry fees are goin' straight into my pocket. So this Bud's for you! Thanks for givin' me a little more spendin' money!"

Most of the men and women standing around their cookers scowled angrily at Jimmy, but no one responded to his taunts. Several flipped him the bird, and one of the women from Adam's Ribbers stuck out her tongue, but the majority of the competitors chose to ignore his boasts.

Jimmy walked back to his cooker, lifted the lid, and began to remove foil-wrapped meat from within using a pair of metal tongs. He whistled while he worked, as if his behavior was perfectly acceptable. James couldn't help but notice Hailey's face as she stood on the RV's steps. Her gaze was fixed on a point somewhere behind James.

Her eyes were wide with fear.

Before James could discover the source of Hailey's dread, Lucy grabbed him by the arm and pulled him away. "Come on, James. We can't keep the future Queen of Hog Fest waiting."

Chapter Six

Pig-Shaped Strawberry Cupcakes

Hundreds of onlookers were gathered around the park's outdoor track to watch the Queen of Hog Fest Beauty Contest.

Gillian, who was already seated in a high-back chair at the judges' table, broke off her animated conversation with R. C. Richter to wave her friends over.

"Look!" she cried, gesturing at their table. "Isn't this elegant? These touches of finery make me feel very appreciated."

The setup was impressive. Their table had been draped with a pink linen cloth and bunting in a darker shade of pink encased the perimeter. Crystal water goblets with matching pitchers had been placed at each judge's spot. Saucers with slices of fresh lemons and limes were positioned next to the pitchers. Gillian poured water into her glass and motioned for her friends to follow her lead.

"We're going to need plenty of pure and refreshing spring water, my friends. The local baker, Mrs. Phelps, has made us a special treat." She smiled, her good humor returning in the face of such royal treatment. "R.C. told me that Mrs. Phelps is bringing us strawberry cupcakes. They're so famous that people have been known to drive down here from DC to buy a dozen."

"Yes, indeed." R.C. smiled with pride. "Mrs. Phelps uses real pieces of strawberry in the icing, and she frosts all the cupcakes upside down so there's more buttercream per square inch." He looked up as a woman in her early seventies carrying a covered tray approached the table. "Here she comes now."

"Welcome, folks!" Mrs. Phelps gave them a hearty smile and placed the tray on the table. With a flourish, she removed the domed top and waited for a reaction.

All of the supper club members murmured appreciative *oohs* and *ahs* when they saw the confections. Five pink cupcakes sat in the center of five china plates drizzled with strawberry glaze. Each cupcake bore a unique pig's face, complete with candy eyes, a cookie nose, and strawberry wafer ears. No two cupcakes were alike, for Mrs. Phelps had added sparkly sprinkle eye shadow, licorice lace eyelashes, a chocolate-chip beauty mark, pursed lips made from

Red Hots, or powdered cheeks created with white gumdrops.

"Enjoy!" she told the judges and winked at R.C. "I've got one for you, too, Mr. Richter. I left it in your office because I figured you were too busy to eat right now."

"Thank you, Mrs. Phelps. I hope you have plenty of extra help this weekend, because after I mention your shop in this evening's announcements, folks are going to be lined up, elbow to elbow, waiting to buy your delicious homemade goodies."

Mrs. Phelps beamed at him. "Oh, I have plenty of help, sir. This festival keeps me alive durin' the leaner months. That's why all of us in Hudsonville are right thankful for your hard work."

"It's my pleasure, Mrs. Phelps." R.C. colored, embarrassed by the compliment.

The baker appeared to be in no hurry to leave. "'Course, I'm sure it's the same for you and your RV business. I bet you get plenty of sales after folks feast their eyes on the fancy trailers you've got on display in the barbecue area." Suddenly, Mrs. Phelps caught a glimpse of her digital watch and gave a little yelp. "Well, good luck, y'all!" she told the judges, took one last look at her baked handiwork, and disappeared into the crowd.

"It sounds like this festival generates good revenue for the majority of the local businesses," James said to R.C.

"Our coffers would certainly be emptier without it," R.C. agreed. "And Hog Fest grows bigger and bigger every year. I'm very proud of its success. Why, Hudsonville has been featured in fifteen national magazines because of our little barbecue party."

"Have you always lived here?" Lindy asked.

R.C. nodded. "My whole life." His eyes passed over the faces in the crowd. "Everyone I love is here. My business is here. My roots are here. The woman I love is here. Yes, this town is *everything* to me," he added passionately before clearing his throat. "Excuse me, but it's time for the contest to get under way. I'm going to make a few announcements and we'll get started. Are you all ready?"

"Bring on those sexy sows!" Bennett declared, and Gillian shot him a dirty look.

"We're all set," Lucy said. She then took a delicate bite of her cupcake. "Wow," she breathed. "Wow! I'll come back and judge every year if I can have more of these."

"What about your protein diet?" James teased.

"Forget it," Lucy said lightheartedly. "I'm on vacation with my best friends. I'm going to eat whatever I want. At least, for tonight."

"Hear! Hear!" Lindy clinked forks with Lucy as R.C. stepped up to the microphone.

After plugging his own business and encouraging the captive crowd to patronize the Main Street Bakery, R.C. introduced each of the supper club members and painted an extremely favorable, if not a little embellished, picture of their role in solving crimes in the Shenandoah Valley.

The audience responded with boisterous cheers and the supper club members were humbled by the attention. With the exception of Lindy, who waved at the crowd like a state dignitary, they were relieved when R.C. invited the first contestant to make her way to the strip of purple carpet emerging from the opening of a large tent. This was where the beauty queen hopefuls waited. The carpet passed by the judges' table and ended in a small pen where the contestants and their owners were required to wait while the judges came to their final decisions.

"Our first contestant is Little Miss Twinkletoes!" R.C. hollered.

The crowd roared as a massive pink pig stepped onto the carpet. She wore a silver skirt and a wreath of silver stars encircled her forehead. Her ears were longer than James had expected, and they flopped up and down as Little Miss Twinkletoes trotted down the carpet. As she came closer to the table, James noticed that her leathery skin was covered with silver glitter. Her owner was dressed in a silver evening gown that revealed a generous amount of cleavage, and her eyelids sparkled with the same silver glitter adorning her pig.

Stopping in front of the table, the woman turned Little Miss Twinkletoes in a circle before the judges and said, "Dance, Twinkletoes!"

The sow lifted up her front hooves one at a time and snorted. Pleased, her owner blew some glitter in the judges' direction and led her pig to the holding pen.

"Damn it," Bennett grumbled after the owner was out of earshot. "That woman got fairy dust in my cupcake." Scowling, he pushed his plate away and made fierce marks on his score sheet.

"Remember, you can't judge the *contestant* based on the behavior of its *handler*," Gillian chided. "Don't pout. You can have some of mine." She cut off a portion of her cupcake and placed it on Bennett's napkin.

The next pig was named Ms. Harley. She was dressed in a leather skirt and a metal-spiked collar. Harley seemed bored by the entire event and had to be dragged down the carpet by her owner, a fearsome-looking lady bodybuilder wearing leather pants and studded boots. Her white ribbed tank top was stretched so tightly over her muscular torso that the judges could see the shadow of a black bra beneath the thin cotton top.

After Harley labored off to the pen, the judges were introduced to Jasmine, an enormous black pig dressed as a hula dancer; Cherub, a brown-spotted pig wearing wings and a halo; Candy, who wore the trademark Playboy bunny ears and tail; and Annie, a spunky sow sporting a cowboy hat and a red bandana.

Bennett's eyes grew into round moons as a pig named Hot Stuff strutted onto the carpet clothed in a gold sequined bikini and a sunbonnet. It wasn't the pig that caught Bennett's attention, however. Her owner, who led her animal using a silk ribbon instead of a piece of rope, wore a matching string bikini that barely covered her bits. Smiling at the barrage of whistles and catcalls from the male members of the audience, the curvaceous woman shook her derriere. As she did so, Hot Stuff wiggled hers, and the crowd broke into raucous laughter, followed by some lewd commentary from a handful of men.

"Where is that woman's dignity?" Gillian huffed, marking her score sheet.

"Remember," Bennett said, poking Gillian in the ribs with his pencil. "You can't judge the owner, just the pig!"

James's favorite contestant was a pig so large that her belly almost swept the ground as she waddled down the carpet. Her name was Barbie Eden, and she wore filmy pantaloons and a veil like the original *I Dream of Jeannie*. Barbie's walk was deliberate and graceful, and when she reached the judges' table, she dipped her head, blinked her eyes, and wriggled her wide snout.

The delighted audience chanted Barbie's name.

Finally, all of the contestants were contained in the holding pen, awaiting the announcement of the victor. The queen would be crowned with a golden wreath, and a sash proclaiming her as the sovereign of Hog Fest would be placed around her neck.

To the immense relief of the supper club members, who had little experience with large swine, R.C. had volunteered to handle these tasks. Once she was crowned, the queen would take a final walk on the purple carpet and then head home for a good night's sleep. The next day, she would ride in the backseat of a convertible from the recreation center to the barbecue contest area. Her arrival would symbolize the official beginning of the cook-off portion of the festival, as well as the first day of her new life as a local celebrity.

James had no trouble tabulating his scorecard. He voted for Barbie Eden to win. Bennett, who sat on his left, chose Hot Stuff. Gillian shielded her clipboard as if it contained the blueprints to a new weapon of mass destruction, but as R.C. held out his hand for her score sheet, James saw that she'd picked Twinkletoes. R.C. collected scorecards from Lindy and Lucy, glanced over all five of them, and smiled.

"We have a winner," he said to the judges, thanked them, and approached the microphone.

"Ladies and gentlemen, we have seen some lovely females tonight. Let's give them all a hearty congratulations." He paused while the crowd whooped, whistled, and applauded for the pigs and their owners. "We've seen talent, creativity, and the beauty of extra pounds this evening. However, only one contestant can be named the Queen of Hudsonville Hog Fest. That lucky lady will enjoy a life of fame and leisure on a local Hudsonville farm, and her owner and a guest will be treated to a wonderful, all-expense-paid trip to Jamaica along with five hundred dollars in spending money. Sounds like the *royal* treatment to me."

He waited, allowing the dramatic moment to build. "Is everyone ready to hear the winning name?" The crowd cheered and R.C. grinned indulgently. "All right, folks, I won't make you wait a second longer. I am proud to announce that the winner of this year's pageant, weighing in at four hundred and forty-four pounds, goes to none other than Miss Barbie Eden."

Barbie's owner shrieked in delight and gave her pig a big kiss on the snout. Barbie grunted in return and calmly accepted her crown and sash. Barbie took another walk on the purple carpet while the theme song for Miss America played on the loudspeakers and camera flashes created a disco-ball effect. As James watched the new queen on parade, he couldn't help but think that the music reminded him of Jimmy Lang and how the loudmouthed barbecue expert had sung the same song during lunch at Fox Hall.

Once Barbie reached the end of the carpet, R.C. removed an envelope from his coat, handed it to Barbie's owner, and thanked the judges once again for their time. As the spectators began to disperse, R.C. returned to the judges' table and indicated that gift bags for all five of them were being held behind the reception desk in the recreation center.

"There's a box of truffles in each bag and I didn't want the chocolate to melt." He gazed up at the star-pocked sky. "Mind you, it's been quite pleasant tonight, but it's going to be a scorcher tomorrow, so be sure to have your water bottles filled to the brim." After wishing them a pleasant evening, R.C. reminded James, Lindy, Bennett, and Lucy to appear for the mandatory food-judging meeting at ten a.m. sharp.

"How long's that going to take?" Bennett asked. "Don't we just say whether we like the food or not?"

"Mr. Marshall, this contest is quite serious." R.C.'s pleasant demeanor turned firm. "There are many facets to being a fair and discerning barbecue judge."

Abashed, Bennett nodded. "Don't worry, I'll follow every rule to the letter. I'm really looking forward to getting an inside view on this whole thing."

R.C. seemed mollified by Bennett's answer. He was about to turn away, undoubtedly to tend to another festival duty, when he seemed to remember something. "You'll also find a red raffle ticket in your gift bags. Most folks pay ten dollars apiece for these, but if you're lucky enough, you could be returning to Quincy's Gap towing a brand-new RV trailer behind your vehicle, courtesy of Richter's RV Sales & Rentals."

"That would get me half a bookmobile," James said to his friends as R.C. vanished into the crowd.

"What are you using for one in the meantime?" Lucy asked.

"Wendell rigged up one of the retired school buses in his yard.

He's basically toting books around in plastic bins strapped to the decrepit seats with bungee cords, but it's better than nothing."

Lindy pulled one of the festival schedules out of her purse. "Okay, fellow celebrities, what do you want to do now? I'd like to check out the rockabilly concert. It just started a few minutes ago. We have free entry to all of the events."

Gillian glanced at her watch. "I'd normally be meditating to clear my head before sleep about now, but I'll go with you. I do like rockabilly music."

"I'm in, too," said Lucy. "Besides, you need me, seeing as I'm your chauffeur." She turned to James, her eyes hopeful. "What about you guys?"

"I'm hitting the trivia books," Bennett said. "But if you want to stay, James, I can hike back to the inn from here. It's only a few miles."

James shook his head. "No need. This heat's made me kind of sluggish. We'll pick up the gift bags and take them back to Fox Hall," James told the ladies, trying not to ignore the disappointment in Lucy's face. He wondered if Lucy planned to cozy up to him over the next few days. After all, Murphy was over a hundred miles away.

He watched Lucy and his other female friends walk away, stopping to chat with the owners of the beauty contestants. Again, he couldn't stop himself from staring at Lucy's streamlined body or noticing how her caramel-colored hair glimmered beneath the strings of white lights forming a canopy over the animal pen. He'd always thought she was smart, interesting, and beautiful, and nothing about their roller-coaster relationship would ever change that fact.

"Hey, man!" Bennett waved his hand in front of James's eyes. "You coming or what?"

"Yeah." James looked away from Lucy just as she turned back to see if he was still standing there.

James and Bennett collected five Hog Fest tote bags stuffed with goodies from the recreation center before heading to the parking lot. The car lot was adjacent to the camper area, and James noticed that more and more people were gathered around their barbecue cookers. Plumes of smoke drifted into the night, and the glow of lit cigarettes made the cooking area seem as though it had been overrun by a swarm of fireflies. Raucous laughter filled the air, and

James guessed that bottles of beer and whiskey were being passed around among the cooking teams.

"They have to stay up all night?" he asked Bennett.

"At least one team member. They want to cook those briskets as slow as they can to make the meat as tender as prime filet mignon." He smacked his lips together. "Brisket has always been a favorite of mine. I can hardly wait to sample all the entries tomorrow. That's what I call a first-class Southern-style lunch. A big pile of meat and not much else. Yessir."

As James gazed down the aisles between campers, he saw the familiar bulk of Jimmy Lang behind one of the larger RVs. He was speaking to a taller man wearing a white T-shirt and cargo shorts. James was too far away to hear their conversation, but both men appeared agitated. The taller man's features were hidden behind a baseball cap worn low over his brow. The cap was black with a silver symbol on the front that was unfamiliar to James. The brim of the hat dipped up and down as the man forcefully bobbed his head. He was obviously trying to drive his point home.

Suddenly, the taller man took a threatening step toward Jimmy, raising his voice to an angry shout.

Jimmy wore his customary expression of amusement, but when the man finished yelling and stomped off, Jimmy's smile immediately vanished.

Unaware that James's attention was elsewhere, Bennett chatted about the festival events that he planned to attend the next day.

"You'd better read that barbecue book tonight," Bennett went on, but James didn't reply. He was too fixated on Jimmy's posture, for the large man had slumped back against the rear of the trailer. He bowed his head and hid his face in his hands.

This Jimmy bore little resemblance to the boisterous and cocksure man James had seen earlier in the day, the man who claimed he would be the festival's champion and be well on his way to a life of fame and fortune. This man seemed tired. He seemed dejected.

Though the barbecue contest had yet to begin, Jimmy Lang already looked defeated.

Chapter Seven

Blue Ribbon Brisket

James had never slept in the same room as Bennett before, and he wasn't sure if he could survive a second night as his roommate. Bennett studied his trivia books until well after midnight. He then fell asleep with the lamp on. Lying flat on his back with his arms stretched out, Bennett's mouth hung open, and the sounds erupting from his throat sounded like the contented snores of a hibernating grizzly bear.

By quarter after six in the morning, James gave up on sleep. Removing the pillows he'd piled over his head, he pulled on a pair of jeans and his favorite William & Mary sweatshirt, slid his bare feet into a pair of worn loafers, grabbed his book on the history of barbecue, and crept downstairs.

The stairs creaked as he descended. The entire first floor of the inn was silent. No one else seemed to be up and about, but James remembered reading that a coffee urn would be placed in the main hall every morning by six thirty.

I have ten minutes to wait, James thought. He hoped Eleanor would be punctual. In the meantime, he decided to take a seat in one of the front porch rockers. The morning sky was gray and a low mist hovered over the summer grass. Robins poked around for worms while jays pecked through the soil of the garden beds. There was a refreshing coolness to the early air that carried a faint hint of autumn.

James inhaled deeply and caught a whiff of rain. His mother always claimed that she could tell that rain was imminent by stepping outside, standing very still, and taking a deep breath. In the days before the Weather Channel, she'd been the family meteorologist and had never once been wrong. James had often grumbled about taking a golf umbrella to school when none of the other children were carrying one, but he also remembered sharing its shelter with the other kids while they waited at the bus stop.

"Rain can't be good for the festival," James spoke to his tranquil surroundings before opening his book to a section entitled "Presidential Barbecues." As he read about Lyndon Johnson's diplomatic dinners, which were conducted as family-style barbecues, James heard noises coming from the room behind him. Swiveling in his chair, he noticed that his rocker was directly in front of the kitchen window and that the window had been left open a crack.

"Coffee time," James murmured contentedly, glancing at his watch. He'd just decided to finish the section on Johnson before claiming the first cup when he heard Eleanor's voice from inside the kitchen.

"Francesca Fiennes! Where on God's green earth have you been?" she demanded angrily.

There was no response from Eleanor's daughter.

"I told you to be home by midnight, which I thought was a mighty generous curfew for a person of your tender years, and how do you thank me? By keeping me up all night, worrying that you'd been abducted or . . . something worse!" Eleanor paused and then cried, "I even called the sheriff, Francesca! I was *that* worried!"

"I was going to call you," Francesca said without a shred of remorse. "But my phone battery died. And then, it got later and later and I . . . just fell asleep. I was hanging out at the festival with a bunch of my friends and we crashed in someone's tent."

"Someone's *tent*?" Eleanor sounded horrified. "*Whose* tent?"

Francesca didn't answer and James heard the rattle of silverware.

"I asked you a question, young lady." Eleanor's tone was strained. "In case you've forgotten, you are still living under *my* roof. I work my fingers to the bone each and every day, and the money from this inn pays for your clothes, your phone with the *dead battery*, and your contest entry fees. So when I tell you to be home by midnight, you'd better be home by eleven fifty-nine!"

"I don't want you to pay for those stupid contests! I never asked you to spend money on them!" Francesca snapped. "I *told* you that I want to spend my free time tutoring disadvantaged kids. I want to be a teacher—not win a stupid modeling contract."

"We've been over this a *thousand* times." Eleanor was exasperated. "You can *be* a teacher *after* you've entered the Miss America contest. The judges will love your passion to help those needy little—" She broke off and then whispered fearfully, "Sweet Jesus! Are those love bites on your neck, Francesca?"

"They're called hickies, Ma. Get with the program."

James heard the crash of dishes.

"That's just great, Francesca! Are you trying to drive me to an early grave? So you were out all night with some boy, doing God knows what, and now your neck is full of those ugly red marks. You're *supposed* to be a princess today — not some roll-me-in-the-hay teenage tramp!" Eleanor drew in a ragged breath. "What boy coaxed you into his filthy, mildewed tent?"

There was a moment of silence and then Francesca calmly replied, "Who said I was with a boy? It could have been a man. An *older* man."

"Good Lord." James could almost visualize Eleanor grabbing the edge of the counter for support. "Please tell me that it wasn't that disgusting barbecue swine, Jimmy Lang."

"I can't kiss and tell," Francesca goaded her mother.

"I'll *kill* him!" Eleanor raged. "So help me, I will! I have plenty of pesticides and poisons to rid this world of that nasty pest! The thought of him touching my beautiful girl fills my throat with bile. Franny, how could you?" Eleanor wailed.

"Don't worry, Ma. I'll still be ready for my car ride with a pig, but I'm not going to follow your life plan for me much longer. I mean it!"

Seconds later, the front door slammed and Francesca appeared on the porch. She looked at James, keenly aware that he'd heard the entire exchange.

"Coffee's ready," she told him nonchalantly before heading toward one of the nature trails.

From inside the kitchen, James could hear the muffled sounds of Eleanor weeping.

• • •

Over a breakfast of sausage rolls, strawberries, and hunks of cheddar cheese, James told his friends about the altercation he'd overheard.

"Francesca and Jimmy Lang?" Lindy gave an involuntary shiver. Glancing around to make sure that none of the other guests were listening, she lowered her voice. "That's too gross to imagine."

Gillian examined the dregs of tea at the bottom of her china cup and frowned. "Do you think Eleanor was serious about having poison around the inn? She seems like the type of person who'd use natural pesticides. Maybe I shouldn't listen to any more of her herbal tea blend recommendations."

"Just because the woman has a nature trail doesn't mean she's down with all that organic, going green hype," Bennett told Gillian.

"Hype?" Gillian regarded Bennett with disdain. "We have *one* planet to call home, and if we don't take care of it—"

"If there's such a thing as global warming, then why is there a wintry chill on an August morning in Virginia? Tell me that!" Bennett asked. He was teasing Gillian, but she didn't know it.

"Because a cool front came down from the mountains. It's supposed to rain all afternoon and into the evening," Lucy informed her friends before Gillian became too upset. "I watched the local news while Lindy was curling her hair."

"Poor R.C.," Lindy sympathized while checking to make sure that her thick black hair was still falling the way she wanted it to. "And all those vendors counting on nice weather. Rain must really cut into their profits."

James swallowed the last of his coffee and set the mug back onto the table with a firm thud. "I hope it *does* rain. I can come back here and take a nap. My *roommate* sounds like a locomotive crashing into a cliff."

"Must've been lying on my back," Bennett said with a smirk. "Just give me a nudge so I roll to the side. I won't make a peep if you do that."

"You could have shared that little detail with me *before* last night," James replied sulkily. His friends laughed.

"Come on, sunshine." Bennett poked James in the side. "We don't want to keep R.C. waiting."

Lucy checked her watch. "Gillian, are you going to hang out here for a bit, or do you want a ride to the festival grounds now? Or I could just leave you my car, and Lindy and I can ride over with James and Bennett."

Gillian folded her hands in her lap and closed her eyes. "I've already been on a most restorative walk through the woods this morning. My soul has been refreshed by the wise spirits of those old trees. Can you imagine all the things they've witnessed since they were young saplings?" Spreading her arms out as if she planned to embrace the air, Gillian opened her eyes and cast a serene glance at Lucy. "I'll join you at Hog Fest because I'm going to watch the dog show. Mr. Richter has given me permission to hand out Pet Palace brochures to the audience members. He's such a generous spirit."

"Since we'll all be eating barbecue for lunch, you can meet us after we're done judging." Lindy held out a map to Gillian upon which she'd drawn a circle. "I checked out the vendor list and there's a Greek food booth near our judging area. You could get a salad and falafels before joining us for the announcement of the winner."

Gillian clapped with delight. "Thank you, Lindy! I've never met a chickpea I didn't like."

Bennett grimaced. "Let's get out of here, James. All this talk of vegetables might put me off my meat."

• • •

R.C. paced inside the tent where the judges would assess the food entries. A series of industrial floor fans spun noisily in all four corners and the tent felt refreshingly cool. Despite the temperate weather both inside and outside the tent, R.C.'s cheeks were flushed. As the four supper club members settled themselves at the table in the center of the room, R.C. pulled back the tent flap and examined the gray sky.

"He must be worried sick over the possibility of rain," Lindy whispered to her friends.

"The festival grounds are packed." Lucy shot R.C. a troubled look. "I really hope the rain will hold off."

As the foursome exchanged weather predictions, a couple in their late sixties entered the tent and greeted R.C. After shaking their hands, he led them to the available seats at the judges' table. He then cleared his throat and straightened his pink bow tie by a millimeter.

"Welcome, judges, and thank you for coming. I see you're all wearing your name badges. That's good." R.C. proceeded with introductions. "Mr. and Mrs. Connelly are seated on Mr. Henry's right. The Connellys own a steak restaurant in Blacksburg. They've judged for us for the past five years."

"We like to break free of the daily grind and come here for some down-home 'cue." Mr. Connelly grinned at James. "This your first time judging?"

When James nodded in affirmation, Mrs. Connelly reached over and patted his hand. "Oh! Y'all are in for a treat! The brisket competition is my personal favorite."

R.C. peeked out at the thick clouds again and coughed noisily. "If I may . . ." The six judges gave him their full attention. Consulting an index card, he began his lecture. "I would like to review the judging guidelines. First of all, please do not consume any alcohol prior to or during the judging session."

"Guess I'd better hand over my flask!" Mr. Connelly kidded.

Ignoring the playful outburst, R.C. continued. "Please do not socialize with the contestants prior to the judging. As of this moment, you should refrain from entering the cooking area. All entries will be placed before you and marked by a number. You will taste the item — in this case, brisket — and score the entry."

"How much can we eat?" Bennett asked.

"That is an excellent question, Mr. Marshall." R.C. looked thoughtful. "Eat enough to be able to score the food, but pace yourself. You'll be consuming a fair amount of brisket this morning, and as you know, brisket isn't light fare."

James raised his hand.

For the first time since their arrival at the tent, R.C. cracked a smile. "Yes, Mr. Henry?"

"Can we talk to each other while we're eating?"

R.C. shook his head. "No. There must be absolute silence during the tasting. We wouldn't want you to influence another judge's decision. You may talk only *after* you've written down the scores for each entry. Now, here are the scorecards. You'll see that you'll be judging the meat based on a scale of one to ten, one being the worst meat you've ever tasted and ten being a bite of pure heaven."

"It says here that we're scoring based on appearance, tenderness, and taste." Lucy looked confused. "How do we judge appearance?"

"If the entry is placed before you and it looks like something you'd like to dig right into, then the presentation should be given a high score. Here's a list of illegal garnishes." R.C. handed each of them a sheet of paper. "If any of the entries are served with these garnishes, they will be disqualified."

James consulted the list of contraband garnishes. It included endive, radish, cabbage, kale, red leaf lettuce, or any other vegetables. The only acceptable garnishes were parsley, green lettuce, and cilantro.

"What the heck does kale look like?" Bennett mumbled in James's ear. When James shrugged, Bennett pulled nervously at his toothbrush mustache. "Where's Gillian when we need her?"

"If the meat's on something green and leafy, then it's probably a legal garnish," James said, but he was beginning to feel anxious about the level of detail required in being a food judge.

R.C. consulted another index card. "If there are no further questions on garnishes, I would like you to recite the judges' pledge located on the bottom of your scorecard. Please read it aloud with me now."

James recited the words: "I, James Henry, pledge to judge today's food with objectivity and integrity. I will abide by all of the judging guidelines and will do my best to ensure a fair and just contest."

"Goodness!" Lindy exclaimed with a nervous giggle. "I feel like I'm under oath in a court of law."

R.C. took a step toward her. "You have a very important role in our festival, Ms. Perez. I'd like to remind you all just how significant the barbecue contests are to the public's general impression of Hog Fest. Hudsonville depends on this event and, therefore, our town is depending on you as a judge."

Lindy's mouth hung open and Bennett mopped his brow with a paper napkin from the pile stacked on the table.

Relaxing a little, R.C. checked his watch again. "Why don't you all chitchat for a few minutes? The first entry should be arriving any moment now."

James was still anxious and turned to the Connellys for reassurance. They promised him that there was nothing difficult about being a food judge, as the scoring was all based on personal preference. They added that the blue-ribbon winner was usually the entry that the majority of judges loved best. It always outshone all the other entries.

"The hardest part is scoring the first entry," Mr. Connelly explained. "Because you have nothing to compare it to. That's why none of the barbecue teams want to go first. It's just the luck of the draw if your team gets picked to go to the head of the line." His face brightened. "And here comes the first brisket now."

James turned to see a pair of attractive young women wearing red-and-white-checked aprons place a foam takeout container in front of every judge. Each container was filled with slices of glistening brisket. James pulled the meat closer, inspected the bed of shredded lettuce, and noted that some of the edges of the garnish had turned an unappealing brown. The bark of the meat was covered in globs of sauce, some of which had dripped onto the lettuce. James felt that the presentation could have been stronger and gave the entry a five in the appearance category.

After spearing a piece of meat with his fork, James popped the brisket into his mouth. The initial taste was that of an overly sweet tomato sauce. In fact, James sensed that there was too much brown sugar or molasses in this particular sauce, though the meat itself was incredibly tender. He wrote down a nine for the tenderness category and a six for taste.

Deciding not to eat another bite, James swallowed some water and then watched as the Connellys and his friends completed their scorecards. After everyone scored the first entries, Bennett sat back in his chair and exhaled in relief. "Whew! That wasn't as tough as I thought it'd be."

"You're right," Lindy agreed. "I guess that's because we all love food, so we're naturals for this kind of thing."

Lucy dabbed at her mouth with a paper napkin. "Maybe we should start a business. Food Judges for Hire. We could judge barbecue contests, pie bake-offs, decide who makes the best fried chicken, chocolate cake, peanut brittle, casserole, food using maple syrup, sweet potatoes, strawberries . . ." She grinned. "Can you tell I'm feeling a bit burned out on my protein diet?"

James returned her grin and was about to compliment her again on her weight-loss success when the second entry was placed before the judges and the room instantly fell silent.

The entry was average overall, and James wrote down sixes for all three categories. The third entry was far superior to the first two. The brisket, which was nicely presented in a fanlike pattern over large lettuce leaves, was extremely tender and covered by a delicious smoky glaze that hinted of black pepper, garlic, and soy sauce.

"That one was really good," Lucy said after their scorecards had been collected.

"Definitely the best so far," Bennett concurred. "Wouldn't you like to know which entry is Jimmy's?"

"If he's as good as he claims, it might have been that last one," Lindy said and then made a zipping motion across her mouth as the fourth entry was brought in. The moment it was placed in front of the judges, Mr. Connelly held out his hand and shouted, "Stop!"

Concerned, R.C. scurried over to the table. "What is it, Mr. Connelly?"

"Well, I hate to say it, but this brisket is sitting on a bed of endive. Isn't that on the list of illegal garnishes?"

R.C. examined the entry and sighed. "You're correct, sir." He gestured to the two girls in the checkered aprons. "Ladies, please remove this entry and bring in the next."

Disappointed that he hadn't had the opportunity to sample the disqualified entry, James anticipated the arrival of the fifth entry. When it was put down before him, he immediately smelled something spicy. As he inhaled deeply, he realized that the brisket had been arranged on a bed of fragrant cilantro. The garnish was a suitable accompaniment for the tender meat because it was distinctly spicier than the previous entries. James chewed, savoring the hints of paprika, cayenne pepper, and onions. The flavor reminded him slightly of chili and was certainly a distinct entry. He gave the entry high scores.

After the score sheets were turned in, Mrs. Connelly drank her entire glass of water and then waved at one of the girls to refill her glass. "I think I got a piece of jalapeño in mine!" She gasped, her eyes watering. "My mouth is on fire!"

R.C. offered her a package of saltines. "Bread is better than water if your tongue is burning." He waited until she'd eaten all of the crackers and seemed to have regained some feeling back in her mouth. "Are you able to continue?" he asked her.

Wiping tears from her cheeks, she nodded. "I'm fine. I just think my piece had some *extra* spice. I'm afraid that mistake is going to cost somebody."

The next entry tasted particularly fruity, but James couldn't pinpoint which fruit he was eating. The blend of the fruit flavors in combination with the meat was interesting, but James wouldn't have ordered the brisket in a restaurant. Like the first entry, it was simply too sweet. Even though he sensed the fruit and added sugars were made less intense by the addition of ginger and a salty flavoring that he couldn't identify, James didn't enjoy the combination.

"What was the fruit used in that sauce?" he asked the other judges once the entry had been whisked away.

"Mango," Lindy said. "I'd know that taste in a heartbeat. My Brazilian mama is wild about mangoes. I really liked that entry."

Bennett snorted. "Why would you go ruining a perfectly fine piece of meat with a mango? Would someone explain that to me? Bet it was that women's team, those Adam's Ribbers."

"That's mighty sexist of you, Bennett!" Lucy's blue eyes flashed angrily. "I think you should apologize. You have a tendency to demean—"

Lucy's tirade was instantly interrupted by the arrival of the final entry.

James instantly approved of the entry's appearance. The brisket had been sliced thin and laid out on a bed of curly leaf parsley. The ruffled leaves of the garnish set off the two-toned meat. Having read up on the entire process of barbecuing meat the night before, James now knew that the reddish-pink shade on the meat was caused by the smoke ring—the chemical reaction that occurred when the nitrates in the smoke blended with the protein in the meat. These brisket slices had a more dramatic smoke ring than any of the previous entries. James scored it a nine out of ten for appearance.

Pulling the meat from the fork with his front teeth, James was shocked by its tenderness. It practically disintegrated after the first chew. And then, there was the taste! James tried to chew slowly, but he simply couldn't. He hurriedly swallowed the first piece and then popped a second into his mouth. There it was again, the perfect blend of garlic, tomato, chili sauce, mustard, and brown sugar. As he shifted the meat over his tongue, he detected a trace of nutmeg and the most delicate hint of honey. In addition to all of these flavors was an underlying layer of Worcestershire infusion along with a breath of whiskey.

This is the best brisket I've ever had, James thought. He scored the entry another nine on tenderness and a ten on taste. He then continued eating, waving away one of the girls when she came to collect his plate.

Bennett did the same. "No, no! This is my lunch," he told the young woman.

R.C. reviewed the scorecards and seemed to tabulate which team had won very quickly. James assumed the champion brisket was the last entry. After all, everyone had kept their portion of the entry and seemed to still be relishing every forkful.

In the space of ten minutes, R.C. and two other men from the Hudsonville Chamber of Commerce had reviewed the scorecards and were prepared to announce the first-, second-, and third-place winners in the Best Brisket category. They asked the judges to exit the tent and join them by the podium, where the trophies and cash prizes would be awarded.

James saw Jimmy and Hailey standing expectantly in the front of the large crowd. Both Jimmy and his girlfriend wore bright red T-shirts that read *The Pitmaster Loves a Tender Butt.* The competing teams wore color-coordinated shirts, hats, or aprons. James noticed that Jimmy's team was the smallest. Most teams consisted of three or four members.

R.C. began his announcements by declaring that the entry from the Tenderizers had been disqualified due to the use of an illegal garnish. The three men in their team, wearing orange aprons bearing a black meat tenderizer in the center, began to shout at one another. Above their discord, the sound of Jimmy's hoarse laughter could be heard.

"Dumb asses!" he bellowed at them.

James thought Jimmy looked even worse than yesterday. His face was more swollen, and there were dark bags beneath his eyes. Of course, Jimmy wore his customary expression of amusement and was boldly launching insults at the competition just as he had the evening before.

"Mr. Lang." R.C. leaned toward Jimmy. Though he spoke away from the microphone, the warning in his voice was clear. "If you cannot behave in a civilized manner, I will ask you to leave the contest area."

"Sure thing, boss. I'll scoot off after you hand me my trophy!" Jimmy opened his arms, displaying a complete view of his enormous belly and sweat-soaked shirt.

Ignoring Jimmy, R.C. announced that the third-place winner, who would be awarded five hundred dollars in cash, was the Marrow Men. The audience cheered as a man wearing overalls and a chef hat embroidered with flames and the name of his team accepted an envelope and a white silk ribbon. R.C. then called for a representative from the second-place team, the Thigh and Mighties. After a middle-aged woman took the ribbon and the envelope from R.C.'s hand, she planted a big kiss on his cheek.

"This is our very first ribbon!" she exclaimed and waved it in the air.

The crowd applauded her loudly and several people shouted congratulatory phrases such as "You go, girl!" and "Cook that 'cue!"

One of the other men from the Chamber of Commerce collected a small trophy with a blue ribbon attached to its base in order to present it to the winner. When R.C. announced that the Pitmasters had been granted the first-place prize, Jimmy hollered with delight. The noise sounded strangled in his hoarse throat, but it was a triumphant sound all the same.

Pumping R.C.'s hand, Jimmy grabbed the microphone and said, "Get used to me, folks. I'm gonna be winnin' all the prizes this weekend." He then blew a kiss to Hailey and stepped to the side of the podium and surveyed the crowd, clearly wanting to bask in his victory a little longer. Trying his best to mask his irritation, R.C. reclaimed the microphone and started to explain the time schedule for the remainder of the barbecue contests.

"I'm gonna get another blue ribbon tomorrow!" Jimmy tried to shout, but the words came out as a croak.

It was at this moment that Gillian appeared in the front row of the crowd. She waved at her friends before her gaze fell on the figure of Jimmy Lang. As James and the other supper club members watched, Gillian stared at Jimmy, her eyes wide with shock. Slowly, as though her body found it difficult to function, Gillian walked toward Jimmy.

By this time, R.C. had completed his announcements and had switched off the microphone. The audience members had mostly dispersed, seeking lunch or their next round of entertainment. The barbecue contestants headed back toward the cooking area and Jimmy, who'd been busy smiling at himself in the reflection of his trophy, finally realized that the show was over. No one except Hailey waited to congratulate him.

When Jimmy saw that Gillian was blocking his path, he paused and grinned at her. "Hey there, Red," he said as though greeting a fan. "You waitin' to shake the winner's hand? Maybe take a picture with the famous Pitmaster?"

Gillian didn't answer. She kept staring at Jimmy, her face drained of all color. Her fists were clenched so tightly that her knuckles were moon-white, but her shoulders sagged as if a great weight had been placed upon her back.

Jimmy cupped the trophy under one arm and scratched his shaved head in confusion. "Do I know you from somewhere?" He waited while Gillian mutely stared. "Well, if you're gonna just stand there like you should be ridin' the short bus, then I'm gone! I'm Jimmy Lang, future champion of Hog Fest, and I have places to go."

Jimmy moved to brush by Gillian when, without warning, her right arm shot out like a hammer. Her fist struck Jimmy square in the nose.

"You know me!" Gillian shrieked as blood oozed forth from Jimmy's nose. She yelled in a voice torn with pain and grief—a voice her friends had never heard before. "And I know you! Not a day goes by that I don't wish *you* were rotting in the ground!"

James spoke Gillian's name, but she didn't hear him.

"How could I *ever* forget you, you bastard?" Tears streamed down Gillian's face. "And you *should* know me! You killed my husband. *You killed my husband!*"

Chapter Eight

Cucumber Tea Sandwiches

James was utterly floored by Gillian's words. He stared at his friend as if he'd never seen her before.

As for Gillian, she'd covered her face with her hands and was crying hard. Her shoulders shook as she drew one ragged breath after another.

James blinked once, twice. But the reality remained unchanged. Gillian had been married. Not only that, but Gillian had just accused Jimmy Lang of killing her husband.

She had a husband. The thought echoed on a loop through James's mind.

Turning to look at his other friends, James could tell from their expressions that they were just as flabbergasted by Gillian's words. Even Hailey was struck dumb. The only person who didn't appear the slightest bit surprised was Jimmy. Cradling his nose with his meaty hand, he backed away from Gillian, grabbed Hailey by the arm, and walked off toward the cooking area.

He never said a word.

Somehow, his departure broke the spell.

James rushed toward Gillian, his right arm extended with an offering of a paper napkin.

"It's okay," he softly whispered. "Gillian. It's okay. He's gone now."

Sensing that someone had spoken her name, Gillian raised a face awash in agony. Her eyes gazed unseeing at the napkin, at James, at the handful of gawking onlookers. Her closest friends stared numbly back at her, still too shocked to speak.

James felt helpless. He couldn't think of how to comfort Gillian. Just when he was about to ask if she'd like to sit down, she abruptly turned and bolted behind the tent, quickly disappearing in the mass of wandering festivalgoers.

"Gillian!" James called after her, but it was too late.

Lindy put a hand on his arm. "What just happened? What did I just hear?"

Instead of answering, Bennett walked back inside the tent where, moments ago, they'd all been happily assessing the virtues and vices of barbecued brisket. The other supper club members watched as he sank into one of the chairs and tugged at his mustache furiously. "Did Gillian actually say she had a husband?" he asked his friends as they dropped into the other chairs.

"Yes," Lucy said. She poured herself a glass of water from one of the pitchers on the table. She drank down the entire glass and then wiped her mouth with the back of her hand. "A husband supposedly killed by Jimmy Lang."

James shook his head. "None of you knew she'd been married?"

Lindy threw her hands wide in a gesture of helplessness. "Gillian never mentioned it before! Maybe there was something in her falafel. Maybe her breakfast tea was spiked! Maybe she hung out with some of those dog people after their show and smoked a . . . I don't know, a peace pipe! But *that*" — she pointed outside the tent as if Gillian still stood there — "that person was *not* the Gillian I know!"

James agreed with Lindy. Gillian was passionate about many topics, but she was also a calm, well-balanced person. The explosion they'd just witnessed, followed by the intense crying and the mad dash into the crowd, were behaviors someone else might exhibit. Gillian, their animal-loving, tree-hugging, orange-haired friend, who enjoyed tie-dying T-shirts or creating homeopathic remedies, wasn't prone to dramatic outbursts.

"What should we do?" James asked. "Whatever's going on, she's obviously distraught. We should look for her — make sure she's okay."

Lucy nodded. "You're right, James. But where did she go?"

"She'd want to get away from all this bustle," Lindy said. "She may head back to the inn."

"Why don't you take the Jeep and see if you can find her?" Lucy said to Lindy. She then turned to Bennett and James. "The three of us should split up. I could ask R.C. where the dog show people are staying and ask them if they saw or talked to Gillian before, well, before she came to meet us."

"Hold the phone, folks." Bennett was still yanking on his mustache. "Can we talk about what Gillian said? What if it's true? She had a man. And her man was killed by this Jimmy fellow." His dark eyes were lit with anger. "I'm going to talk to that loudmouth

SOB and see what he has to say for himself. You notice that he was quiet after Gillian blasted him. He didn't deny a thing."

"Well, she *did* clock him in the nose," Lindy pointed out. "I think he was trying to stop the blood flow."

"Hell of a shot too," Bennett said in admiration. "But I saw the big man's expression. I think that arrogant hillbilly recognized Gillian."

James couldn't shake the sound of the abject pain in Gillian's voice or the anguish etched on her face. "I'm going with you, Bennett. Let's get to the bottom of this whole thing right now."

Lucy held up her cell phone. "Call me if you guys find out anything," she said and hurried off.

As James and Bennett walked toward the cooking area, the sky mirrored their mood. Dark clouds, swollen with unshed rain, massed over their heads. A light wind, which foreshadowed the coming storm, pushed at flags, banners, and pinwheels. There was an urgent feeling among the crowd that hadn't been there an hour earlier. People moved more quickly, hoping to reach their next destination before the rain, and James noticed that some of the cooks had stowed their barbecue equipment. They were now equipped with windbreakers and coolers of beer. Gathering in groups, they sat on folding lawn chairs or the stoops of their campers and gossiped, sharing bottle openers and bags of potato chips while watching the sky.

For the professional teams, however, the weather was irrelevant. Their cookers were stoked, the smoke was rising, and the team members were huddled in earnest conversation. By this time, no doubt, word of the drama that occurred immediately after Jimmy won the brisket competition was spreading through the rows of RVs, folding campers, and travel trailers like a brushfire.

"I don't think we can just waltz up to his door and demand an explanation," James said. He felt a surge of his customary sense of caution return as soon as Jimmy's RV came into view.

"He might be outside." Bennett shook a festival schedule. "The chicken and rib contests are coming up tomorrow. If he plans to be the champion, he could be practicing different sauces and infusions already."

"Let's just peek around the back of his camper," James

suggested. As the two men approached the RV with as much stealth as they could muster, it was obvious that Jimmy and his girlfriend were not holed up inside the vehicle. In fact, Hailey was demanding to know the reason behind Gillian's allegation, and she wasn't keeping her voice down. James was sure most of the neighboring campers could hear her shrill, rapid-fire questions.

Jimmy, on the other hand, replied to the barrage in a bored tone. "I told you, baby, that woman's soft in the head. I don't know nothin' about her."

"But you did fifteen years, Jimmy. You told me that when we met durin' those counseling sessions for folks who wanted to turn their lives around. You was just like me, Jimmy, 'cept I was doin' time for possession of marijuana You said you'd done time for dealin'." She paused. "We were battlin' the same demons. Drugs. It's what we bonded over."

"That's right, doll, and we're both clean as rocks polished by the river, so can we have a beer and get on with mixin' up the mop for the chicken?" James could barely understand Jimmy, as his voice had grown even more hoarse.

"Forget the beer," Hailey said testily. "That woman seemed a little wacko, but seein' *you* is what made her come all unhinged. You'd better be straight with me, Jimmy, 'cause if I find out you're lyin' to me about why you were in jail I'll—"

"You'll what?" Jimmy snarled at her. "You'll take your fat, Bible-readin' ass off elsewhere? I'd like to see *that*! Who would want you?"

James and Bennett exchanged startled glances.

"Ouch," Bennett whispered.

"Man, what a charmer," James murmured.

"Lots of men would! 'Specially barbecue cooks!" Hailey spluttered angrily. "You'd never win a single contest without my help!" After Jimmy offered no comeback, she sniffed and then walked toward the camper's door. "I'll be inside readin' my *In Touch* magazine. If you want help on that chicken mop, and you know you're gonna need it, you can come get me. And when you do, it'd better be with an apology and the truth about that redhead on your lips! Otherwise, stay out there and kiss your blue ribbons goodbye."

James and Bennett heard Hailey's heavy tread on the RV's steps followed by the muffled footsteps of her moving around inside the vehicle.

"Hush up, woman!" Jimmy made his way to the closed door and hit it with what sounded like a metal cooking tool. "You talk like that again so's folks can hear and I'll shut your big mouth for good! I can take those blue ribbons or leave 'em. I got a whole 'nother reason for bein' at this festival!"

Hailey didn't answer, but James could hear cupboards being opened and forcefully closed again. A few seconds later, a radio was switched on. James, Bennett, and half the campground could easily catch every note of the Christian praise hymn.

"Sounds like Jimmy may not be the real Pitmaster," Bennett whispered to James.

James took a quick glance around the corner of the RV. Jimmy was standing near his cooker, his face tilted toward the sky. Muttering angrily, he rubbed his arms.

"Stupid redheaded bitch," he said, spitting on the ground in a way that reminded James of the angry action taken by the female dog owner the day before. "Of all places for her to turn up." He rubbed the skin on his arms vigorously and then turned back to the RV.

"Hailey, baby. I'm sorry." Jimmy mounted the first step, causing the RV to keel slightly, and knocked at the locked door. "Could you please gimme my flannel shirt? It's gettin' chilly out here. Come on, baby. You know I'm nothin' without you. Open up. I'll give you a nice backrub." He knocked harder. "Hailey!"

After a pause, the door opened and Hailey said, "You want a shirt? You want a mop for the chicken? You want lots of stuff. Then it's time to repent, Jimmy Lang. Come inside and confess your sins."

Grumbling, Jimmy hesitated for a moment before disappearing into the camper. No more sounds were heard above the harmonious voices of a large choir.

"Guess that's the end of Jimmy for a while," James said derisively.

"Is that guy nuts?" Bennett asked once they had left the cooking area. "I know the sun isn't shining and there's a breeze blowing, but how can he be cold? It's August, and Jimmy's got enough extra layers to keep an Arctic walrus nice and snug." He squeezed his own belly. "I know I have plenty to spare, but I'm not like that man. I hope I never will be."

James felt a stress headache approaching. "Jimmy's a strange one. You saw how volatile he was with Hailey. Maybe he *has* killed someone."

"We'll have to get the truth from Gillian. I have a feeling Jimmy would only lie to us anyway," Bennett said. "I don't know what made me think he'd just spill the whole story to us."

"Well, Jimmy obviously knows Gillian. You heard what he mumbled to himself. And what about confessing and repenting to Hailey?" James asked cynically.

Bennett rolled his eyes. "I think Hailey is being hand-fed a serious tall tale right about now."

"Come on." James quickened his stride as they headed toward the parking lot. "Those clouds are getting ready to open up on us."

"Looks that way," Bennett agreed. "Let's go back to the inn, have some coffee, and sit down with the ladies. I bet they've already straightened out this whole mess and have a logical explanation for Gillian's going off the deep end."

"I have my doubts about everything being sorted out, but there should be coffee at any rate," James said wearily.

• • •

James knocked on the door of the room shared by Lindy, Lucy, and Gillian, but no one answered. Shrugging, he retraced his steps back to the first floor and dialed Lucy's cell phone number.

"James?" She sounded breathless.

"Did you find Gillian?" he asked.

"No." The word was infused with disappointment. "We're just coming back from the walking trails behind the inn. Where are you?"

"Standing in the lobby," he said. "We spied on Jimmy a bit, but we didn't actually talk to him. We still have no idea what's going on."

"Me neither. The dog people weren't much help, though most of them received Gillian's brochure and are dreaming about doggie palaces. They all told me basically the same thing—that Gillian was pleasant and *very* enthusiastic. Sounds like she was her normal self." Lucy sighed. "Apparently, she and that lady who spit on Jimmy's cooker yesterday were quite chummy, but I couldn't track that woman down."

"So no leads from that group at all?"

"Meet us on the back porch. We can continue talking there," Lucy said. "Eleanor is serving afternoon tea. She said lots of people come back from the festival to relax before returning for dinner and an evening of entertainment, which means you'd better claim a table for us." She paused. "It's going to rain any second now. Maybe Gillian will just show up when it starts. We can have her favorite tea ready and waiting."

James followed Lucy's advice. He and Bennett returned to their room, scooped up their books, and hustled downstairs to the back porch. James did his best to concentrate on a chapter entitled "The Great Meat Debate," which examined the East Coast notion that pork was the superior meat to use when barbecuing, versus the Kansas City and Texan claims that beef made a better choice. Bennett seemed absorbed by his trivia book, but when Eleanor stepped onto the long porch bearing a tray laden with sandwiches, he snapped his head around at the sound of her footfalls.

"The cakes aren't quite done yet," Eleanor said with a tired smile. "You're welcome to some sandwiches if you're feeling peckish."

James observed the proprietor as she fanned out a pile of cocktail napkins. He wondered if Eleanor and her daughter were on speaking terms yet. He knew that the pig parade was scheduled to begin at eight p.m. and that it would be followed by a fireworks display. Hopefully, the weather would cooperate or there'd be no pyrotechnics, and the makeup covering the marks on Francesca's neck would need to be waterproof.

This day hasn't turned out to be very festive, James thought. Between Eleanor and Francesca's fight, Gillian's eruption, the demonstration of Hailey and Jimmy's conflicted relationship, and the rain that was sure to send R.C. into a state of panic, the feeling of celebration had turned rather dour.

Bennett scraped his chair back and closed his book, interrupting James's ruminations. "I can't focus," he declared and jerked his thumb at the buffet table. "Want some grub?"

"Sure," James said. "Looks like cucumber sandwiches up there. Can you get me a couple? They seem kind of small."

In fact, each sandwich was easily consumed in two hearty bites. James wolfed down three and licked his fingers. "These are terrific. I like how one piece of bread is rye and the other one's white. I think I taste fresh chives in the cream cheese, too."

Bennett nodded. "Nothing like good food to take your mind off your troubles."

At that moment, Lindy and Lucy arrived. Both women were pink-cheeked from their brisk walk on the nature trail. James watched as the hopeful light in both of their faces was extinguished as they noted the three empty chairs at the table.

"She hasn't come back?" Lindy's question was rhetorical. Instead of responding, Bennett handed her a plate of sandwiches. While the group concentrated on their food, Eleanor appeared on the porch with an urn of tea, followed by a woman wearing a maid's uniform who carried a platter bearing tiny cakes and homemade oatmeal chocolate-chip cookies.

"The tea has a subtle hint of almonds," Eleanor announced to the guests gathering on the porch. "It's very refreshing."

Bennett served himself a steaming cup and several desserts. At their table, he picked up the cup, blew on the surface of the hot tea, and then placed it back in the saucer without taking a sip. "Here we are, eating a vegetarian snack and drinking herbal tea, and the one person in the world who would be tickled pink by this spread isn't with us."

The supper club members exchanged glum looks and quietly ate their food. In the distance, thunder rumbled, and the treetops beyond the pool shifted back and forth in the strengthening wind.

"Maybe the rain will bring her back," Lucy murmured.

But when the downpour began a few minutes later, causing excited shrieks from some of the other guests, who scrambled to move their chairs farther away from the open air, there was still no sign of Gillian. Her friends stared into the curtains of rain and silently waited.

Chapter Nine

Falafel Tent Gyro

The rain pelted down all afternoon. By early evening, it softened to a light drizzle, hinting at the possibility of ceasing altogether. The storm had mottled the ground with patches of muddy puddles, and small twigs, dislodged from the trees by the wind, were scattered everywhere.

James had napped for nearly two hours. His lack of sleep from the previous night, combined with the steady rhythm of the rain, made a nap impossible to resist. At first, he'd gone to his room, intending to read until Gillian returned. Four sentences into the chapter on marinades, his lids grew heavy as anvils. It was easy to surrender to the darkened room and the absence of the sonorous noises produced by his roommate.

When he woke, he felt a stab of guilt that he'd slept while Gillian might have been wandering, alone and distraught, in the unrelenting downpour. He hoped that she'd made herself cozy in one of the town shops, and that she was now safely back at the inn, ready to explain everything to her friends over dinner.

At quarter to six, just a few minutes after James sat up in bed and ran his fingers through his disheveled hair, Bennett burst into the room. "We're going to the festival grounds. Gillian still hasn't come back. The girls have spent the last hour combing through every store in town, but no dice. She isn't there." He checked his reflection in the mirror and tucked his shirt deeper into his pants, eyeing his paunch critically all the while.

James rubbed the sleep from his eyes and grabbed his wallet and the room key from the nightstand. "Is it still overcast?"

Nodding, Bennett pulled a windbreaker out of his leather satchel. "I thought I was packing like a little old lady when I stuffed this in my bag. Who knew that an August evening in southern Virginia could cause goose bumps?"

Lindy and Lucy were waiting for the men by Lucy's Jeep. Lucy wore a Shenandoah County Sheriff's Department sweatshirt, and Lindy was decked out in a black sweater trimmed with a faux fur collar. James paused when Lucy opened the back door and indicated they should hop in. Noting his hesitation, Lucy gave James a push on the back. "Don't worry, James. I cleaned it before we left Quincy's Gap."

James blushed, for Lucy had guessed that his hesitation was based on the fact that the inside of her car tended to resemble an overturned garbage can and often smelled just as bad. Her sloppiness had been one of the things that troubled him when they'd been dating. Her home, her yard, and her car were always in a state of disarray. And though James didn't care if things were a little untidy, he drew the line at rotting food, surfaces sticky with soda splatter, or flattened pieces of chewing gum mottled with dog hair. Thinking of his failed relationship with Lucy reminded him that he should check in with Murphy at some point, but that could wait until after Gillian was found.

The four friends rode to the fairgrounds in silence. As they approached the parking area, Lindy unfolded a piece of paper containing a listing of the evening's events. "I'm trying to figure out if Gillian would be interested in any of tonight's entertainment," she told the others. "There's the parade, of course, followed by a country music concert. Other than those two things, it's just the usual rides and carnival games and stuff."

"No animal shows?" Lucy asked.

Lindy shook her head. "No. The dog show took place this morning, and there was a SpongeBob production for kids this afternoon, but I really can't see Gillian sitting through that."

"I don't get that SpongeBob cartoon one bit," Bennett mumbled. "No wonder kids are so mixed up. How are they supposed to learn life lessons from a bunch of ugly aquatic invertebrates?"

"Which cartoon *do* you think teaches life lessons?" Lindy raised her plucked eyebrows in curiosity.

"I'm a Peanuts fan. Charlie Brown could teach us all a thing or two," Bennett said as Lucy pulled into a parking space.

James said, "Looks like the lot is still full. I guess the rain only scared folks off for a short while." Inhaling the refreshing evening air, he listened to the cacophony of sounds coming from the festival grounds. There was music, a rumble of unintelligible announcements coming over the PA system, and the ever-present buzz of the crowd. James gazed at the rows of lights in the distance. "Where should we go first?"

"Let's find R.C. He might be able to contact his staff with his walkie-talkie and ask if anyone's seen Gillian," Lucy suggested.

"Brilliant idea." James smiled at her. "We're lucky to have a sheriff's deputy with us."

Lucy's face glowed with pleasure.

The foursome walked to the recreation center with care. The mass of humanity had reappeared with the break in the weather, and hundreds of feet had flattened the wet grass and expanded the stretches of mud. Every now and then, a child would break free from his parents' grasp to splash in one of the numerous puddles. As the supper club members passed the petting zoo area, a little boy missing both of his front teeth sprayed James's khaki pants with brown water. Examining his dirt-splattered pants in dismay, James wondered why he hadn't had the foresight to change into jeans before leaving the inn.

Lindy chuckled at his distress. "See? You should have brought extra outfits like I did. You'd better hope Fox Hall has a washing machine."

By the time they made their way to the recreation center, Lindy's good humor had vanished. Her new wedge sandals were caked with mud and several petals from the fabric flowers attached to the center of each shoe had vanished.

"Damn it!" Lindy frowned unhappily at her footwear. As they entered the building, she did her best to wipe the mud on the doormat. "These are totally ruined!"

R.C., who was seated behind the receptionist's desk, examining the document spread before him, looked up in alarm. "Did you say rain? It hasn't started again, has it?"

Lucy hastily assured the frazzled director that the sky was free of precipitation. She then asked for his assistance in locating Gillian. When he didn't jump to help, she told him what had happened after the brisket competition had ended.

A crease appeared on R.C.'s brow. "Yes, I heard about what your friend said to Mr. Lang. I have to admit that I find the whole story very disturbing." He rubbed the crown of his head, where James imagined a strong headache was blooming. "At one time, Jimmy was good for this festival. His, eh, larger-than-life persona used to be a draw. His cooking skills were above average, but it was the way he made such a big show of everything he did that had people gathering around his grill." He mopped his forehead with a bandana. "Now, I fear, he's become more of a detriment to this festival, especially if he's a convicted felon."

"Um," Lindy stammered. "We're not completely sure that our friend's accusation is true. She —"

"No matter what Gillian said, Jimmy Lang *has* been to jail," Bennett interrupted. "He and his girlfriend met in some ex-con, talk-about-your-feelings session."

R.C. gave Bennett a searching look. "How do you know that?"

Bennett suddenly launched into a coughing fit.

"Um, we overheard Jimmy and Hailey talking outside their camper," James explained cryptically. "We all split up to look for Gillian. Bennett and I were searching the campground area when we stumbled on Jimmy and Hailey," he added, stretching the truth. "That was hours ago. There's been no sign of Gillian since."

Picking up a pen from the desk, R.C. said, "I know your friend has light skin and reddish-orange hair, but what other details can I add to her description?"

"Her full name is Gillian O'Malley," Lucy said. "She's approximately five foot six. Forty years old. Thin legs. Barrel-chested. Wearing a long silver skirt, lime-green T-shirt, and an armload of silver bracelets. Carrying a hemp purse stitched with butterflies." Lucy turned to her friends. "Did I leave anything out?"

The other supper club members shook their heads as R.C. relayed her words verbatim via his walkie-talkie to the large group of workers running the festival. When most of them reported back that they hadn't seen a woman matching Gillian's description recently, R.C. requested that they all keep a sharp lookout for her and immediately report any sighting to him.

Lucy thanked R.C. and handed him her cell phone number. "Please call me if anyone spots her."

R.C. noticed the concern on Lucy's face and responded by squeezing her lightly on the shoulder. "Why don't you all get something to eat? By the time supper is over, I'm sure someone will have run across your friend."

The four friends wandered down the muddy and water-streaked road flanked by the merchants' booths and the food vendors. No one spoke up as they passed one illuminated sign after another advertising fried chicken, beef hot dogs, Angus burgers, barbecued ribs, turkey legs, seasoned cheese fries, and personal pan pizzas. They were too focused on looking at the faces in the crowd to concentrate on any particular food.

"Let's go to that stand where Gillian had lunch," Lindy suggested. "Who knows? Maybe she really liked it and will go back there for dinner."

"They better serve somethin' besides chickpeas," Bennett muttered.

"They have gyros or chicken souvlaki platters," Lindy assured him.

When they reached the vendor's booth, entitled the Falafel Tent, they each ordered the gyro platter and a large Coke. Lucy found an empty picnic table nearby, and they sat down to eat, keeping their eyes on the passersby.

"Is this meal a good choice for the protein diet?" James asked Lucy. He wasn't particularly interested. He was just trying to jump-start a conversation.

"If you stick to the lamb and the salad only. That rice isn't necessary. I probably should have gotten the souvlaki platter, as chicken is a much leaner meat than lamb, but I've been eating lots of chicken this summer. Shoot, I'll start clucking if I swallow another piece of poultry." Lucy took a bite of seasoned lamb and a glob of yogurt sauce fell onto the skin just below her necklace pendant. James watched as she dabbed at the sauce before quickly looking away, embarrassed by an unbidden memory of a time when he ran his fingers over her body.

"So here we are. Friday night at the fair," Bennett mumbled, checking his watch.

"That's right, it's Friday!" James wiped his mouth with his napkin and pulled out his cell phone. "I need to check in with the Fitzgerald twins and see if that nonsense with the high school kids is really over. Be right back."

"If they've been making fake IDs, I'll to want to know their names." Lucy issued him a stern look.

"I don't have any hard proof," James said, getting up from the table. "The IDs just seemed like the most logical explanation. If my theory is correct, then the kids won't be hanging out at our branch anymore. I'll have scared them off."

"But that doesn't mean they won't *use* the IDs they've *already* made," Lucy replied heatedly.

"Oh, I doubt they're any good." Excusing himself, James wandered into the empty judging tent and dialed the circulation desk's extension. Scott answered right away.

"I had a feeling you might call, Professor." Scott sounded as cheerful as ever.

Assuming from Scott's tone that all was peaceful at the library, James asked, "So is everything as it should be this evening?"

"Not quite." Scott's enthusiasm instantly deflated. "The kids are back. The ones from last week and some new ones, too."

"What?" James was shocked. "What are they doing?"

"Same thing. Paying homage to that brute Martin and messing up all the magazines. And they're definitely less willing to listen to Francis and me," he confessed ruefully. "We're not having much success keeping them quiet."

James struggled to keep his irritation from coming through in his voice. "How many non-teenage patrons are there?"

"Only two. Mr. and Mrs. Schroeder. They're picking out a pile of books to take to the beach next week."

Visualizing the teenagers creasing magazines and talking too loudly while they conducted their illicit activities nearly drove James insane with frustration. He wished he could teleport to Quincy's Gap and have Lucy appear inside the library, dressed in her uniform and tapping her gun holster. He knew she'd frighten some common sense into the group of teen miscreants without uttering a word.

"Okay, this is what you're going to do," he told Scott. "First, turn off the A/C. As soon as the Schroeders are finished checking out, make an announcement over the intercom system that, due to technical difficulties with the air-conditioning system, the library will be closing early."

"Seriously?" Scott asked after a stunned pause. "Can we do that?"

"Oh, we're doing it!" James shouted and then felt guilty about taking his ire out on his employee. "Really, Scott. This thing with the kids is getting out of control, and I can't help you from here. I should apologize for assuming that I had the problem all figured out."

"No worries, Professor," Scott said. "Francis and I know that you'll get to the bottom of this mystery sooner or later."

James grinned. "Thanks for the vote of confidence. Now, close up shop and go to a movie or something. You guys deserve a break after putting up with that group again."

Stuffing the phone into his pocket, James picked his way through the muddy grass to where his forlorn friends pushed food around on their plates.

"I can't stand this!" Lucy declared, suddenly standing up. "It's time to split up and search every inch of this park, from the campground area to the face-painting booths. I can't sit here for another second!"

Bennett got to his feet and cleared the table of their unfinished meals. "Come on, James. We're not going back to that inn without Gillian."

The four friends scoured the festival grounds until almost ten at night. They interrogated anyone carrying a walkie-talkie, poked their heads into magic shows, animal pens, tents in the camping area, and port-a-johns. They questioned merchants, entertainers, and any crowd members wearing Birkenstock sandals or trailing a dog on a leash.

Finally, exhausted and dirty, they reconvened at Lucy's Jeep. When James and Bennett heard that Lindy and Lucy had no better luck in finding even the slightest trace of Gillian, they grew very disheartened. At a few minutes past ten, R.C. called to say that his network of festival workers had had no success either.

"I'm sure she's waiting for you at the Fox Hall," he said in an attempt to console Lucy.

But back at the inn, Gillian's bed was empty. Her belongings were untouched.

"Before I go to bed," Lucy said wearily to her friends, "I'm going to call the local sheriff."

"Let us know if there's any news," James said.

Lucy promised that she would phone them and closed the door to their suite.

Following Bennett as he shuffled off to their room, James

thought it would be impossible to fall asleep. What with worrying about Gillian and the goings-on at the library, his mind was on overdrive. However, the moment he closed his eyes, his body seemed to melt into the bed and he immediately drowned in dark waves of sleep.

The ringing phone jolted James from a dream in which he and Murphy were at the beach. The sun was burning his pale cheeks and forehead into a crisp red, but he couldn't move a muscle. Looking at the incoming surf, he realized that Murphy had buried him neck-deep in sand and had run off to interview a man who claimed that his surfboard had just been bitten by a twelve-foot shark.

Blinking the dream away, James switched on the bedside lamp. Bennett answered the phone. As his friend croaked out "Hello," James pulled the digital clock within inches of his nose. It was three minutes past seven.

Bennett listened to the caller for several seconds, and James tried to read the mixed expressions passing across his friend's face. He sensed that whatever Bennett was hearing was completely unexpected, for Bennett's eyes widened into black pools as he nodded mechanically.

"I see," Bennett finally said in a leaden voice. "We'll meet you downstairs in ten minutes." He waited, listening again, and then sighed lugubriously. "Yes, of course I'll tell him."

Replacing the receiver, Bennett reluctantly glanced at James. "That was Lucy. She didn't have good news, my man. Jimmy Lang was found dead this morning—inside his camper."

"Jimmy's *dead*?" was all James could think to say.

"Yeah. The local sheriff wants to meet us in the judges' tent in fifteen minutes. He wants to question us about yesterday." He shook his head in dismay. "It gets worse, James. Gillian was there when Hailey found Jimmy's body. The sheriff and his deputies have taken her into custody."

"Who?" James asked, trying to fathom what Bennett had just told him. "Gillian or Hailey?"

"Gillian," Bennett said as he grabbed his jeans from the closet. "They think she murdered Jimmy Lang."

Chapter Ten

Sheriff's Department Coffee

James plied Bennett with a thousand questions as they sped toward the festival grounds, but his friend could offer little in the way of new information.

"I'm in the dark, man!" Bennett finally shouted when James kept asking how Jimmy Lang had met his end.

"It must have been a violent one, or Gillian wouldn't be sitting in a holding cell right now," James said anxiously. He zoomed into an empty parking space next to Lucy's Jeep, turned off the engine, and opened his car door with so much force that his Bronco shuddered. When he saw that Bennett's mini recorder had fallen from his friend's pants pocket, he scooped it off the passenger seat, shoved it into his own pocket, and slammed the Bronco's door.

"Where are we supposed to go?" James frantically looked around. "To the crime scene?"

"Hey, there's Lindy." Bennett pointed at a figure heading toward them. "Maybe she can give us some answers before we both crack apart like eggs."

Lindy was jogging straight for them, her unfettered hair forming a black tornado around her head as she ran. As she grew closer, James could see that tracks of black mascara lined both of her cheeks. She'd also buttoned her blouse incorrectly. Stopping in front of her friends, she paused to catch her breath.

"Lucy's in with the sheriff right now. I'm supposed to take you straight to them," Lindy panted, her brown eyes pooling with tears. "Isn't this awful? Do you think Gillian really could . . . ?" She trailed off and shook her head fiercely. "No! She's no murderer!"

James held out his hands in a plaintive gesture. "Please, Lindy! Tell me what the hell is going on! How can I help when I don't know anything?"

Struggling to regain her composure, Lindy took several deep breaths. "Okay, here's what I know. I overheard the sheriff telling Lucy that Jimmy Lang died of propane poisoning. He went to sleep last night with a portable heater turned on high and the window vents fully open. Apparently, someone taped over the window vents, the plumbing pipes, and even climbed onto the roof and covered the roof ventilators with several layers of duct tape. Jimmy couldn't get a lick of fresh air if he wanted to. Over the course of the night, he just slipped away."

"And they think Gillian did this? *Gillian?*" James spluttered and turned to Bennett. "Is it possible to get a propane overdose from some rinky-dink heater?"

Bennett nodded as the three friends started walking. "Sure, man. Some of those suckers run off full propane tanks. They can pump out thirty thousand BTUs an hour."

"In laymen's terms, Bennett," Lindy said with reproach. "And why do you know facts about propane tanks?"

"I camped out all the time as a kid, and I was an Eagle Scout," Bennett replied testily. "BTU stands for British Thermal Unit. It's the quantity of heat needed to raise one pound of water by one degree Fahrenheit. And I know *that* from studying acronyms to prepare for *Jeopardy!*"

"I still don't understand, but I don't care about the scientific definitions. Can you just explain how a heater can kill someone?" Lindy asked with uncharacteristic impatience.

"The heater eats up oxygen at the same time it produces carbon monoxide." Bennett rubbed his mustache. "That's not good. Without a source of oxygen, the carbon monoxide can suck away your last breath. You'd never know what was happening. Carbon monoxide doesn't have a distinctive odor. That's why they call that gas the silent killer. Doesn't happen fast either, so someone must have taped the vents pretty soon after Jimmy went to sleep."

"Wouldn't manufacturers make a safety switch on those heaters if they're that dangerous?" James puzzled.

"They did after a bunch of folks died from carbon monoxide poisoning." Bennett slowed as they approached Jimmy's camper. "A few years ago, I read an article about accidental deaths caused by those portable heaters in an issue of *Outdoor Life*. If Jimmy had one of those older models, it would've kept right on pumping out the bad gas until someone turned it off."

"But Gillian doesn't camp!" Lindy cried. "How would she know to use a heater as a weapon? And for crying out loud, why did

Jimmy have the heater on, anyway? Couldn't he just wear a sweatshirt or use a blanket or something?"

James nudged Bennett. "He was cold yesterday. Remember how he asked Hailey for another shirt? I also saw goose bumps on his arms when he came up to the stage to receive his prize. That's not normal."

"I wish I had some answers, friend, but I don't." Bennett stared gloomily ahead.

A cluster of deputies from the Hudsonville County Sheriff's Department turned at the sound of Bennett's voice. Lucy stood among them, an unreadable look on her face. When she saw James, her eyes betrayed the seriousness of the situation. She slowly raised her hand to wave at her friends while offering a timid smile, but James saw genuine fear written on her face. Gillian was in real trouble.

Stepping away from her fellow officers, Lucy approached her friends and steered them a few yards farther away from Jimmy's RV.

"They've already removed the body," she said, trying to sound detached. She rubbed a business card between her fingers until James was certain the ivory card stock would turn to ribbons. "Hailey claims that she had no idea Jimmy's life was in danger. Apparently, she was in charge of keeping an eye on the ribs for today's contest. According to her statement, one or two people from each cooking team must pull an all-nighter on what they call Rib Night." She glanced down at the business card before stuffing it in her pocket. "Hailey admits that she spent the hours between one and three hanging out with the Marrow Men—coming back to check on the cooker from time to time. She then went to catch a few hours of shut-eye in the back of her SUV. She says that lately, Jimmy had been keeping the camper too hot for her, so she slept in the car."

"How does Gillian fit into this scenario?" James asked impatiently.

Lucy pursed her lips as if she wasn't sure how to answer his question. "Hailey woke up at five thirty and saw Gillian on the camper steps. She thought Jimmy and Gillian had been messing around, so she burst into the RV and found Jimmy stone dead on the sofa. She called the cops and told Gillian to stay put."

"And Gillian listened to her?" Lindy sounded surprised.

Lucy bowed her head, clearly avoiding eye contact. "She didn't say a word. Hailey claims that Gillian was smiling like a deranged clown the whole time they waited for the sheriff and her crew to get here."

Bennett scratched his head. "Smiling? And . . . did you say the sheriff is a she?"

"Yes." Lucy glanced over her shoulder. "Here she comes now, and she doesn't look happy."

The conversation among the group of deputies abruptly came to a stop as a petite woman with skin the hue of warm toffee and close-cropped dark hair marched toward the supper club members.

"Sheriff Jade Jones," she said, shaking hands all around with a brief but firm grip. "I'm sorry you had to start your morning off in such an unpleasant manner, but I need to take statements from each of you regarding Gillian O'Malley's interactions with Jimmy Lang."

"There was only *one* interaction!" Lindy cried. "We didn't even know that she *knew* him until yesterday. And we had no idea what she was talking about when she accused Jimmy of killing her husband. But I'll tell you one thing I *do* know. Gillian didn't murder anyone. She's a deep believer in that what-goes-around-comes-around stuff. She doesn't even kill spiders! She *relocates* them to the plants on her front porch. Does that sound like someone capable of an act of cold-blooded violence to you?" Immediately following this outburst, Lindy began to cry.

Something that might have been respect for Lindy's loyalty flitted across Sheriff Jones's face for a millisecond. She then shifted her muscular body and gazed intently at each of the supper club members. "We're investigating all angles, ma'am," she said to Lindy. "Miss O'Malley has not been formally charged with a crime, but we're interested in discovering how she was acquainted with Mr. Lang."

"So are we!" Lindy retorted. "Has she said anything yet?"

Sheriff Jones shook her head. "No. She hasn't spoken a word."

James eyed the crime scene tape fluttering in the morning breeze. "Jimmy seemed to enjoy rubbing people the wrong way, Sheriff. Just because Gillian was at the scene doesn't mean she was involved." But his words sounded unconvincing, even to his own ears. Did he completely believe in Gillian's innocence, or had her bizarre behavior from the other day caused him to doubt her character?

The sheriff stared at him curiously. "And which people did he rub the wrong way? Mr. Henry, is it?"

When James hesitated in order to gather his thoughts, Lucy jumped in. "The woman who runs the Inn at Fox Hall, for starters. Eleanor was pretty irate when she discovered that her *teenage* daughter had fooled around with Jimmy on Thursday night." She pointed at James. "He even saw the evidence on Francesca's neck. That's Eleanor's daughter, and Eleanor was pretty livid. Francesca has to maintain a spotless reputation if she wants to become the next Miss Virginia."

"Francesca doesn't give a fig about the upcoming pageant," Lindy added. "But her mother certainly does."

The sheriff tilted her chin at the nearest deputy, who immediately produced a pad of paper and began taking notes.

"Mrs. Fiennes isn't the only other possible suspect," James said. "Bennett and I also overheard a heated exchange between Hailey and Jimmy yesterday. I don't know what Hailey told you about their relationship, but from what we heard, it wasn't what I'd call harmonious. In fact, it seemed downright volatile. Right, Bennett?"

James turned to his friend, but Bennett was deaf and dumb to everything other than the attractive sheriff. Casting his eyes back and forth between Bennett and Sheriff Jones, James realized that the pair was close in age and roughly the same height. The comparison ended there, however, for although Jade had a boyish haircut and an air of intensity about her, she possessed a regal beauty that had clearly struck Bennett to the core.

James elbowed Bennett in the ribs, and he was pleased to hear his friend come to his senses and join the conversation. "James is telling the truth, Sheriff." Bennett glanced at his friends. "And let's not forget the dog lady, folks. That crazy woman spat on Jimmy's cooker and called him all sorts of names. I'm sure she'd liked to see him sleeping with the fishes. That was a seriously unhappy woman, yessir." Bennett cleared his throat in embarrassment. "Uh, I mean, ma'am."

Assessing Bennett with calculating eyes, Sheriff Jones addressed the deputy taking notes. "Harding, I'd like this group to be transported to the station immediately. I'd like separate statements from each of them concerning Jimmy Lang—and I mean down to the tiniest detail—about what they know to be fact, have heard as hearsay, or witnessed with their own eyes." She pointed at Lindy and Lucy. "I'll take the ladies with me. The two gentlemen can ride in your car."

"Will we be able to speak to Gillian?" Lucy demanded.

Sheriff Jones considered the question before nodding. "I'll allow you to be present for her questioning, Deputy Hanover. You're an officer of the law as well as Ms. O'Malley's friend. The combination may prove fortuitous."

Bennett watched the diminutive woman march toward the parking lot. Every deputy she passed stood a fraction taller and several of the men touched the brims of their hats in deference as well. If the sheriff noticed the demonstrations of respect, she gave no indication.

"Now, *that's* a woman," Bennett said a little breathlessly. "Holy smokes."

"Get a hold of yourself, Casanova." Lucy gave Bennett a pinch on the arm. "Gillian needs us. Instead of daydreaming about Jade Jones, use your time in the car to think of specific statements to take the heat off Gillian. We need to shine a spotlight on other suspects until we can start our own investigation." She smiled at James. "You know, that was really clever of you to throw doubt on the theory that Gillian is the killer by mentioning Eleanor and Hailey. I brought up Felicity earlier—that's the dog trainer's name—but I was only able to speak to the sheriff for a few minutes."

"What are you going to say to Gillian when you see her?" Lindy asked Lucy while attempting to gather her tangled hair into a rubber band.

"I don't know, but if I can't scare her into piping up and defending herself, it's going to look really bad for her." Lucy glanced at the sheriff, who was issuing orders to the deputies working in and around Jimmy's RV. "Silence won't win her any points. It makes her look guilty."

As Deputy Harding gestured for James and Bennett to accompany him to his cruiser, James quickly grabbed Lucy's hand. "You can do it, Lucy. You can help Gillian. I know you'll find a way."

He gave her fingers a soft squeeze, relieved to see a look of firm resolve enter Lucy's eyes.

Inside the patrol car, James and Bennett took Lucy's advice to heart. They both concentrated on their encounters with Jimmy Lang, trying hard to remember each and every detail.

James thought about R. C. Richter's passion over seeing both Hog Fest and the town of Hudsonville meet with success. He decided that R.C.'s displeasure over Jimmy's offensive behavior was worth relaying to Deputy Harding.

Harding was polite but formal. As they arrived at the small brick building that housed the sheriff's department, he directed James and Bennett to a conference room and stiffly offered them coffee. Both men readily accepted and then frowned when they tasted the bitter brew.

"You need more sugar?" Harding asked. His tone seemed to suggest that they weren't macho enough to drink the incredibly strong coffee that he gulped down as if it was chocolate milk.

"Heck, yeah, I need more sugar! How about a dump truck full of it and a gallon of cream, too?" Bennett replied, unfazed by Harding's judgmental glare. "Shoot, man! When the oil in your car runs low, do you use this stuff instead of Quaker State?"

"We use Pennzoil," Harding said flatly. He gestured at the deputy who'd entered the room during Bennett's tirade. "This is Deputy Neely. He'll be taking your statement, Mr. Marshall. Mr. Henry, you'll be staying here with me."

Bennett shot James a thumbs-up and trudged off behind Deputy Neely, who was so tall and thin that it wouldn't have surprised James to learn that his law enforcement colleagues referred to him as Deputy Needle.

"Let's start at the beginning," Harding said, uncapping a pen and settling back in his chair. "When was the first time you became aware of Jimmy Lang's existence?"

"Within a few minutes of arriving in Hudsonville," James said readily, recalling their delicious lunch on the back porch of the inn and how Jimmy had sat down at their table. "I'd say it was a little after one o'clock that Thursday afternoon."

Harding scribbled something on his notebook. "What was your initial impression of Mr. Lang?"

James took a sip of his coffee and grimaced. It was still early in the morning, and though shock had startled him into wakefulness, he could feel his body crying out for its daily dose of caffeine. Still, he'd have to track down coffee later, as the contents of his cup were simply undrinkable. Pushing the foul liquid away, James looked at Harding. "I thought Jimmy Lang was a loudmouthed pig. He was the kind of guy you might find amusing at first, but within seconds, all you want to do is get away from him. The man was large and crude and I found him a bit repulsive." He pointed at his cup. "Kind of like this coffee."

An hour passed as Harding asked question after question and took careful notes on his pad. Finally, when they'd reviewed James's statement several times, Harding capped his pen and slid it into his shirt pocket. At the same moment, James's stomach gurgled loudly.

"You hungry?" Harding asked James, who nodded honestly. "Be right back," the deputy said, and he left the room.

Harding returned a few minutes later carrying a ceramic American flag mug and a paper plate containing three biscuits. James gratefully accepted a biscuit and, even though it was cold and hard, scarfed it down in four bites.

"This is the coffee we drink on a regular basis." Harding grinned slightly, pointing at the mug. "We only give folks that other stuff before we interrogate them." He grinned. "It kind of sets a tone."

James doctored his coffee with cream and a sprinkle of sugar, not completely trusting Harding, but the hot brew was good. It was smooth and rich, and it brought him some comfort after what already seemed like an endless morning.

"I ran into the sheriff in the kitchen." Harding picked apart a biscuit, took a small bite, and frowned. "These were much better two hours ago. Still, middle-aged bachelors like me will eat just about anything." He brushed crumbs from his hands. "Your friend the deputy isn't having much luck getting Ms. O'Malley to talk."

The last bite of James's biscuit stuck in his mouth. When he tried to swallow, his throat closed and he inhaled most of the biscuit into his windpipe. James gasped for air and finally guzzled his hot coffee in an attempt to move the glutinous mass of biscuit down his throat.

"That's not good," James said in a hoarse whisper. When he could finally speak normally again, he asked, "Do you think the sheriff would let me talk to Gillian?"

Harding rubbed his dimpled chin in thought. "You think you could do better than a trained officer of the law?"

Sensing that Harding wasn't threatened by the possibility that a civilian might be able to provide assistance with their investigation, James nodded. "I think I know exactly what to say to get Gillian to talk."

Harding pushed back his chair. "In that case, come with me."

James was brought into a stark room containing a table and two metal chairs. A recorder sat on the middle of the table, along with a plastic pitcher of water and a stack of paper cups.

"Have a seat," Harding directed and then turned on the recorder and murmured into the speaker. When he was done, he leaned toward James and said, "I'm going to stand off to the side and be unobtrusive." At the sound of footsteps outside the door, Harding jumped forward to open it. He ushered Gillian inside and James gave an involuntary cry at his friend's appearance.

He rushed forward and put his arms around her. "Gillian!" He held her while casting an angry glare at Harding over her shoulder. "Why is she wearing this orange jumpsuit?"

Harding, looking slightly abashed, said, "Her clothes were wet and dirty, and she was shivering with cold when we picked her up. We thought she might be more comfortable in this."

James released Gillian and forced a smile for her benefit. "Well, at least it matches your hair."

Gillian kept her green eyes locked on the floor and James remained silent for a moment, simply standing close to her and keeping a loose hold of her hand. "I know you didn't hurt anyone, Gillian," he whispered softly, observing the bluish half circles under her eyes. The skin around her nose was bright red, probably a result of catching cold combined with hours of crying. Her chilled fingers trembled within the embrace of his hand.

"That man got to you. I can see that." James gently rubbed Gillian's back. "You thought you were done grieving over something that happened in the past, but you're not. He brought all the memories back, didn't he?"

Tears rolled down Gillian's freckled cheeks and she uttered a little whimper. It was the first sound she'd made since being brought into the room.

James lifted her chin. "Don't give in to grief, Gillian. Your friends need you to be strong. Your employees need you to show up at work on Monday. He felt a prick of guilt for dragging her beloved cat into the conversation, but it couldn't be helped. "And what about the Dalai Lama? He couldn't live without you. Who would play his bird DVDs or fix him plates of organic tuna fish?"

The tears came faster, and though Harding held out a pocket-sized packet of tissues, James ignored him. He sensed that he'd struck a nerve by mentioning Gillian's tabby, so he pushed on. "You're his mother, Gillian. You can't just give up and rot in jail for a crime you didn't commit. Think of Dalai, and tell me where you've been."

Gillian slipped her hand from James's and used the sleeve of her jumpsuit to wipe her face.

"I spent the night with a woman named Felicity," she mumbled, her voice a ragged croak. "She was hired to put on several dog acts at Hog Fest." She sniffled and James accepted the tissues from Harding and handed them to Gillian. Harding covertly produced his pen and paper. "After I saw . . ." Gillian trailed off, unable to utter the name of the man she despised, so James said it for her.

"Jimmy?"

"Yes. *Him!*" She rubbed her eyes with a tissue and continued in a pained voice. "I just had to get away. I ran to the very end of the campground area, and then, I was too tired to keep running. My body is weak. I haven't been doing my yoga lately, and I've been sitting around too much after work, drinking tea and meditating." She sank down into one of the two chairs, never once looking in Harding's direction. She fastened her eyes on James as if he were her lifeline. "Anyway, I ran out of steam by the river, at the place where it runs parallel to the campsites."

"Is that where you met up with Felicity?" James gently prodded.

Gillian nodded. "She'd brought the dogs down to the river as a treat for performing so well. They were running and jumping and barking, and Felicity was sitting on a big boulder, watching them. She looked so content. She recognized me from the dog show and invited me to sit with her." Gillian balled the tissue in her hands. "I heard her, but it was like someone was shouting my name from a long way away. I just stared at the dogs. I . . . I wanted to jump in the water with them. Get lost with them." She lowered her voice to the faintest whisper. "So I did."

"You jumped into the water?" James asked and Gillian made a noise of assent. "And afterward, Felicity took care of you?"

"Yes," Gillian said. "I felt arms pulling me to the bank, and I was wrapped in a blanket. I remember her humming to me, and then I slept for a long time. When I woke up, I told her everything. Felicity and I talked long into the night. I . . . we . . . drank, too."

James was surprised. Gillian hardly ever consumed alcohol. "Well, you were pretty distraught."

"I am in agony, James," Gillian said without any of her usual dramatic flare. "That strawberry wine helped dull the pain, but that's all. When I woke up, I hoped that I'd dreamed the whole thing." She finally gazed at Harding. "But I knew that I hadn't. After thanking Felicity for her kindness, I went to *his* camper. I wanted to know if he was sorry for what he did so many years ago." Her eyes filled with tears again. "He never told me he was sorry. Not once. I wanted to hear the words, so I could consider granting him forgiveness."

"Did you talk to him?" James asked quickly.

Gillian shook her head. "No. I sat on the camper steps, trying to work up the courage to knock on the door, when that *awful* woman pushed me away and went inside. She then came right back out and started yelling at me." Gillian pulled a fresh tissue out of the packet and blew her nose. "I couldn't understand most of what she said because she was shouting in double-time, but I caught on that Jimmy was dead. When I heard that, I couldn't move. It was like getting punched in the stomach."

James eased himself into the chair across from her. "What do you mean?"

"I'm not sorry that he's gone to the other side, but *I* didn't send him there." Gillian put her head in her hands. "I wouldn't have wanted him to leave this life until he apologized to me. I needed to know that he felt regret over what he did."

James was almost afraid to speak the words that had formed on his lips, but before he could contain them, they came tumbling out. "You wanted Jimmy to apologize for killing your husband?"

Gillian issued the briefest nod but did not look up.

"How did it happen, Gillian? How did Jimmy cause your husband's death?"

Shoulders shaking, Gillian wailed into her hands. "He ran over him. That son of a bitch deliberately ran over my husband."

"With his car?" Harding asked from his corner.

"No." Gillian lifted her head, her green eyes rimmed with red. Sorrow had etched lines in her skin and cast shadows across her face. "With a chicken truck."

Chapter Eleven

Spaghetti Bolognese

An hour later, Gillian had finished her story. The telling of it drained her so completely that afterward she asked to be returned to her cell because she longed for quiet and solitude. With a sympathetic nod, Deputy Harding handed Gillian off to the officer waiting in the hall. When she was gone, Harding gestured for James to leave the room as well.

"Are you going to release her?" James asked.

Harding shook his head. "She's still a suspect, Mr. Henry. She has a strong motive, so we can't let her go until we've gathered more information."

"But she didn't hurt anyone!" James wearily protested. "She just wanted to confront the man who killed her husband."

Harding turned the corner at the end of the hall at the same moment Sheriff Jones stepped out of her office. Standing directly in his path, she gazed at him inquisitively.

"Ms. O'Malley has provided us with a complete statement," Harding informed his superior.

Jones was pleased. "Excellent. Let's talk in my office." She turned her tawny eyes on James. "We have your contact numbers, Mr. Henry. Why don't you and your friends return to the inn and try to relax?"

"We can hardly *relax* while Gillian is being held in suspicion for a crime she didn't commit," James said, his voice taut with anger.

"Understood, Mr. Henry," said the sheriff calmly. "We're going to examine every angle, I assure you. My deputies are canvassing the campground area and conducting interviews as we speak. We don't operate under assumptions in this department. We search for evidence and allow the facts to guide us." She placed a hand on his arm and steered him toward the lobby. "I'll review Ms. O'Malley's statement immediately. In the meantime, I'd like you and your friends to refrain from involving yourselves in our investigation. Ms. Hanover has my contact numbers, and I've also asked her, as one professional to another, to step aside so that we can gather information during this critical time. As she knows, the first twenty-four hours following a crime of this nature are crucial."

When they reached the lobby, the sheriff released James's arm. James met the distressed stares of the other supper club members. They all looked tired and uncomfortable as they waited on a wooden bench. Bennett perked up slightly upon seeing the attractive sheriff, but Sheriff Jones ducked back into the inner hallway without glancing his way.

Seeing James, Lucy raced over and threw her arms around him. "What happened back there?" she murmured into his neck.

In the circle of her arms, James inhaled the fruity scent of her shampoo. "I feel like I've been hit by a bus," he said. Gently pushing her away, he walked over to Lindy and Bennett.

"Did you see Gillian?" Lindy sagged against the side of the bench, hugging her purse to her chest in search of solace.

"She didn't kill Jimmy," James said and heard his friends exhale loudly in relief. "But I could see why she'd want to. Let's find a place where we can talk. I don't want to share her story here."

"The deputy taking my statement mentioned a place called the Old Hollywood Diner," Bennett said. "He said the decor's a little cheesy, but the food can't be beat."

"I can't believe I could eat at a time like this," Lindy moaned. "But I could use some comfort food. A big bowl of macaroni and cheese, maybe."

"Or pie," Lucy said. "Warm apple pie. With ice cream on top." She glanced at James. "And big mugs of coffee with loads of half-and-half. Come on, guys, we should get energized. Gillian is going to need us to be at our best if we're going to prove her innocence."

"In that case, I'm getting the biggest piece of meat on the menu." Bennett helped Lindy up from the bench. "I need something to wash away the taste of that foul coffee. No wonder those deputies arrested the wrong person—their brains have turned to mush from drinking that sludge."

● ● ●

The Elvis section of the Old Hollywood Diner was full, so a waitress wearing a lemon yellow dress and squeaky white sneakers led them to the Elizabeth Taylor section. Below a poster of Liz flashing a predatory smile in her role as Cleopatra, the supper club members perused a menu that was as thick as an anatomy textbook.

The waitress passed out ice water in amber cups and flipped open her pad. "Y'all wanna hear the specials?" she asked, slowly chewing a large piece of gum.

As James formed an image of a cow lazily chewing a long piece of grass, the rest of the group told her they'd be delighted to hear the specials. After the waitress mechanically recited them, she drifted away to care for other customers.

Bennett was the first to close his menu. Gazing at the poster above their table, he said, "Did you know that Elizabeth Taylor was born in England? Her parents were art dealers from St. Louis and went over there to open a gallery. She met Richard Burton, aka husband number five, while shooting that film. She actually got paid a million clams to star in that movie. That's a ton of dough in today's money, let alone 1963. Liz won two Oscars as well, but not for playing Cleopatra."

"I take it your current trivia book is about Hollywood," Lucy said sourly.

Bennett shook his head. "Nope. I'm done brushing up on that category. And don't go getting punchy at me just because you're hungry and worn out."

Lucy murmured an apology just as the waitress appeared to take their order.

"How's the Brando Bolognese?" James asked, his stomach rumbling expectantly.

Their waitress, who wore no name tag on her spotless uniform, shrugged. "Pretty good, I reckon. I don't eat them foreign foods, but other folks seem to like it fine." She jotted James's order on her pad. "'Sides, I don't care for that Brando fella. He couldn't talk right. Sounded like a goat chokin' every time he opened his mouth."

Having no idea what a strangling goat might sound like, James nodded in agreement. The rest of the supper club members ordered and the waitress left. She returned a few minutes later bearing a pitcher of root beer, even though no one had ordered soda. "I know y'all wanted tea, but we make it fresh, and it's still brewin'," she explained. "This here's the best birch beer you'll ever taste. It's a house special."

"What *isn't* a house special at this place?" Bennett said. He took a sip of soda and the caramel-colored foam flecked his mustache. "All right, James. I can't stand it anymore. We have time before our food arrives, so tell us what happened at the station. How'd you get Gillian to talk, and what did she say?"

James removed Bennett's tiny recorder from his pocket. "I hope you're not mad, but I've had this with me since it fell out of your pocket in the Bronco. Something just told me to press the Record button, so I did. I think I taped over most of your statistics. I'm really sorry, Bennett."

"It's okay, man. You made a good call. Now, put that thing on the table and let's all listen to what you heard."

After rewinding the tape, James pressed the Play button. Gillian's voice fizzled out of the machine's tiny speaker.

"To tell you how Jimmy killed my husband, I have to go back a few years, to a time I've tried really hard to put out of my mind and out of my heart.

"I married Walden O'Malley when I was twenty. We met doing volunteer work at the local animal shelter and fell in love quick as a lightning strike. My hometown was so small that the post office and grocery store were in the same building. There was one place to eat, a bank, and two churches. Most folks worked at the local poultry plant. Walden's family had just moved to town because his father had gotten a job at the plant. That's why I'd never met him before the day at the animal shelter.

"Walden enrolled in the local community college. He took agriculture classes because he wanted to own a small farm and raise livestock. We dated for six months and were married on the courthouse steps. No party, no gifts — just us declaring our love for each other with our landlord as witness. It was perfect."

There was a pause while Gillian accepted a glass of water from Deputy Harding.

"Walden really loved animals, so he asked his father what the conditions were like in the factory. For the birds, that is. His father told him that the conditions for the workers were fair and that was all that mattered. He got really angry and told Walden to be thankful that they had enough money to pay for his classes.

"Walden's family had moved from Pennsylvania because mills and factories across the state were closing. Families were turned out in the cold with no means of paying for mortgages or car loans or food. Walden knew his father had been lucky to find work, but he still wanted to know how the chickens were handled once they were delivered to the factory, so he asked one of the line workers to give him a tour. That's how it all started."

"How what started, ma'am?" Deputy Harding asked.

"Walden's interaction with Jimmy Lang. Jimmy was a driver. He picked up the birds from farms all around western Virginia and brought them to the plant. He was a cruel soul. He actually enjoyed bringing the birds to their deaths. And the more they suffered, the more he was entertained."

"But the chicken factory was a processing plant, right?" Harding sounded genuinely perplexed. "That's what they do – process poultry for the rest of us to eat. It's a dirty job, but someone's got to do it, or no one would be eating fried chicken for supper. Does that really make a person bad?"

"It wasn't what they did but how they did it!" Gillian raised her voice. "The birds were stuffed so tight into cages on Jimmy's truck that they couldn't move. Then, Jimmy would unload them with a forklift and dump them on the conveyer belt. He didn't care if some of them fell off, got crushed by machines, or died from exposure on the road. He'd keep track of the number of casualties on each load and mark them in a notebook. He and two of the factory workers held a secret bet over who had the highest number of 'accidents' each month.

"At the time Walden went on that factory tour, we'd only been married four days. We didn't have any money except what we both earned working part-time at the grocery store, but Walden promised me a honeymoon week in Philly as soon as we could afford it. He wanted to introduce me to his grandparents and show me the city of his childhood. He never got the chance."

James noticed their waitress bearing down upon them with a laden tray and hit the Pause button.

Bennett received a mammoth bacon and Monterey jack burger accompanied by a mountain of French fries and a dish of baked beans. A platter of fried catfish and hush puppies was slid beneath Lindy's nose, and Lucy was given slices of turkey resting on pillows of mashed potatoes and stuffing, a bowl of cranberry sauce, and a small pitcher of thick brown gravy. A basket of corn-bread muffins was set in the center of the table for everyone to share.

"Be right back with your Brando, hon," the waitress said. She returned without delay carrying an oversized plate of spaghetti noodles drenched in a thick meat sauce. In addition to his pasta entrée, James was given a small basket of garlic bread.

"Y'all need anything else?" the waitress asked as her customers gaped at their plates.

"You got a wheelbarrow?" Bennett looked at her. "We're going to need one if we eat so much as half of this stuff."

"No one ever leaves the Old Hollywood hungry." The woman smiled. "Gimme a holler if your drinks run dry."

After twirling a strand of slippery spaghetti around and around on his fork, James gave up and began to cut the saturated noodles with his knife. He took a bite of pasta and felt some of his tension dissipate as he savored the rich meat sauce and the supple noodles. Sighing with satisfaction, he prepared another forkful.

"I hear you, man," Bennett said, holding his mammoth burger aloft. "Just what the doctor ordered."

Lindy squeezed a fat piece of lemon over her catfish filet, creating a crooked line of drizzle over the deep brown crust. While Lindy cut into her fish with the side of her fork, Lucy scooped a gelatinous spoonful of cranberry sauce onto a slice of turkey breast. She gestured at the recorder. "Keep going, James."

James pushed the play button and Gillian's voice floated from the speaker.

"Walden got his tour. What he saw forever scarred him.. He came back to our apartment and cried. He put his face in his hands and let his emotions flow out of his body. Oh, how I loved him for that. But he told me such horrible things that day. Things I'll never forget! He said that after the chickens were unloaded from the truck, they were hung upside down and dipped into an electrified stunning tank. This makes them confused, but not unconscious, before they're finally killed. It's so cruel!

"And the conditions on the farms were too much to bear! Those chickens spent six weeks crammed into an enclosed structure, standing and sleeping in their own waste. Genetically modified, they grew so fat so fast that tons of them had heart attacks or complete organ failure because of the sheer mass of their bodies.

"If they managed to live the whole six weeks in those conditions, then Jimmy would come for them. Whether it was pouring rain or ninety-five degrees beneath a sweltering sun, he'd stuff them in their metal cages and take long lunches while the birds endured the weather. One day, he bragged to his buddies at the plant about how a bunch of boys threw rocks at the chickens and the birds were too dumb to realize they were being pummeled in the face by stones. It's not like they could have moved!"

Gillian paused again, but obviously only long enough to calm herself.

"Walden was desperate to secure humane treatment for the poultry, so he started an activist group. You can only imagine how unpopular that made him! The only people who'd join were college students or bored retirees."

There was a grunt from Harding.

"After all, the plant employed most of the town. When Walden began picketing outside the plant's front gates, his father threatened to cut all ties with us. But Walden and his group didn't stop. Workers threw chicken feet and other body parts at us. They called us traitors and names I'd rather not repeat. We tried to get the press on our side, but the local papers weren't sympathetic to our cause. Finally, Walden got a reporter from Washington to come to one of our rallies. This journalist interviewed Jimmy, and the story of the chicken's mistreatment got picked up all over the region. However, the story was quickly replaced by the news of a missing hiker who happened to be a distant cousin of the governor.

"Nothing changed at the plant or at the farms. The only thing that the publicity did was make Jimmy Lang furious! He'd been portrayed as the malicious cad he was, and his boss heard about Jimmy's monthly bet over the dead chickens. From that point, Jimmy was told that his pay would be docked for every dead bird. Jimmy was furious. The plant had always taken all his birds before – alive or dead. Suddenly, they changed their policy and he wanted revenge. So one day . . . "

Gillian fought to compose herself as she neared the most difficult part of her tale.

"Walden always rode his bike to campus. The college was about four miles from our apartment. He rode on the shoulder of a two-lane road that ran parallel to the interstate for about three of those miles. That's where Jimmy spotted him. Jimmy was headed to the plant with a load of birds, and he'd left the interstate to visit a decrepit truck stop that served beer. He was

far from sober and had smoked a joint before getting back into his rig."

Seated at their table in the Old Hollywood Diner, James and his friends had stopped eating and were staring at the recorder as though it were a coiled snake.

"Jimmy swerved that big truck and laid on the horn, hoping to give Walden the scare of his lifetime, but once his rig started to skid, Jimmy couldn't regain control of the truck. It flipped over, sliding down the highway. Walden was pinned under it.

"The doors to the chicken cages burst open and birds went everywhere. They were strewn all over the asphalt, the embankment, the wildflowers growing alongside the road . . .

"The state police arrived at the scene and took Jimmy away. He was uninjured. I went to the courthouse every single day of his trial. He was given fifteen years for vehicular manslaughter under the influence of alcohol and drugs. That's it! Fifteen years in exchange for the malicious act that ended Walden's life."

Another silence. Lindy dabbed at her wet face with her napkin.

"I thought I'd continue Walden's fight against the inhumane treatment of those poor birds, but after the incident, the other activists were too frightened to protest. I became a pariah. Everywhere I went, people muttered jokes about chickens crossing the road. It was awful. I made it through my final exams at college, graduated, and moved away. I've never been back to that town. I've never even visited Walden's grave. I thought I could pretend that that part of my life never existed. It all happened so long ago. But when I saw Jimmy — alive and laughing, I felt like my husband had been killed all over again."

The sound of weeping echoed from the recorder.

"But I didn't hurt that man, Deputy Harding. Much as part of me would have liked to, I didn't. That would have dishonored Walden's memory. He was a pacifist. He was a gentle, giving soul. I wanted an apology from Jimmy. I needed to know that he regretted what he'd done — that he was sorry for shattering our hopes and dreams. Now, I'll never know. There'll never be closure for me."

More silence. Finally, the sound of a defeated exhalation.

"I'm tired, James. These memories . . . they weigh so much. May I be alone now, Deputy Harding?"

James turned off the recorder.

"There it is." He sighed. "That's her story."

His friends were stunned.

"No wonder she's a vegetarian," Lindy mumbled after a long silence, pushing her plate of half-eaten fish away. Lucy and Bennett followed suit. As they sat, digesting their heavy food and Gillian's tragic narrative, their waitress returned, wearing a look of concern. "Somethin' wrong with your dinners, folks?"

"No, no," Lucy hastily assured her. "We just wanted to save room for dessert. We have some serious thinking to do, and for that, we're going to need some sugar. Apple pie à la mode for everyone. And coffee, please. Lots of coffee."

The waitress nodded and cleared their plates. She wiped their table clean and came back a few minutes later with four servings of apple pie topped with vanilla ice cream. She then handed out white coffee mugs and placed a steaming carafe of coffee in the center of the table. She retrieved a dozen individual creamers from her apron pocket and sprinkled them in a loose circle around the carafe.

"I'll check back on you folks in a bit," she said, bustling off to take the order of a family of six seated in the James Dean section.

Lucy dug a small notepad from her purse, uncapped a pen, and gave her friends a penetrating stare. "We're going to make a list of those people we need to interview in order to find Jimmy's *real* killer. I think we should start with Felicity, the dog lady."

Lindy frowned. "But Lucy, you're a deputy now. Won't treading on the sheriff's territory get you into trouble?"

"This is *Gillian* we're talking about." Lucy's blue eyes flashed. "I don't care what rules I break, we have to find the solution to this mystery before the festival ends!"

"You're right," James said. "We need to get answers from Felicity, Hailey, Eleanor, and anyone else who might have a clue as to what really happened last night." He touched Lucy's hand. "But we have to be discreet, or we might get sent back to Quincy's Gap."

"And that won't do Gillian a lick of good," Bennett said.

As the four friends stared at the names on the list, James plowed his fork through the golden crust of the apple pie and scooped a generous bite into his mouth. The apples were so soft that they practically dissolved after contacting his tongue. Sugar, cinnamon, and a hint of nutmeg coated his taste buds, and he greedily took another bite. Next, he collected a forkful of the smooth and creamy ice cream and ate it slowly, blissfully, licking every drop from the tines.

Lucy jabbed a finger at the list. "At this point, our suspects are all women."

"Makes sense. It's a bit easier for me to picture a woman climbing up that skinny metal ladder to that camper roof to tape over the vents," Bennett said, wiping ice cream from his mustache.

"But a man could do that just as easily," Lindy argued, splashing cream into her coffee.

"Like that pale-skinned guy with the black baseball hat I saw arguing with Jimmy," James said. "He and Jimmy had a serious fight. We should keep our eye out for this guy."

"It won't be easy without the rest of us having seen him and no name to go by, but if he's *that* pasty, he should stick out in a crowd." Lindy twirled a coffee stirrer around her finger. "I also don't think we should forget about the barbecue competition."

"You believe someone would murder Jimmy just to be known as the barbecue champion of Hog Fest?" James asked.

"Not so much for the title as for the contract with Heartland Foods," Lindy replied. "That kind of offer could change a person's life."

"Good point, Lindy." Lucy scribbled on her notepad. "We need to see which of the other team leaders might be pinched for money. They'd have the best access to Jimmy's camper, after all."

"And didn't that Hailey girl say she'd spent a few hours fraternizing with one of the enemy teams?" Bennett pointed his fork at his friends. "In the middle of a competition? Doesn't that strike you as peculiar?"

Everyone nodded in response.

"Maybe Hailey's been looking for greener pastures. With Jimmy as my boyfriend, I sure as heck would be," Lindy said.

Lucy signaled for the check. "We'll start with Felicity. Hailey will be tied up at the sheriff's department for a while. And James is right. We need to find the guy Jimmy fought with if we can." She glanced at her watch. "When is the barbecue rib contest over, Lindy?"

Lindy dug her folded schedule from her red leather purse and scrutinized it carefully. "It should be done by now. The next food category is Poultry. The judging begins in less than two hours."

"Perfect. We'll just have time to interview Felicity before we start talking to the cooking teams." Lucy looked up as the check was placed in front of her. She slid across the table to Bennett. "What's the damage?"

Bennett eyed the check and performed an instant calculation. "Fourteen dollars and thirty-three cents per person." He reached into his wallet and pulled out a ten and four singles. "That includes the tip."

After settling their bill, they climbed back into Lucy's Jeep and drove toward the festival grounds. At one point, Lucy stopped at a red light that seemed interminable. Finally, a sheriff's department cruiser shot across their path, followed very closely by a car that looked strangely familiar to James.

It can't be, James thought. Panicked, he leaned forward in his seat and peered intently at the moving car, hoping to catch a glimpse of the license plate. He couldn't be certain, but he was relatively sure that it read THESTAR, an abbreviation standing for their hometown paper, the *Shenandoah Star Ledger.*

It appeared that Murphy had ditched her stories on fancy felines and yodeling in order to drive to Hudsonville, and James had the distinct feeling that she hadn't changed her plans just to spend quality time with him. She must have heard about Jimmy's murder.

"What's up?" Bennett whispered from the seat next to him. "You look like you saw a ghost."

James rubbed his temples. "Not a ghost. Just more trouble."

Chapter Twelve

Barbecued Cornish Hen

Felicity was practicing with her dogs at the far end of the campground. A pair of Jack Russell terriers leapt through a series of hoops in blurs of white fur as they raced one another. At the end of the obstacle course, the dogs barked and smiled, their tongues lolling and their stumpy tails wagging fiercely as Felicity lavished them with praise.

Two border collies performed their routine next. They dashed through tunnels, climbed steps, and wove in between flexible poles with lightning speed. Felicity encouraged her animals by calling their names and blowing shrill notes on a small silver whistle. She had a long, blond braid and wore a baggy white cotton shirt embroidered with small flowers. With her black skirt and mud-covered clogs, Felicity looked like a Dutch milkmaid.

"I was wondering if y'all were going to track me down," she said by way of welcome. "The news about Jimmy's death has spread like germs on an airplane. I heard about Gillian, too. I even asked to see her after they finished questioning me at the station, but they wouldn't allow it." She picked at the end of a coiled leash in agitation. "How is she?"

"Not so great. But she had someone to confide in before her arrest, thanks to you." Lindy took both of Felicity's hands in her own. "We are so grateful to you for taking care of Gillian last night. We were frantic with worry over her disappearance."

"It was nothing." Felicity waved off Lindy's gratitude. "Plus, I made a new friend. That doesn't happen too often at our age, does it?"

One of the border collies trotted over to Bennett and began to sniff the cuffs of his pants. Bennett shifted his feet and backed away from the curious canine.

"He's harmless," Felicity assured Bennett.

"Everybody says that about their dogs," Bennett muttered. "But I'm a mailman. I've seen the *nicest* dogs turn into savage, postal-carrier-hating maniacs in my presence." He eyed the dog fearfully. "This dog's going to eat me, isn't he?"

"Parson might lick you to death, but that's it." Felicity placed her hand on the head of the black and white collie sitting calmly beside her. "And this is Vicar. The terriers are Minister and Clergy. My father was a preacher. He passed away years ago, and now, these guys are my only family."

"Is your show still set for tonight?" Lucy asked.

Felicity nodded. "Nothing on the schedule's been altered despite this morning's, uh, discovery. That's why we're practicing. Besides, I wanted to get my mind off my trip to the sheriff's. It was a very intimidating experience. I felt guilty even though I haven't done anything wrong."

"Believe me, we've all felt that way before," James said and Felicity shot him a grateful smile. "We can promise you that Gillian's innocent of Jimmy's murder as well."

"I'm sure Felicity made it clear to the authorities that Gillian was too inebriated to have been able to find her way to Jimmy's camper and climb onto the roof," Lucy said.

Felicity fidgeted with Vicar's collar. "I told them what happened. Plain and simple. We both drank wine and fell asleep. When I woke up this morning, Gillian was gone." She shrugged in resignation. "I don't think I made a very good alibi for Gillian. She could have left anytime during the night, and I wouldn't have been the wiser."

The supper club members exchanged glum looks.

Felicity ruffled the fur on Vicar's neck and sighed. "I'm sorry."

Lucy touched the trainer on the shoulder. "Don't be. All you did was tell the truth."

"Did Jimmy have something against dogs?" James asked abruptly.

Felicity narrowed her eyes for the briefest of seconds. "I have no idea. Why?"

James's friends shifted their gazes so that none of them were staring at Felicity as he pursued his indelicate line of questioning. "We were standing with him yesterday when you, er, shouted rather passionately at him." He held out his hands in supplication. "I'm sure you had every reason to be angry at the guy. We'd only talked to him for a few minutes, but it didn't take us long to figure out that he was a louse."

Lindy nodded. "He was rude and crude."

"A loudmouthed jerk," Bennett said.

"Don't forget chauvinistic hillbilly," Lucy added.

Felicity studied James and then sat on a folding chair positioned between her tent and a row of roomy dog cages. She gestured at a picnic blanket spread out on the ground beside her. "Why don't y'all take a seat and I'll tell you how that demon disguised as a human being caused me to end up here, performing like a circus monkey and sleeping in a tent."

The moment the supper club members settled down on the picnic blanket, the two Jack Russells made a beeline for Bennett. After covering the back of his hand with wet kisses, they stretched out on either side of his legs and closed their eyes.

"Looks like you have a pair of bookends," Lindy teased.

Bennett rolled his eyes in response. "Why me?"

"They must've detected the scent of a fellow carnivore," James said before turning his attention back to Felicity. "So you travel around with your dogs? Doing shows?"

"That's right. Festival after festival for about eight months of the year. When we're back home in South Carolina, I pick up extra money doing doggie birthday parties and performing for nursing homes and day cares and such." She stroked Vicar's head and the dog blinked his liquid brown eyes at her in adoration. "But this didn't used to be our life. My dogs were competitors, and for several years, they were the best in the Southeast. I used to teach classes at one of Columbus's top kennels, too. That was all before Jimmy came along and ruined everything."

"What did he do?" Lucy glanced at Parson in alarm. "He didn't hurt the dogs, did he?"

Felicity shook her head. "No, though I wouldn't have put it past the bastard. Two years ago, my camper — this was back when I had a pretty nice one — was parked next to Jimmy's at the Memphis Brews and Barbecue Festival. My dogs were competing in the agility trials, and I was also asked to help judge the jumpers event, since my dogs never competed in that category."

"Do the dogs earn pretty good prize money?" Lindy leaned forward, curious.

"It's not bad," Felicity said evenly. "Top prizes could earn you a thousand dollars here and there, as well as food and supplies and stuff like that. We won quite a bit, but I made my money giving lectures and demonstrations. Back then, folks saw me as an expert in the field. My reputation paid my bills." She scowled. "That's how Jimmy got to me. He tarnished my reputation to the point where people wouldn't want me to clip their dogs' toenails, let alone enroll in my agility training or obedience classes."

"How? He's just a tow-truck-driving barbecue cooker." Lucy gave Felicity a look of bewilderment. "How could his opinion matter to anyone in your field?"

"His opinion mattered when he lied to the head judge at our competition in Memphis. Jimmy claimed that I was giving my dogs illegal substances so they'd have more energy. He said that he removed pills from their food bowls because he was worried they might be dangerous for my animals. Turns out they were illegal steroids—the kind men use to bulk up their muscles. He even claimed to have found the empty pill vial in my garbage!" Felicity slapped her hand on her leg. "As if I would ever put the lives of my dogs in jeopardy. They're my closest friends!"

"But the judges believed him?" Lindy asked.

"Maybe they did, and maybe they didn't, but they *were* concerned about having a scandal connected to their event, so they disqualified my dogs, canceled my lectures and demonstrations, and found another judge to replace me. After that, I was blackballed in the dog world because everyone *assumed* I was guilty. And now"— she waved her arm around the campground—"here I am. Barely scratching out a living."

James stroked Parson's soft fur. The canine blinked his eyes in contentment. "Why did Jimmy go after you?"

"He complained that my dogs barked too much in the early morning when he was trying to sleep," Felicity said. "He told me that it was their fault he didn't win his cooking contests that day, and if 'my beasts' weren't quiet the next night, he'd teach them, or *me*, a lesson."

Thinking of how Gillian had described Jimmy's cruelty to the chickens he delivered to the poultry plant, James believed that Jimmy's threats against Felicity and her dogs were issued in complete seriousness.

"Did you relocate to a different place in the campground?" Bennett wanted to know.

Felicity sighed and shook her head. "No, and not a day goes by that I don't regret that decision. I was too proud and stubborn to realize that one man could change my life with a single lie." She shrugged helplessly. "He taught me a lesson all right."

"I'd like to hurt the guy for what he did to you, but someone beat me to it!" Lindy said.

"Like I told the sheriff, it wasn't me," Felicity continued. "When I woke up this morning alone, I was a bit confused. I saw the blanket I had given to Gillian folded neatly in a corner of my tent, and I knew that she hadn't been a figment of my imagination, but she wasn't there anymore." Felicity gazed at her four pets lovingly. "I'm not sorry that Jimmy's dead, but it wasn't by my hand. If I were sent to jail, who would take care of my dogs? It may sound silly, but they're my reason for living, and I'd never risk their future like that."

Lucy chuckled. "That's not silly at all. Want to see my babies?" She removed a color photograph from her wallet and unfolded it for Felicity to view. "Here are my darlings. Bono, Benatar, and Bon Jovi. I named them after my favorite rock stars."

"Gorgeous!" Felicity exclaimed and showed the photo to Vicar. "Look at these German shepherds, Vic. I bet you guys would have a great time playing together." She handed Lucy the photograph. "Would y'all like to watch our show tonight? We'd be proud to have you in the stands."

"We'll come if we can," Lindy promised and got to her feet. "But right now, we have to do everything possible to help Gillian."

"Of course." Felicity slipped a leash around Vicar's neck. "Please let me know if there's anything I can do. After all, she barely knew me, and yet she offered me a job. She said she's been thinking of expanding her grooming business into a full-fledged dog obedience school and kennel. Oh, what was the name of her business? The Yuppie Puppy! She said that I could run the new business with her, as a partner. Just like that, she was giving me that chance to go back to my old way of life. She believed in my talent and integrity."

"That's our Gillian," Bennett said proudly.

Lucy touched Felicity's shoulder. "But you drew her out of the water, put a blanket around her, and let her unburden herself to you. And *she* was a stranger to you when you did those things. You're a good woman, Felicity, and you're now a friend to all of us." Lucy put her hands on her hips in the determined posture James had seen many times in the past. "We're going to straighten this all out, and when Gillian is back with us, we're all going to celebrate together, okay?"

Overwhelmed by emotion, Felicity could only nod in response. The supper club members said goodbye to Felicity and the dogs and wished them good luck at their show. "We'll keep you in the loop," James promised as they walked away.

"Thank you!" She waved and Vicar barked in accompaniment.

The foursome navigated through the campground area and came to a stop in front of a lemonade stand.

"I don't think she's our killer," Lindy said in a low voice.

"Me either, but we can't cross Felicity off our list yet," Lucy said. "She had both motive and means. And she's camped next to Jimmy before, so she might have known that he used a propane heater." Lucy's eyes scanned the crowd. "Still, she doesn't strike me as a murderer. We'll just move her name down to the bottom for now. Let's go ahead and question the other barbecue teams next. And don't forget to keep our eyes open for the pale guy James saw arguing with Jimmy. Who knows? He might even be on one of the teams."

"We'd better split up," James suggested. "There's not much time left before their next category is due in to the judges."

"Wait a sec." Lucy held up a finger as though to stop her friends from moving forward. "If the other barbecue guys are anything like Jimmy, they won't spill their guts to the two of us." Lucy looked at Lindy. "You men might need to break the ice with them."

"You have a point. Let's have a gander at the team names again," Bennett said, and the four friends quickly divided the teams between them. Lucy and James paired off and headed toward the cooking area. The first group they planned to talk to was the Adam's Ribbers.

"Better let *me* take the lead with these gals," Lucy said, her eyes sparkling in anticipation of prying information from the four women.

The teammates were huddled around the grill, engaged in a debate over which sauce to brush on the Cornish hens they had chosen as their entries in the Poultry category.

A large woman wearing a pink-and-white-striped apron and a white golf visor slapped a pair of tongs against the top of her cooker and shouted, "No more fruit sauces, damn it. They're not working!"

"But it's just a *hint* of orange juice!" a woman dressed in a denim skirt and T-shirt reading *I Love Johnny Depp* argued.

"No. We're goin' with the spicy sauce this time," said a third woman in a firm but gentle voice. "Thelma's got this sauce just right. It's a winner for sure."

"Men prefer spicy," the fourth team member, a skinny redhead, declared and then noticed James standing near their grill. "Isn't that right?" she asked him.

"I'm partial to spicy sauces over fruit sauces, yes," he answered truthfully.

The woman in the Johnny Depp T-shirt said, "Hey! You were one of the brisket judges. Now that the contest is over, can you tell us what you thought of the mango sauce we entered in that category?"

"I thought it was a bit too sweet and fruity to complement a piece of red meat." James shrugged. "I'm sorry, ladies. I'm not trying to offend you, but if your friend Thelma made a spicy sauce, I'd go with that one."

"Would you try it for us?" The Johnny Depp fan gave James and Lucy eager looks. "We're using it on Cornish hens."

"Sure thing," Lucy agreed. "As long as it's not against the rules."

"If you're not judging that event, then you're just tasting this sauce as a food lover, not as a judge," the woman said. "I'm Zoe, by the way." She smiled and handed them a paper plate bearing a half of a hen. Though still stuffed from their enormous late lunch, James and Lucy took a bite of Cornish hen, chewed thoughtfully, and then took a second bite in order to convince the ladies that their sauce was being carefully assessed.

Lucy set her plate down on the card table next to the grill. "It's good."

"But not great?" The woman in the striped apron gave Lucy a piercing look and then turned her sharp gaze on James.

"The spices are a bit too subtle for my taste. I think you need more crushed red pepper," he said. "But the texture is perfect. It's thick and savory. As soon as you get the spice factor down, I think you'll have the perfect sauce."

Thelma and Zoe beamed while the other Adam's Ribbers thanked James and Lucy.

"Can we get you some tea?" Thelma asked.

Lucy accepted and settled down at their card table, trying to appear as relaxed and casual as possible. James followed her lead.

"Who's the one to beat in the Poultry category?" She directed her question at Zoe.

"The Tenderizers are good at everything," Zoe said. "We could beat them in this category if their team doesn't get extra help."

"What do you mean?" Lucy frowned in confusion. "Are you referring to what we just did?"

Thelma sprinkled several ingredients into a large bowl of barbecue sauce. "No. You just tasted our food. We're talking about someone actually *makin'* their food. We heard a rumor that Jimmy Lang's girlfriend was the person who came up with all his secret sauces, rubs, and mops. We also heard that two of the other teams were tryin' to get her recipes from her."

"You'd think they'd let the woman alone!" Zoe growled in disgust. "Jimmy seemed like a nasty piece of work, but he was still her man. People can be such vultures."

"Did you gals know Jimmy well?" Lucy asked.

They all shook their heads.

"We've only been in one other contest with him, and that was almost a year ago," Zoe said. "That was our first time cooking competitively, and we were too busy scrambling to get our entries in to pay him much mind."

"Good thing we *didn't* bother with him," Thelma added. "I'd have had to smack that boy with the business end of my spatula if he carried on to our faces the way he did at the brisket contest yesterday. What a horse's ass!" She dipped a spoon into the sauce and licked it. Grinning, she winked at James.

"Still, there are men like him all over the place," one of the other women said with a shrug. "You gotta just leave them in your rearview and do your own thing. That's how we all got together. We left jobs run by overbearing, butt-pinching jerk-offs. Now, we run our own gourmet food market and do these contests as a hobby." She raised her glass to her friends. "We're havin' a blast and we're gettin' better with every entry."

The women exchanged high fives.

"Sounds like tons of fun." Lucy finished her tea and smiled at the women. "We'd best be on our way. Good luck to you all in the next contest." She patted the grill lightly. "I think you have a winner here."

Thelma handed James a handwritten recipe. "Just in case we win, I want you to know what was in the sauce. Just keep it hidden until the contest is over."

Surprised by Thelma's generous gift, James blushed and thanked all four women.

"I don't see any motive there," Lucy said as they headed for the next cook site. "They don't need money, and they weren't really affected by Jimmy's death."

When James didn't respond, she turned to look at him and realized that he'd stopped walking. "What are you looking at?" she demanded and then gaped in astonishment.

Murphy Alistair had appeared from behind one of the RVs and was making her way toward James in hurried strides. When she was close enough to touch, she dropped her briefcase on the ground and kissed him on the lips.

"Poor you!" she whispered tenderly. "I'm so sorry about Gillian! How are you holding up?"

James gently extracted himself from the embrace. "I'm okay," he responded, keeping his emotions guarded. "How did you find out about what happened?"

"You know I have contacts all over the valley. I got an email from a colleague in Charlottesville, and when I recognized that the murder had taken place in Hudsonville, I called my friend and learned that the victim had been killed at the festival." Her hazel eyes were filled with concern. "I had to come see that you were all right."

Unable to stop himself, James asked, "So you're just here for me? Not to write a story about this?"

Murphy scooped her briefcase off the ground. "I'll cover the story, of course. Our readers would want to know about a fellow town member's involvement in the case."

"Are you referring to Gillian?" James tried to control his rising anger.

"I'm talking about all of you, actually." Murphy issued a brief nod at Lucy.

James took Murphy's arm and pulled her several yards away. "Look. You don't know the full picture. Gillian is innocent. Once we get her name cleared and take her back home, she's not going to want to see her ordeal in print in the *Star*. And her friends don't want people gossiping about her. You need to keep her out of your paper."

"I can't leave out pertinent information like that. She's half the story!" Murphy protested. "And people in Quincy's Gap know her and will care deeply about how this whole thing unfolds for her."

"*Unfolds!*" James spluttered. "She's not a piece of laundry! She's my friend and a damned fine person." He lowered his voice to a hissed whisper. "I'm warning you, Murphy, leave her name out of your piece."

Murphy was stunned by his ferocity, but she quickly recovered. "Why not tell me what's going on in your words, then?"

"You're unbelievable, you know that?" James snarled at her. "You're not here for me at all. I'm secondary to this—the *big* story!" When Murphy didn't deny this, he turned away from her in a fury. "I have to go. Lucy and I are trying to do some *good* before Gillian is forced to spend the night in a jail cell."

Grabbing his arm, Murphy pleaded with him. "I could help, too. When I interview people, I could discover information that would throw doubt on Gillian's guilt."

"That would finally put your prying ways to good use, then," James snapped and then relented a fraction. "We'll talk later, okay? I'm short on time."

"And on kindness," Murphy muttered stormily and stomped off in the opposite direction.

"Let's tackle the Tenderizers," James growled when he reached Lucy's side. "I'd love to have an excuse to take out my anger on some smart-ass, beer-swigging, butt-scratching SOB."

"I love it when you talk tough," Lucy said, looking unexpectedly happy.

Chapter Thirteen

Tie-Dye Sno-Cone

If James and Lucy hadn't been so distracted by Murphy's sudden appearance, they might have paid more attention to the noticeable lack of activity near the Tenderizers' commercial-sized grill. Instead, they took a cursory glance around and assumed that the team must be gathered inside one of the nearby RVs.

"This one's the biggest," Lucy said, jerking her thumb at the RV parked closest to the grill. She knocked lightly on the door, waited a moment, and turned the knob.

As the door swung inward, James caught a glimpse of two horizontal figures on the camper's pullout sofa. He saw a tan thigh, a flash of large breasts, and the round white hills of a man's hairy rump. It took both James and Lucy several seconds to realize that the many-limbed creature they were staring at was, in actuality, the entwined bodies of Jimmy's girlfriend Hailey and a man James didn't recognize.

"What the—!" the man shouted as he swiveled his head toward the open door.

Lucy pivoted so abruptly that she lost her footing on the camper's step and fell onto James, knocking him to the ground. They lay there for a moment, stunned.

By the time James stood up and brushed loose grass and dirt from his soiled pants, Hailey had appeared in the camper's doorway. Clutching the hand of a middle-aged man wearing a pair of faded jeans and an embarrassed grin, Hailey descended the two metal stairs. Her cheeks were spotted with red, and her two-toned hair looked like an unraveled ball of yarn.

"Ever heard of knockin'?" she demanded angrily, adjusting her low-cut T-shirt so that it barely covered the lacy cups of her turquoise bra. Finally, satisfied that the perfect amount of cleavage was visible, Hailey placed her hands on her hips.

"We knocked," Lucy said. "I'm sorry. I guess it wasn't loud enough."

"It sure wasn't!" Hailey pointed a magenta nail at James and Lucy. "And before you go judgin' me, bein' that Jimmy's not even in the ground yet, I want you to know that Bob here is my *real* man. We've been together, at a distance like, for almost a year now."

The man stepped forward and held out his hand. "I remember y'all from the brisket judgin'. Damned endive." His face clouded over at the memory, but he shrugged it off with a forgiving grin. "Name's Bob Barker. Not the game show host, but the contractor with the most. Pleased to meet you."

Bob's slogan gave James pause, but he shook the man's hand all the same.

"I just asked Hailey to marry me," Bob said, smiling. He removed a black velvet box from his front pants pocket and opened it. "Cost me more than my first truck," he told James and Lucy and angled the box so that the sunlight glinted off the diamond solitaire. "But my Hailey's worth it."

"It's beautiful," Lucy said, ogling the ring.

James glanced at Hailey. Though she gazed at the piece of jewelry with pride, he wondered why the ring was still in its box and not on her finger.

"Why pretend to be with Jimmy if you and Bob have already been together for a year?" Lucy asked Hailey without glancing away from the diamond.

"Well, I didn't know if Bob was really gonna leave his wife, but he did. He showed me the legal papers last night. This was all after Jimmy fell asleep with that dumb heater on. It's why I spent the night with Bob. I knew it was all over between Jimmy and me. I was gonna tell Jimmy about Bob this morning." She paused and inspected her nails. "But I had some personal business to work out with him first."

Before Lucy could ask what kind of business Hailey had to complete with Jimmy, Bob Barker took a step forward, as if to shield Hailey from additional questioning. "I think Hailey's been through enough, don't you?" His tone left no room for argument. "She's just gonna help me polish up the mop we're usin' on the Tenderizers' chicken entry, and then she's gonna take a nice, long rest."

Hailey frowned. "Don't forget that I'm entering this category, too, Bob." She stared at him. "I told you I was gonna let everyone see who the *real* Pitmaster is. This is *my* chance to shine, and I ain't gonna pass up the chance to be the champion."

"Sure, why not? After this competition, you'll be Mrs. Bob Barker, and you'll be one of the Tenderizers." Bob lowered his voice. "A behind-the-scenes member, of course, seein' as we *are* a male team." He rubbed Hailey's lower back fondly. "We're gonna win all over the country with you as our secret weapon."

Hailey wasn't pleased. "I don't think I wanna be any man's secret weapon anymore. I'm tired of folks not knowin' that I'm just as good as the rest of you when it comes to 'cue."

Bob seemed to consider his reply carefully. "Don't get yourself upset, darlin'. Come on back inside and try our chipotle chicken mop, and then we can talk some more *in private* about when we're gonna tie the knot."

Hailey glanced at Bob, clearly in no rush to taste the Tenderizers' mop. "You go on. I'll be just a sec. I wanna have a smoke, and I know you don't like the smell of cigarettes inside the camper."

Hesitating again, as though fearful that his future authority as the dominant partner was being put to the test, Bob stared at Hailey. There was a long moment of awkward silence. Then, he smiled sheepishly at James and Lucy and said, "I hope you'll come to see the results of the Poultry category. It's gonna be neck and neck between me and my lovely fiancée."

When Bob was back inside the camper, Hailey pulled a pack of Virginia Slims from her pocket. She shook a cigarette loose from the packet but made no move to light it.

"That's a gorgeous ring. Have you accepted Bob's proposal?" Lucy asked while pretending to study the cauliflower-shaped clouds overhead.

"Not yet." Hailey also raised her face skyward, her cigarette dangling limply from her right hand. "Men have been bossin' me about my whole life. First Daddy, then a druggie boyfriend, then Jimmy. It might be nice to be on my own for a bit."

"Do you have a job back in Fort Worth?" James asked.

"Not really. I spent most of my time doin' church stuff and cleanin' and cookin' for Jimmy." She flicked her eyes at James. "Now that he's gone, I don't wanna cook and clean for anyone else."

James nodded. "I don't blame you."

Lucy was watching Hailey closely. "Did you tell Sheriff Jones about Bob?"

"She doesn't know about the ring, but she knows we were knockin' boots when someone taped the vents shut on Jimmy's camper. The sheriff lady told me that the murderer must have done that around midnight. I reckon it takes a long time for that propane stuff to kill someone Jimmy's size." Hailey's eyes grew misty. "'Least he died peaceful after comin' clean with me. We'd had a big fight earlier that day about that redhead and why he's been hid—" She stopped and glared at Lucy. "Why are you askin' so many questions?"

"Because the woman under suspicion is not only innocent, but she's a dear friend of ours," Lucy said plainly. "Did Jimmy tell you anything about Gillian?"

"The redhead is your friend?" Hailey looked away quickly. "Jimmy mentioned somethin' about a truck accident. He said that he didn't hurt anybody on purpose."

"Yes, he did. It's why Jimmy spent fifteen years in prison," Lucy said. "He was convicted of vehicular manslaughter. Jimmy ran into Gillian's husband with his truck. It was a deliberate action."

Hailey's face drained of all color and she touched the dove tattoo on her chest. "Sweet Jesus! That son of a bitch lied to me! He said he was in jail for dealin' drugs."

"Well, Jimmy was both high *and* drunk when he hit Gillian's husband, so there *were* drugs involved, but he wasn't in jail for dealing," Lucy said softly.

Hailey snapped her cigarette in half. "He promised he was givin' me his full confession. His hand was on my Bible! That bastard!" Her pupils grew small with rage. "He lied to me about *so* many things! Why he was in jail, about his incredible cookin' skills, his secret hidin' places for ca—" She suddenly stopped her tirade and issued an insincere chuckle. "I guess I made the right decision to wait for Bob to get divorced. At least, he don't lie. He's a gentleman. He never even touched me until last night because it wouldn't have been right."

Ignoring the list of Bob's attributes, Lucy continued her interrogation. "You told the sheriff that Gillian was *inside* your RV when you returned to the vehicle after spending time with Bob last night. But Gillian *wasn't* inside, was she?" Lucy moved closer to Hailey. She put her hands on her hips and planted her feet shoulder-width apart. Her blue eyes bored into Hailey's. "She was sitting on the camper steps. Isn't that right?"

Hailey looked everywhere but at Lucy. "It was real early, okay? I got confused about the details."

Lucy's hand shot out like a snake and grabbed Hailey's plump arm. "You'd better get clear on the facts *really* fast. If my friend has to spend the night in jail because you found it *convenient* to say she was inside the camper instead of *outside*, I'm going to hound you for the rest of your time here." Lucy shook Hailey's arm. "Do you understand me? I'll be by your side, hanging on you like a leech, every minute of the day. I'll be so close that we're going to breathe the same air.   How do you think Bob would enjoy that? Just the three of us, together for the rest of the festival?"

Hailey cast James a glance of appeal, but he folded his arms and tried to appear as menacing as possible. It was difficult for him to look away from Lucy. He wanted to freeze time, to simply stand there and drink in the sight of her. With her bright blue eyes ablaze and the sun illuminating her hair and her creamy skin, James couldn't keep his heart from swelling with affection. He glanced between her and Hailey, who seemed to have shrunk while Lucy seemed colossal—an Amazon warrior fighting for truth and justice.

"All right, all right!" Hailey jerked her arm away. "The redhead was on the steps. I remember now. I didn't think they'd haul her in just because I said she was inside with Jimmy." She clasped her hands, her magenta nails flashing. "You gotta understand where I was comin' from. I've been to jail. I knew they'd take one look at me, see the hillbilly girlfriend with a juvie record, and they'd pin Jimmy's death on me faster than a lightnin' strike."

Lucy gave a small nod. "I understand your being scared, Hailey. But you don't put someone else's head on the chopping block just to save your own. You need to call the sheriff and set things straight." When Hailey hesitated, Lucy added, "She's a good woman, our Gillian. You have to do the right thing."

Hailey absently touched the tattoo on the top of her left breast. "Yeah, okay. I'll call her." She closed her eyes as she made her promise. "But not now. I've gotta get my barbecued turkey legs to the judges in fifteen minutes. Be a miracle if I make it in time. I'll call the sheriff lady after I've won another blue ribbon."

As Hailey hustled off, her wide hips swaying in another pair of too-tight shorts, Lucy watched her through narrowed eyes. Within moments, Hailey disappeared between two campers, but Lucy continued to stare into the distance. Blinking, she observed the crowd for a moment and then swung around and took James by the elbow.

"Please tell me you got all that on tape."

James removed the mini recorder from his pocket and hit the rewind button. They heard Hailey's voice going backward in a speedy whine. He waited a few seconds and then played the recording. Hailey's recitation of the actual events of that morning, when she discovered Jimmy's body, was captured clearly.

"*She was on the steps,*" Hailey's voice intoned.

Lucy beamed. "Time to call Sheriff Jones."

Bennett, Lindy, and James treated themselves to sno-cones while Lucy called the sheriff.

"Aren't you going to interview her again?" Lucy spoke forcefully into the receiver. Listening to the response, she shifted impatiently.

"If Hailey didn't tell the truth about Gillian being inside the camper, who knows what else she lied about? For all we know, *she* could have killed Jimmy any time that night. Plus, she started to talk about something hidden, and I think the word was *cash.* She also mentioned having unfinished business with Jimmy, so why isn't Hailey your prime suspect?" Taking a frosty bite of his sno-cone, James watched as Lucy blushed. "Oh, I see." Shaking her head, she reiterated her demand that Gillian be released based on the statement James had recorded.

"What flavor did you get?" Bennett asked Lindy while Lucy continued arguing in the background.

"Honeydew. You must have the lime. Your lips are all green."

Bennett scrutinized his half-eaten cone of shaved ice. "I got kiwi, but I wish I hadn't. I don't like it very much." He smiled and pointed at James. "Man, take a look at those lips! You have blue, red, *and* green all over your face. You look like the flag of Azerbaijan."

Seeing the blank looks on his friend's faces, Bennett clarified. "It's a country in southwest Asia. Sound familiar?" He waited. "Guess not. It's between Iran and Russia, and borders on the Caspian Sea. Do any of those names ring a bell?"

"We're not all trying out for *Jeopardy!* you know." James wiped his mouth and grimaced at the stained napkin. "This is what happens when you order a tie-dye sno-cone. Instead of green apple, cherry, and blue raspberry, I should've gone with coconut."

Removing her wallet from her purse, Lindy returned to the sno-cone stand. She waited until Lucy slid her cell phone into her pocket before handing her a cone.

"Thanks." Lucy took a small bite of the shaved ice. "This is good. What flavor is it?"

"Passionfruit. I figured it would match your mood," Lindy said.

"Shoot. You'd be blushing too if you heard what Sheriff Jones just told me."

Bennett lowered his sno-cone. "What did she say?"

Lucy smirked. "You're totally smitten with that woman, aren't you, Bennett? Maybe *you* should try to talk some sense into her." She bit off another piece of her treat. "Hailey's intimate activities with Bob provide them with a solid alibi. Seems they were rather vocal in the back of Bob's camper around eleven thirty and carried on for quite some time after that. All of the Tenderizers, as well as several of the Thigh and Mighties, heard Hailey praising Bob at the top of her lungs between the hours of midnight and two a.m."

Bennett grinned. "Maybe Hailey likes passionfruit too."

Lucy wasn't amused. "The sheriff also pointed out that Gillian has no alibi. Whether she was inside the camper, on its steps, or hiding behind one of its tires, she was still found at the crime scene this morning. That's the bottom line, and the sheriff has no plans to release Gillian. We need to find out who's responsible for Jimmy's death, and soon!" She glanced at Lindy. "Did you two have any luck?"

"None. We can rule out the Thigh and Mighties. They're a group of elementary school teachers, and this is their first contest. They had no idea who Jimmy was until he took their designated parking and cooking space. They mentioned the matter to Jimmy, who ignored them. They also complained in passing to R.C., but they weren't too worked up about the whole thing." She turned to James. "And none of the team members were really pale-skinned or wearing a hat with a tuning fork on it. Sorry."

"The Finger Lickers are not the murdering types either," Bennett said. "They're a bunch of dental hygienists who get together to drink beer, barbecue, and avoid their wives and girlfriends. They all thought Jimmy was a hoot and didn't bear him an ounce of ill will." He balled up his paper cone. "They're also from North Carolina, and have only seen Jimmy at two other festivals besides this one."

"Maybe location has something to do with Jimmy's death." James grew pensive. "He was from the Fort Worth area, right?" He directed his question to Bennett, whose knowledge of geography was excellent. Bennett nodded in assent. "Were any of the other teams from Texas?"

"The Marrow Men are from San Antonio." Lindy handed over the sheet listing the barbecue teams, the names of their members, and their hometowns.

"The Tenderizers are from Kansas, and the Adam's Ribbers are all Georgia peaches." James read from the list. "So only Jimmy, Hailey, and the Marrow Men are from the same state. How far apart are Fort Worth and San Antonio?"

"About two hundred and fifty miles," Bennett said.

Lucy threw her hands into the air in exasperation. "We're grasping at straws! Texas is a big state. However, we need to give the Marrow Men a look-see. Then, it's time to go back to the inn and get some answers from Eleanor. She could have easily snuck down to the campground. Keep in mind that she thinks her precious daughter swapped spit, and possibly some other bodily fluids, with our dead guy."

"That's a charming image." Lindy eyed her melting sno-cone with distaste and tossed it into the nearest garbage can.

James checked his watch. "They should be announcing the winners of the Poultry category. Let's wrap things up so we can go back to Fox Hall. I'd really like to take a shower and change out of these pants while you guys are cross-examining Eleanor."

"You might be dirty, my man, but at least you're not wearin' an orange jumpsuit." Bennett gestured at the mud splatters and grass stains on James's khakis.

"We'll have Gillian back in her own clothes by the time this festival is over," Lucy vowed. "We've solved tough mysteries before, and Gillian has all four of us working on her behalf." She cocked her head sideways and muttered loud enough for her friends to hear.

"Five, if you count the extra help we're getting from an unexpected source."

Bennett and Lindy stared at her in confusion while James quickened his pace. Still, he couldn't escape the sound of Lucy's voice as she added, "That's right, friends. Murphy Alistair, the voice of the *Star*, is here in Hudsonville."

Chapter Fourteen

Tomato, Mozzarella, and Basil Salad

The barbecue teams were already gathered in front of R.C.'s podium when the supper club members arrived. Having decided to split up to better blend in with the crowd, James meandered to the outskirts of the audience and scanned the throng. The barbecue teams were easy to spot because they stood near the front. Again, they were wearing colorful aprons, shirts, and chef hats.

The Marrow Men, who wore the matching chef hats embellished with orange and yellow flames, were holding cans of beer. James was close enough to the group that he could read the text on the red foam can coolers. It said, *Bad to the Bone.* James could see that the men spent a great deal of time outdoors. The sun had burned their foreheads, cheeks, and the tips of their noses a faint red. Their fourth team member, the man James suspected of being pale as a phantom, was nowhere in sight.

R.C. stepped up to the microphone and tapped it with his finger. As the crowd's murmuring grew quieter, James felt sorry for R.C. He couldn't begin to imagine the stress the poor man must be under. If R.C. had appeared haggard yesterday, he looked downright cadaverous today. His hair and clothes were slightly disheveled, and his eyes were dull with fatigue.

James wondered how Jimmy's death would affect the festival. Judging from the knot of people swarmed in front of the podium and walking around the fairgrounds, Hog Fest hadn't suffered a depletion of visitors. Yet.

It'll take a few more hours for the local press to run inflamed stories about the Hog Fest tragedy, James thought. *But surely, the area news channels had begun covering the story within hours of the sheriff's arrival at Jimmy's trailer.*

"I guess rain's worse for this festival than murder," James muttered to himself and turned his attention to the pretty brunette arranging prize ribbons and white envelopes on a table near the microphone stand.

"Thank you all for the most memorable poultry entries we've ever had the pleasure of tasting," R.C. began with a tired grin. "And a special thank-you to our judges for their time and expertise." R.C. inclined his head gratefully to the familiar figures of Mr. and Mrs. Connelly, as well as a group of four adults who, based on their features and coloring, were undoubtedly related.

R.C. paused and appeared to stare at Hailey. Clearing his throat, as though trying to decide what to say, he blinked and shifted his gaze. If he planned to say anything about Jimmy's passing, the moment had passed.

"Without further ado," R.C. continued. "Let's announce our first winner."

Cheers erupted as R.C. awarded the white ribbon and cash prize to the Tenderizers. James spied Bob Barker whistling as his teammate shook hands with R.C. before waving the third-place ribbon in the air. Hailey stood next to Bob, their shoulders touching. She still wore her Pitmasters T-shirt.

After the member of the Tenderizers departed with his awards, R.C. announced a tie between the Finger Lickers and the Marrow Men for the second-place prize. James smiled when a young man with a mouthful of dazzling white teeth bounced up to R.C. to collect the red ribbon and envelope of cash. When he turned to wave at his friends, James noticed that his yellow apron was embroidered with a white tooth partially smothered in barbecue sauce. The tooth had been given a smiling face and the text in the bubble above its head read *Eat 'Cue, Floss, Repeat.*

"I guess those dental hygienists know how to grill," a woman to James's left remarked to her friend. "They're mighty cute, too."

The Marrow Men representative appeared from the opposite side of the crowd and James drew in a sharp breath when he stared at the unnaturally pallid skin of the middle-aged man. The man accepted the prizes from R.C. with mumbled thanks. On the way back to his friends, the man ducked to avoid one of Hog Fest's signature pig balloons, and the movement jarred his chef hat loose. James watched with keen interest as the man stooped to retrieve the hat. Instead of replacing it on top of his thinning hair, he pulled a black baseball cap from his back pocket and settled it on his head with the brim facing backward. Once again, James caught a glimpse of the strange symbol that resembled a silver tuning fork.

Spotting Lindy, James skirted around people sipping homemade lemonade or gnawing on rib bones or barbecued chicken legs until he reached her.

"Lindy!" he cried. "I saw the pasty-skinned guy! He's with the Marrow Men, and he's wearing the hat I told you about. If we can't get close enough to take a pic with our cell phones, can you draw the symbol so we can look it up online?"

Lindy nodded. "Sure. I have a pen and some scrap paper in my bag. Where's the guy?"

Keeping his hand at waist level, James pointed to the left. "They're the ones with the flaming chef hats. Except for the guy I saw with Jimmy. His chef hat fell off so he put his baseball cap on. It's black."

"Good Lord, I've seen fish bellies with more pigment than that. He must work inside all day," Lindy said and moved off.

By the time James turned back to the podium, R.C. was ready to announce the winner of the Poultry category. The members of the remaining teams grew tense with anticipation. A few rows in front of him, Bob Barker placed a proprietary hand on Hailey's shoulders, which she shrugged off in the pretense of having to scratch her lower calf. By the time she straightened, R.C. had called a name other than the Pitmasters. Adam's Ribbers had earned the first-place prize.

Zoe, who'd changed out of her Johnny Depp T-shirt in favor of a hot-pink tank top that read *The Adam's Ribbers: We'll Rub Your Butt,* squealed all the way to the podium. When she reached the microphone, she threw her arms around R.C. and kissed him noisily on the cheek. R.C.'s face turned as pink as Zoe's shirt. She then jogged back to her teammates and the entire group exchanged high fives and hugs.

Still blushing, R.C. reminded the audience that the Anything Butt and Beef Rib contests would take place the next day, and he cautioned the crowd not to miss the blueberry pie-eating contest as well.

"We'll announce the name of the Hog Fest Barbecue Champion during tomorrow's closing ceremony, so don't miss it!" he informed the crowd with as much enthusiasm as he could muster.

The crowd issued a final cheer and began to disperse. James happened to find himself walking behind a family preoccupied with tearing apart of a blue cloud of cotton candy. After they finally peeled off from the main throng in search of napkins, James was right on the heels of Bob and Hailey.

"Too bad you didn't win that money, darlin'," James heard Bob say. Rubbing Hailey's back in a gesture of consolation, he sighed. "Now that I've got alimony payments to make, I've got less to spend on us. Every bit of cash we get will mean a nicer honeymoon."

Hailey shrugged. "That cash prize was small change. 'Sides, I've got money of my own."

After purchasing two bottles of Budweiser from a nearby vendor, the couple veered in the opposite direction, undoubtedly heading back to the cooking area. James stared after them, noting how Hailey detached herself from Bob's possessive arm.

"Doesn't look like she wants to be Mrs. Bob Barker too badly," James said to himself and wondered why Hailey seemed so unperturbed over not winning the cash prize. She didn't receive a paycheck, so unless she had another source of income, she and Jimmy had survived on his salary as a tow truck driver along with his barbecue contest winnings.

As James pondered this riddle, he spied Bennett cresting a slight rise up ahead. Jogging around a clot of slow-moving festivalgoers on their way to the parking lot, James caught up with his friend.

"Lucy and Lindy are checking on R.C.," Bennett said as they walked toward Lucy's Jeep. "Lindy was concerned about the guy's overall health and well-being, but Lucy seemed more interested in getting a read on him. Says he could be a suspect seeing as Jimmy offended people left and right at this fair." He snorted. "She's one dogged deputy."

James shook his head. "I don't see the logic in viewing R.C. as a suspect. After all, he wouldn't seek negative publicity for Hog Fest, and nothing garners bad press faster than an act of violence." He shielded his eyes from the glare of the afternoon sun. "R.C. must have called in every favor to keep the fact that Jimmy's death was a murder under wraps, but the story will break soon enough. After that, the festival's reputation could really suffer."

"Speaking of stories, is your girlfriend going to be one of the people giving R.C. a heart attack? She does have a nose for drama. I guess that kind of writing helps sell papers, eh?"

Noting the hint of irritation in Bennett's voice, James couldn't help but recall how many articles Murphy had written about his friends and their efforts to shed some extra pounds. She often revealed too much information in the opinion of the supper club, and though Murphy tried to redeem herself by touting their crime-solving skills, the personal information she'd disclosed about them would not easily be forgiven.

"I don't know, Bennett," James admitted. "I had no idea she was coming to Hudsonville."

"Communication is the key to a successful relationship," Bennett quipped. "I'd like to *communicate* a few things to Sheriff Jade Jones."

A few minutes later, Lucy and Lindy returned, and the four friends clambered back into the Jeep. On the way back to the Inn at Fox Hall, James asked Lindy to show Bennett the sketch she'd made.

"Does this look familiar to you?" James asked.

Bennett took one look at her drawing and began to chortle. "You really need to watch more sports, my man." He took the picture from Lindy's hands. "This isn't a tuning fork. This is a spur, my friend! As in the San Antonio Spurs? The basketball team? Please tell me that you've heard of the NBA."

"Yeah, yeah," James replied irritably. "So I don't watch professional basketball. It's just a bunch of guys with huge egos and inflated salaries tossing a ball around. What am I missing by watching PBS instead?" He pointed at the drawing. "The pale guy is one of the Marrow Men. He was wearing this baseball cap. Did you all notice him when he went up to the podium?"

His friends nodded.

"Hard to miss with that shark-belly skin," Bennett joked.

"That's that man who argued with Jimmy," James said. "Both men are from Texas, and that guy obviously had a bone to pick with 'the Pitmaster.' Jimmy definitely reacted to this guy's threatening body language. I saw his face. He was scared. I think we need to spend some time with the Marrow Men."

Lindy sighed. "I'm tired of smoking grills and barbecued meats. If we're coming back to do more snooping, then let's have dinner elsewhere. Something light. Like a vegetable plate."

Bennett's lip curled.

"I'm with you," Lucy said as they turned down the tree-lined driveway leading to the inn. "Maybe I can ask Eleanor if I could cook us omelets or something. We could all use a rest before we get back to work."

Lucy parked and the foursome made their way to the front door, walking in weary silence. It wasn't until someone spoke his name from a front porch rocker that James realized Murphy was sitting there. Bennett and Lindy gave Murphy a polite wave before entering the inn.

"See you later," Lucy mumbled to James. She ignored Murphy completely. She closed the front door behind her, and the fox head knocker clacked noisily.

James sank down in the rocker next to Murphy's and closed his eyes.

"Long day?" she asked in a soft voice.

"Yes, and it's far from over."

Murphy slowly rocked back and forth. "It's so peaceful here. It's probably really romantic when it's not so booked up. Might be nice to come back in the winter."

Opening his eyes, James took in the shadows stretching across the expanse of lawn. "I was out here yesterday morning, too, though it seems like a year ago now. I don't think I can appreciate the beauty of this place while Gillian's in a holding cell."

"Do you want to tell me where you guys are in your investigation?" Murphy asked casually, but James knew that every cell in her body was squirming in anticipation.

"I just want to sit and rest for a bit, okay?"

"I'm not asking you to get details for my story," she said testily. "I have what I need. As a matter of fact, I may have discovered something helpful."

James closed his eyes again. "I'm all ears," he mumbled tiredly.

"I discovered the name of the garage where Jimmy Lang worked," Murphy said. "And I called his boss. The man didn't even know Jimmy was dead. Guess Jimmy didn't have any family in those parts, and so no one in Waxahachie knows what happened. I didn't find out too much from this Mr. Leggett—just that Jimmy ran his mouth all the time. However, he was a responsible worker, and the customers seemed to like him just fine." She rustled some papers. "What *I* find strange is that Jimmy was able to purchase a recreational vehicle two years ago that cost nearly a hundred grand. He makes about thirty thousand a year at his job, and a few extra thousand in prize money, so how could he afford that camper?"

Murphy waited for James to provide a theory, but he was too worn out to think of anything creative. "He must have taken out a loan."

"That's what I thought until I called the RV dealer!" Murphy cried. "Jimmy paid for the whole thing in cash. No financing, nothing. Brought in a duffle bag of greenbacks and drove that monster off the lot. Doesn't that strike you as odd?"

James recalled Hailey's reaction to losing the barbecue contest's cash prize. He opened his eyes and sat up. "Hailey acts like she has plenty of money, too, and she doesn't even have a job. I get the impression she came into some cash after Jimmy died."

Her hazel eyes sparkling, Murphy leaned forward. "What makes you say that?"

"She started talking about how Jimmy had lied to her, and about these hiding places he had in the camper. She then started to say the word 'cash,' in reference to what he was hiding, but cut herself off. *And* she has this boyfriend—"

"Bob Barker."

James nodded, grudgingly impressed with how much information Murphy had gathered since her arrival. "Yes, Bob Barker. But she seems to be cooling toward him as the festival wears on. She told us that she'd like to live without a man for a while. I wonder if the newfound cash has something to do with her desire to remain single."

"I believe the answer to this whole mystery lies in where that extra money came from." Murphy smoothed the printouts on her lap. "If Jimmy was hiding money in his camper, maybe he meant to buy something on his way to or from Hog Fest."

"Or while he was here," James mused aloud. Suddenly, he jumped out of his chair in excitement. "That's it! When we first met Jimmy at this inn, he bragged about his ship coming in. Maybe he wasn't talking about landing a contract with Heartland Foods at all! Maybe he had some other kind of deal in the works!"

Murphy smiled. "If you can discover what that deal was, I bet you'll find the killer. Jimmy probably screwed someone over, and that someone wanted revenge."

James immediately thought of the ghostly-white limbs of the man with the San Antonio Spurs cap.

"I may know the person Jimmy argued with," James boasted and then felt his ego deflate. "But I have no idea what the argument was about."

"You have time." Murphy placed a reassuring hand on James's arm. "Remember, it's just a lead until you find evidence."

"I know, but it gives me hope." James squeezed her hand. "Look, I'm sorry I was so short-tempered before."

"It's okay. I was being pretty bitchy myself. I always get that way when I think of you spending time with Lucy. I know she still has feelings for you, and I'm the jealous type."

"You have nothing to worry about," James said, but the words didn't feel completely genuine. He'd enjoyed working with Lucy again, and some of his old feelings for her seemed to be resurfacing despite his efforts to suppress them.

Gently extracting her hand, Murphy gazed out into the twilight. "Speaking of leads, I went to see Gillian soon after I got to Hudsonville, but she wasn't up to receiving visitors."

James swiveled in his seat and stared at Murphy. "Why did you go? To interview her for the *Star*?"

"Of course. I'm a journalist, James," she said flatly. "She's still the primary suspect."

Trying not to judge Murphy too quickly, James took a moment before calmly asking, "You already knew her story, so why go?"

Murphy broke eye contact and pretended to examine the potted fern alongside of her. "I wanted to hear her version of the events. If someone ran down *my* husband, I might be prone to seek revenge."

James clenched his fists, anger coursing through him. "Well, *Gillian* wouldn't!" He slapped the arm of his chair and Murphy jumped. "You think she might actually be a murderer. She's my *friend*, Murphy!"

"I know." Murphy's voice was quiet. "And like I said, I believe that money is the source of the crime. Still, Gillian *could* be involved, and your judgment might be clouded because of your friendship with her. If I could review Gillian's testimony, I could then check the facts as an *objective* investigator."

"What you mean is that you could determine if she were lying!"

James felt like moving his chair away from Murphy's. He had never found her so unattractive as he did right now. "All for some article for our little hometown paper? Is the front page of the *Star* really worth this, Murphy? Because you've put our relationship on the line by questioning Gillian's character." He drew in a breath and glowered at her. "But I suspect you realized you'd get this reaction from me before you ever drove down here."

"I'm *not* just writing a *little* article!" Murphy shouted. "And I'm glad we're having this discussion, James. It finally gives me the opportunity to tell you something I've been keeping to myself for weeks. Right before I met you at the beach for our weekend getaway, I signed a contract with a major publishing house in New York." She looked down at her hands, clearly struggling between wanting to brag about her accomplishment and delivering her news with an iota of sensitivity. "I've been meaning to tell you, James, but I wasn't sure how you'd take it. I'm not certain if you can handle being in a relationship with someone who might become more of a celebrity than you and the Flab Five."

"You're not writing a book about how we've all blown our health routines by gorging on barbecue and funnel cakes, are you?" he asked wryly.

"No." Her laugh sounded false. "My book's not about your dieting ups and downs. It's a thriller, actually, only *loosely* based on how you and your friends have solve cri—"

At that moment, the screen door burst open and Francesca appeared on the porch. Her mouth was set into a smile and she was humming a zippy tune. Seeing James, her smile grew even wider, and she removed her lime-green earbuds.

"Hi!" She wiggled her fingers in greeting. She then leaned against the porch railing as if she intended to linger for a while. "I wanted to say sorry about yesterday morning. I know you heard me being ugly to my mom." Darting a glance at Murphy, she toyed with the headphone wires and gazed at James from beneath her lashes. "We've been arguing all the time lately, which is sad, because she used to be my best friend."

"I'm sorry to have been in the wrong place at the wrong time," James said gallantly.

Francesca dug her hands into the pockets of her skimpy jeans shorts and continued to look at him. "Anyway, I was pretty horrified by my behavior."

Sensing that she'd suddenly become a third wheel, Murphy rose and handed James the printouts containing the information she'd acquired on Jimmy Lang's finances. "If you'll both excuse me, I'm going to rustle up some supper in town."

Francesca waited until Murphy had closed the front door before asking, "Is that your girlfriend?"

"Yeah," James answered quickly. Desperate to change the subject, he pointed at Francesca's neck. "I see you were able to cover that mark."

Instead of being embarrassed, Francesca looked positively jubilant. "Mom's lucky it's only a hickie and not a tattoo! I'd like to climb to the roof and tell everyone how I feel about my boyfriend!"

Observing the dreamy look in Francesca's eyes, James began to laugh. "It *wasn't* Jimmy. He wasn't the guy you were hanging out with, right?"

Francesca was clearly mortified by the idea. "Lord, no! I was just pushing Mom's buttons." She arched an elegant eyebrow at him. "Do you really think I'd let that overblown Cro-Magnon touch me? Gross!"

"I was having a hard time picturing it, but I did see him, ah, touch you in a familiar way at the festival," James confessed.

Francesca blushed. "And the only reason I didn't smack his face was that Mr. Richter was nearby. My mom is kind of sweet on him, and I didn't want to cause a scene."

James watched the fireflies illuminate the shadowy bushes. Crickets sawed, and a chorus of bullfrogs added their sonorous croaking to the evening's cacophony. "Your mom likes R.C.? That's cool." James began to lazily rock in his chair. "So are you going to tell her about your boyfriend?"

Delighted to talk about her love interest, Francesca settled down on the porch swing and pushed it with the tips of her toes. "He's a year older than me, and we didn't hang out in school because he was really involved with academic clubs and all these community service activities." She hugged herself. "That's what I love about him! He has such a *huge* heart! Anyway, he just got back from a mission trip to Africa and we started hanging out at the Tastee

Freez. He's going to be involved in the county's Head Start program next fall, and I totally want to be involved, too. That's why I don't want to waste time on these pageants. I want to help kids."

"Well, I think your guy sounds like a fine young man," James said, feeling that his praise must have sounded rather old-fashioned. "And I bet your mother would be happy to know you've fallen for someone so generous and kindhearted. It might be nice to tell her about him, so that she doesn't think you were really with Jimmy the other night."

Francesca waved the suggestion away. "Oh, you don't have to worry about that. I left her a note on the refrigerator, like, an hour after our argument. I mean, she might have actually poisoned the man if she thought I'd slept with him." She shivered in distaste. "Sorry. I guess I shouldn't talk about him that way now that he's dead. Mr. Richter called and told my mom all about it. I never knew you could die from inhaling too much propane."

"Me either." James was relieved to hear about the note. It meant that Eleanor had no motive to kill Jimmy. He'd hated to think that she could be guilty of murder.

Despite his late afternoon snack, James's stomach came to life as he pondered Eleanor's culinary skills. It gurgled, loud enough to be heard over and above the sounds of the bugs, frogs, and the creaking rocker.

"Whoa, was that you?" Francesca's eyes grew round. Then, she giggled. "You must be hungry!"

James tried to camouflage his expansive belly with his arms. "Oh, I don't need anything."

Hopping off the swing, Francesca grabbed James by the hand. "We have lots of goodies left from today's tea. Most of the guests were too busy at Hog Fest to eat here, and my mom would be unhappy if her food went to waste. She usually gives R.C. late-night snacks, but he's too wiped out to come over tonight."

"Is there enough for my three friends?" James asked sheepishly.

"Of course!" Francesca led him into the kitchen, where the other supper club members were already installed at the kitchen table. Eleanor flitted around them, chatting and pouring glasses of sun tea. Lucy gestured at the note tacked on the fridge and winked at James.

"Francesca told me all about that," he whispered in her ear.

"Thank goodness we didn't interrogate Eleanor," Lucy whispered back, "or we might not have been given such a lovely dinner." She ladled a spoonful of tomato and mozzarella salad onto an empty plate. "The fresh basil on this salad is delicious. There are deviled eggs and fresh blueberries, too. This meal is just what we need. All of this protein will give us the necessary energy to move ahead in our investigation."

"I hope so." James listened as Lindy told Francesca about the ups and downs of being a schoolteacher. Eleanor began rinsing dishes and placing them in the dishwasher, but James could tell that she was interested in what Lindy had to say.

Outside the window, the night fell in full force, though the summer darkness was softened by a firefly glow. The laughter and companionable conversation reverberating around the kitchen allowed James's anger over Murphy's behavior to ebb away. As he stared at the reflection of their cozy group in the window, he felt that he was a part of a circle of love and trust that would never fail him.

A few minutes later, Eleanor poured coffee into oversized mugs and placed a tray of warm brownies in the center of the table.

"If only Gillian were here, this would be a perfect night," James said.

Lucy touched his hand and, selecting the largest brownie from the basket, she put it on his plate. "Buck up, James. We've made good headway today, and no one's giving up on Gillian. I'm not going back to Quincy's Gap without her."

James gazed at Lucy so tenderly that her cheeks turned pink. "What's that sappy look for?" she teased.

"I'm just appreciating your loyalty," James said. He bit into his brownie. "And that goes for you, too." He gestured at Bennett and Lindy. "You guys are my family, and I'd do anything for you. I've never told you before how much you mean to me, so I'm telling you now."

Lindy dabbed at her eyes with her napkin. "Oh, James! Pass me those brownies. If I don't have a suitable distraction, I'll cry off the rest of my mascara!"

Chapter Fifteen

Jim Beam (Straight Up)

James and his friends trudged over the festival grounds in search of the Marrow Men and their pale-skinned teammate. Eleanor's nourishing dinner coupled with cups of strong coffee had given them much-needed energy, but there was something about the multicolored lights, the aggressive movements of the crowd, the thick scent of fried foods, and the constant noise pouring from the loudspeakers that quickly sapped the group's enthusiasm.

"I could never live this life," Lindy said, gesturing at one of the game vendors. "These people will pack up tomorrow, drive to another town, and get ready to face a new crowd. We must all look the same to them after a time."

Under a sign reading *Bonzo Bazooka*, a group of men occupied three of the eight metal stools positioned in front of water guns. James recognized the game. After all, this game, or one just like it, was a fixture at every fair he'd ever attended. The object was to shoot a concentrated stream of water into the gaping mouth of a deranged-looking clown and blow up the balloon inflating over his head. Whoever popped the balloon first was the victor.

James had won the game once as a boy, but the nightmares he'd had the night after the county fair about a monstrous clown spitting a mouthful of brackish water back into his face weren't worth the plush banana he'd won as a prize.

"We need a fourth to play!" a man with a weathered face called out to James as he passed by. "Come on, mister. Win a giant snake for your girlfriend!"

James turned away. Who *was* the giant snake in his relationship? Him? Murphy? She'd come to Hudsonville to write an article on Jimmy's death, but that was her job, and the cause of death *was* unusual. Was he angry with Murphy for seeking the truth about the murder or because she didn't share his conviction that Gillian was innocent? And what about this book she'd written? Before Francesca appeared, James could have sworn that Murphy was about to explain that her novel was a fictionalized account of the supper club's role as amateur detectives, but why would a publisher be interested in a book like that? They were just ordinary people.

Lost in thought, James paid little attention to where he was walking. As a result, he had a direct collision with a biker carrying a funnel cake in each hand. The funnel cake in his left hand was topped with powdered sugar and fudge sauce, while the cake in his right hand was loaded with a puddle of strawberry jam. In a flash, James's white polo looked like a Jackson Pollock painting.

James looked down at his shirt in horror.

The biker growled.

"I'm so sorry, I wasn't watching where I was going," James spluttered in apology.

"No kidding." The giant of a man took a menacing step toward James. "Ya know, I've been lookin' forward to eatin' those since I hit the road at *five* this mornin'. Now you're *wearin'* them instead."

James dug his wallet out of his pants and shoved a twenty into the biker's meaty hand. "Here. Take this for your trouble."

Scurrying away, James's friends had no choice but to follow as he plowed through the crowd toward the Marrow Men's campers. He finally stopped at their cooking area, puffing in exertion, and disgusted by his own cowardice.

Bennett caught up to James and slapped him on the back. "My man, there are times when you have to cut and run. That was one of those times."

Behind Bennett, Lindy and Lucy hid giggles behind their hands.

The cook site had a deserted feeling to it, so the four friends spread out. They each knocked on the door of an RV bearing a Texas license plate, but no one responded.

Perplexed, Lindy consulted her schedule. "Right after Felicity's dog show, Humphrey the Hypnotist will perform, followed by tonight's main event, a magician called Ivan the Illusionist. Apparently, Ivan travels with a harem of scantily clad assistants. I've seen his poster around the fairgrounds, and if the women are wearing what they have on in that picture, that's probably where the Marrow Men are at this very moment."

Bennett rubbed his eyes. "What time is it over? I don't feel like hanging around much longer. I'm doggone tired."

"I'd say the show will run until at least eleven," Lindy said. "There's a fireworks display, too."

Lucy checked her watch. "It's almost nine now." She ran her hands through her hair and sighed. "I feel terrible saying this, but I'd like nothing better than to collapse in my bed at the inn."

"Well, we can't do much more for Gillian tonight if we're unable to interview the Marrow Men," James said. "I vote for bed."

His friends mumbled their agreement and headed back to the parking lot. The campground area was very quiet. Here and there, a couple sat quietly talking, but for the most part, the sound of an announcer's voice murmuring through distant speakers was the only invasive noise.

The hum of several small generators added to the drowsy peacefulness of the night, and James couldn't wait to take off his soiled clothes and his sticky belt, and step under a stream of hot water. Even Bennett's rumbling snores would have no effect on the powerful lethargy that had permeated every inch of his body. He couldn't remember a time when he'd been so desperate to pull on his pajama bottoms and his favorite William & Mary T-shirt and hit the sack.

As the foursome drew close to Jimmy and Hailey's monstrous RV, they heard a clanking sound near the front of the vehicle. Instinctively, they stopped and exchanged curious looks. Even though they had yet to walk past the camper, they could sense that there were no lights lit near the cooker, but that's where the odd noise had come from.

"Around back," Lucy whispered and pointed at the neighboring camper, which would shield them from view as they investigated the source of the sound.

Walking on tiptoes, they crept behind the camper parked next to Jimmy's and poked their heads around the corner. James experienced a strong feeling of déjà vu from two days ago, when he and Bennett had eavesdropped on the spat between Jimmy and Hailey.

Because a thick cloud layer covered the half-moon, James had trouble distinguishing the shapes arranged alongside the RV. Having seen the area during the daytime, he was able to recognize the forms of two folding chairs, a side table, and of course, Jimmy's commercial cooker. A movement near this rectangular black shape caught James's eye, and he nudged Lucy in the side and pointed. Nodding silently, she put her fingers to her lips.

James watched as the person near Jimmy's cooker bent over to retrieve something from a bag at his feet. He assumed that the stranger was a man by his height and build. When the unknown person suddenly fired up a small welding torch, James saw that his assumption had been correct. The light cast from the blue flame illuminated a pale masculine face, though the eyes remained hidden behind a pair of mirrored sunglasses. After the man adjusted the flame, he applied the torch to an area in the underside of the lid. Jimmy's grill was so large that it actually had two separate cookers, but the man with the torch appeared to only be interested in the right-hand cooker.

"This guy has a *big* pair of ba—," Bennett began, but Lindy covered his mouth with her hand.

"What?" Bennett whispered. "He's destroying a dead man's property right out in the open! He's either desperate or crazy."

"What should we do?" Lindy hissed. "Should we stop him, or wait to see what he finds?"

"Let's wait," Lucy said, and the group fell silent again.

Sparks flew from around the cooker and disappeared in the surrounding blackness.

"Hey!" a man's voice suddenly shouted from the shadows behind the man with the torch. "What the hell do you think you're doing?"

Bob Barker stepped into the illuminated strip of road leading back to the main fairway. He hesitated, as though unsure whether it was a good idea to apprehend a man dressed entirely in black who happened to be brandishing a welding torch. Glancing left and right, Bob seemed to be searching for other signs of life in the campground.

"He needs to know that he's not alone," James whispered. Without thinking about his actions, he stepped out from behind the shelter of the camper and waved. "Howdy, Bob," he said as the man in black swiveled around to face James and his friends.

Realizing that he was trapped, the prowler threw the welding torch directly at Bob's head. Uttering a surprised squeak, Bob raised his arms to protect his face. The stranger slipped past him and sprinted into the shadows beyond the cluster of campers.

The torch, which had missed Bob's head by a few inches, landed in a patch of grass near his feet. When he leaned over to retrieve it, Lucy shouted, "Don't touch that! The murderer's fingerprints are probably on here!"

"Murderer?" Bob stared in the direction where the man in black had disappeared and then moved closer to the welding torch, as though to shield it with his body.

After urgently conferring with Lindy, Lucy unzipped her large purse, turned it upside down, and unceremoniously dumped its contents into Lindy's. Using a paper napkin, Lucy picked up the torch and slid it into her bag. The tip of the torch brushed against her hand as she zippered her purse.

"Ow! It's still warm!" She shook her hand back and forth in the air. "That crazy bastard! What was he looking for?"

"Who knows? That grill is black and it's nighttime." Bennett was obviously disappointed. "Wait! Didn't I see a flashlight rolling around in your Jeep?"

Lucy turned to Bob. "Does Hailey keep one in the camper?"

Bob shrugged. "I've got no clue what's in there. More important, I've got no idea where Hailey is. I was supposed to meet her at the entrance to the pavilion, so we could watch the show together, but she never showed. She's been actin' right strange all day, so I came to see if she was avoidin' me." He gestured at the RV. "She said she wasn't gonna sleep in this thing ever again because Jimmy died in it, but I had to check."

They all glanced at the large vehicle as though assessing whether it now possessed a sinister aura, but it seemed completely innocuous. James stepped up to the door and knocked. While Bob and his friends looked on, he turned the knob and pushed it open.

"Hailey?" he called. Feeling along the wall, he flipped a light switch, producing a soft glow from two brass fixtures hanging in the dining area. The camper was a mess. Sofa pillows were scattered on the floor, their fabric marred by angry slashes. White polyester filler oozed through the gaping holes. The contents of the cupboard had been strewn everywhere. James sensed that a search had been conducted with both urgency and fury. He noticed that the vandal had emptied an entire box of Frosted Flakes onto the carpet. Nearby were piles of flour and sugar; their torn paper bags thrown carelessly into the sink.

"What do you see, James?" Lucy asked. "Is Hailey in there?"

"No." James swiveled on the steps. "I think our intruder was in here, but didn't find what he was looking for. The cushions are torn, there's food all over the floor, and the plates are smashed. The radio's been ripped right out of the dashboard. If Hailey walked in on someone doing this, she would have told someone, and the cops would be here."

"So where is she, then?" Bob asked frantically. "Where's my girl?"

Lindy placed a comforting hand on Bob's shoulder. "I'm sure she's fine. She's probably off looking for you."

James knew Lindy well enough by now to know that she didn't subscribe to this belief. The clouds had released a wash of pale moonlight that served to emphasize the fearful look in her round eyes. She gazed up at James as he stood, frozen with foreboding, on the camper steps.

"Time to call Sheriff Jones," James told Lucy. She nodded solemnly and dug around in Lindy's overstuffed purse until she found her cell phone. As she spoke in a low, rapid voice, Bennett examined the damaged cooker.

"Can you dig the Jeep keys out of there?" Bennett asked Lindy as he pointed at her bag. "I'm afraid if I put my hand in I might never get it back."

Scowling, Lindy rummaged around in her purse until she came up with Lucy's key chain, a polished steel German shepherd.

"This would make a good weapon in a pinch," Bennett said. "Be right back."

"Oh, brother." Lindy sank into one of the folding chairs as Bob began pacing around the cooker.

By the time Lucy had finished her call, Bennett had returned from his trip to Lucy's car. He was breathing hard. "I need to have a look in that cooker before the fuzz show up."

Lucy frowned. "I wouldn't recommend referring to the sheriff that way."

"That fine woman? Wouldn't dream of it. 'Goddess of Justice' suits her better." Bennett smiled and pointed the beam of the flashlight into the black cavity of the cooker lid. Bennett then partially closed the lid, clearly trying to judge the overall thickness of it.

"There's plenty of room to hide something in here," he said, tapping on the metal until they could all hear a hollow echo. "Not only that, but the way this thing's designed, the heat would never enter this chamber. There's no air flow to the right side of the cooker and this top part here—where our Man in Black was cutting—is covered by a thick heat shield, so it wouldn't be affected by the drafts coming from the left side."

"How do you know how this cooker works?" Lindy asked in amazement.

"I peeked at James's history of barbecue book. It includes a diagram on how air flows through these commercial cookers. Both times we saw Jimmy and Hailey using this cooker, they grilled on the left side only. I bet this whole upper right lid has stayed nice and cool. The dripping pan is clean as a river rock, and there isn't a single wood pellet in here." He angled the flashlight into the crack created by the welding torch. "So if Jimmy didn't use it for cooking, what was he storing in here?"

"Bet it's drugs," Bob suggested.

Lucy's eyes grew large. "What makes you say that?"

"Jimmy was just too damned jolly. Didn't matter what was wrong in his life, he acted chipper to everybody but Hailey. And all that extra weight he's gained over the last few months? He's twice the size he was at the last festival. On top of that, his skin looked bloated and rubbery. He was also cold when no one else was, but he'd start sweatin' buckets five minutes later. Wasn't normal."

"Mr. Lang exhibited those symptoms because he had an advanced case of hypothyroidism," said a deep voice from behind Bob. Deputy Neely ran a hand along the sloped hood of Jimmy's trailer and examined the front tire like he was considering purchasing the vehicle. "This medical condition also accounts for the puffy appearance of his face, sensitivity to cold, hoarseness in the throat, flaky skin, and hair loss. The victim had no traces of medication in his body, or in his recreational vehicle. Therefore, we assume he was unaware that he suffered from hypothyroidism. He was in the late stages of the illness."

"Thank you, Deputy." Sheriff Jones appeared beside Neely and shot her subordinate a look that could freeze an avalanche. Without a word to anyone else, she opened the door to Jimmy's camper and went inside. Deputy Neely followed, looking subdued.

Deputy Harding had also arrived with the sheriff. He issued James a polite nod. James remembered how Harding had allowed him to speak with Gillian, and he felt confident enough in the man's capacity for compassion to prod him for information while the sheriff was out of earshot.

"Guess you guys got the medical examiner's results," James said casually.

Harding muttered, "Yep," took a Maglite from his belt, and began to inspect the cooker.

"We have the welding torch he used to bust into that grill," Lucy declared. "You might want to check it for fingerprints."

Harding eyed Lucy expectantly. "Where is it?"

Lucy gave her purse a smug pat while Harding pulled on a pair of latex gloves. Without saying a word, he reached out for Lucy's bag. After a moment's hesitation, she reluctantly passed it to him. Harding placed a pair of sunglasses over his eyes, started the torch, and deftly continued cutting the cooker lid where the man in black had left off.

It was fascinating to watch the white and orange-tinged flame chew through the metal. Harding worked patiently, his hands steady and firm as they guided the torch. Within several minutes, Harding had created a C-shaped panel. Switching off the welding torch, he pushed his sunglasses high on his forehead and tugged at the separated section of metal. He was only able to lift it a few inches, but it was enough to allow the light of his flashlight to penetrate the lid's cavity. Harding grunted, and James and his friends couldn't help but gather around the cooker to see what the deputy had found.

Harding was too consumed in his task to notice that he had an audience, but when he wriggled a small, plastic-wrapped bundle free from the opening he'd made, Lucy gasped, and he suddenly realized that he was being observed.

"Is that marijuana?" Lucy stood on her tiptoes to get a better look. "Is there more?"

Torn between continuing with his search and spending his time shooing away the onlookers, Harding dropped the bag to his side and bent over the cooker again. He removed bag after bag until a mound of plastic-wrapped bundles had been laid out on the grass in a neat line.

"Sheriff!" Harding called once the cooker had been totally emptied of its secret cache. "I think you'd best come out here!"

The sheriff exited the camper and squatted down in the grass. She squeezed the bundles, sniffed them, and turned them over while Neely held a flashlight for her. Finally, she whispered some instructions to Neely before turning to Bob Barker and the supper club members.

"We'll need to take statements about what you witnessed here this evening," the sheriff said briskly. "Did any of you recognize the intruder?"

"I think he was one of the Marrow Men," James said. Noting the look of doubt on Harding's face, James continued. "I know it's dark, but when the torch lit up his face, I was sure it was the guy I saw arguing with Jimmy before his death."

Sheriff Jones glanced up at the sky, where lumps of ash-colored clouds formed a barricade over the moon. Only trace amounts of weak light escaped from the cloud cover. "But are you certain it was him?" She turned her penetrating gaze on James. "Would you swear to this man's identity in a court of law?"

James felt doubt assailing him. "Ah . . ." He turned to his friends in search of support, and they gave him brief nods to assure him that they also believed that the intruder was the man who wore the San Antonio Spurs baseball cap. "Yes," James replied. "I don't know his name, but I could show him to you."

"It was Mitch Walker," Bob said firmly. "No doubt about it. And this fellow's right. He's one of the Marrow Men. I looked right at his face, Sheriff. It was Mitch."

Silence followed Bob's statement. The deputies turned their attention to the bundles on the ground, but Sheriff Jones kept her eyes locked on Bob.

To everyone's surprise, Bennett stepped forward and inserted himself between the sheriff and her deputies. He gestured angrily at the cooker. "Do you still think Gillian O'Malley is involved in *this*?

You think a dog groomer from Quincy's Gap is trafficking pot? That she's dealing in illegal drugs with a tow truck driver from Texas who killed her husband?"

Bennett slammed his palm against the cooker and everyone jumped, except for the sheriff, who didn't react at all. "This is about drugs and money. Where'd Jimmy get this fancy camper? Who are these drugs for? Who was Jimmy going to sell them to? Did he screw somebody over?" Bennett jabbed his finger into his temple. "*These* are the pertinent questions that have to be asked, and Gillian has no answers for you, so give the woman back to us. I'm not providing *any* statement until she's free." He slapped the cooker again. "I'm tired! We're *all* tired!"

After a few moments in which James was afraid to breathe, Sheriff Jones blinked. "Are you finished?" she asked Bennett.

"Just give her back to us," Bennett repeated softly, but with the same level of passion. He let his hand fall back to his side.

"Ms. O'Malley has been free to leave since this afternoon. She's been most cooperative, and there was no reason to hold her any longer," the sheriff replied evenly. "However, she fervently requested that I allow her to remain in her cell overnight. She said that she needed a few more hours of solitude." For the first time that evening, kindness softened her eyes. "I don't run a hotel, and I think Ms. O'Malley would appreciate being picked up first thing in the morning, as our breakfast isn't exactly on par with the Sunday spread laid out at Fox Hall, but I couldn't say no to such a simple request." Her face grew stony again. "Not all demands are so easily met, Mr. Marshall."

Bennett shifted on his feet. "I apologize, ma'am. I let my head get the better of me. I had no idea that crazy woman *wanted* to be in a cell, but now that you mention it, I can picture her sitting cross-legged and meditating while humming."

The sheriff smiled. "She said something to that effect. And your apology is accepted. Ms. O'Malley is fortunate to have friends like you, but now that she's free to go, you need to steer clear of this investigation. I don't expect to see any of you again unless you're fulfilling your judging duties or enjoying the activities of this festival."

"But what about Hailey?" Bob interjected. "She doesn't know

anything about this mess, I'm sure of it. And we've got to find her! Maybe she's been kidnapped!"

The sheriff gestured at one of the lawn chairs. "Why don't you have a seat, sir? I'll speak with you in a moment. As for the rest of you, I think you should go back to the inn and get some sleep. We'll need to take your statements, but I'm short-staffed at the moment and we have our hands full here, so they can wait until morning." The sheriff gestured at the bags of drugs and then winked at Bennett with such subtlety that James wasn't even sure he had seen it. In a low, husky voice, she said, "I'll expect *you* bright and early, Mr. Marshall."

Though they had clearly just been dismissed, James thought Bennett might float away with the next breeze. He practically danced to the parking lot.

"We did it, friends!" Lindy clapped her hands. "Gillian will be out tomorrow. We can judge the blueberry pie-eating contest and get the hell out of this town!"

"No, we can't. The case is still unsolved!" Lucy protested. "Hailey could be in danger *or* she might be involved in this whole drug scheme. We have a responsibility to help."

James climbed into Lucy's Jeep, grateful to finally sit down. "It's true," he said. "If we hadn't snooped around tonight, the drugs could have just disappeared and the sheriff would never have known about them. I know she wants us to butt out, but we may as well keep our eyes and ears open while we're here."

Lucy beamed at James in the rearview mirror.

"I guess you're right." Lindy sighed. "Besides, if we don't keep investigating, how else will Bennett find a way to hit on Sheriff Jones?" She reached around from her position in the passenger seat and poked Bennett on the top of his foot with one of her long fingernails.

Bennett, who'd just popped a piece of chewing gum into his mouth, was extremely ticklish. When Lindy brushed the skin on the top of his foot, he jumped backward and inhaled the piece of gum. Coughing and spluttering, he wheezed and gasped for air until James became genuinely alarmed.

"Should we pull over?" James asked.

Bennett shook his head and finally coughed the piece of gum

into his hand. "With my skin tone . . ." he said and panted, "could be mighty tough to tell if I was turning blue or not." He balled the piece of spent gum into its empty wrapper. "Lindy, I have half a mind to stick this in your hair instead of putting it in the garbage."

"Sorry." Lindy slunk down in her seat.

"You guys are getting punchy," Lucy said, smiling. "I'd better put you all to bed."

"Amen to that, sister!" Bennett croaked. "It'll just be me and my sweet dreams of Sheriff Jade Jones. She winked at me. Yessir, I think she feels it. There's something magnetic brewing between us." He turned to James. "And you'll be dreaming of Murphy, unless you're staying with her tonight."

"Fox Hall was booked, remember, and I have no idea where she's staying," James mumbled. "And I'm too damned tired to dream. I'm going to fall asleep the second I close my eyes."

• • •

"Are you *still* tossing and turning over there?" Bennett asked in the middle of the night. "You're like a damned kayak going over rapids!"

James pushed his glasses onto his nose and eyed the clock. "Three thirty," he groaned. "Why can't I sleep?"

"Might be that love note you got from Murphy," Bennett suggested grumpily. "Got you all riled up."

James eyed the crumpled missive lying on his own nightstand. "It wasn't exactly a love note. All Murphy wrote was that she had to drive back to Quincy's Gap to make sure that the next edition of the *Star* went out on time, and to call if I had any updates on Jimmy's case."

Bennett was silent for a moment. "You're right, that isn't much of a love letter."

"You're on target about the riled-up part because every time I close my eyes, I start thinking about what Murphy started to tell me earlier today."

"What's that?" Bennett sat up in bed.

James hesitated. "She wrote a book about us."

"You and me?" Bennett sounded surprised.

"All of us. The Flab Five." James squeezed his eyes shut. "And she already has a publishing deal."

Again, there was silence.

Bennett switched on the lamp. His dark eyes flashed angrily. "Say that again."

"The book's about the supper club members—how we've helped solve murders in the past," James explained. "She said it's not about our attempts to lose weight."

Bennett rose stiffly from the bed and walked slowly over to the TV cabinet. He opened the small fridge hidden behind one of the lower doors, pulled two bottles from the honor bar, and went into the bathroom. When he returned, he handed James a tumbler filled with an inch of light amber liquid.

Tossing back his drink, Bennett sank down onto his bed. "Go on, man, or you'll never get to sleep."

"What is it? Whiskey?" James sniffed the contents.

"Jim Beam." Bennett swung his legs onto the bed and stared up at the ceiling. "That's some bomb to drop on a guy in the middle of the night. So Murphy's writing a tell-all book. Man oh man. There's no way I'm going to sleep without a little medicinal aid. You won't either, my friend, trust me."

"It's not a tell-all," James protested weakly, gripping the tumbler loosely. "It's fiction."

"Right." Bennett snorted and shook his head in disgust. "And no one in Quincy's Gap is going to know who the black, crime-solving mailman in Murphy's work of *fiction* is, or who the crime-solving librarian living with his daddy is. I can already hear the talk down at Dolly's Diner." He put his arms behind his head and rearranged his pillow, punching it violently into place. "We're not going to be able to show our faces without folks mentioning your *girlfriend's* book. Whether we like it or not, that book is going to change our lives." The sound of the cool air rushing through the vents in the floor followed Bennett's statement, but James didn't know whether he felt more chilled by his friend's words or by the air-conditioning.

"Oh, Lord." James moaned and then swallowed his drink in three gulps. The whiskey burned on its way down his throat, and warmth spread through his belly. He felt his clenched hands relax and some of the tension ebb from his knotted shoulders and neck.

Scrunching his toes in the thick rug next to his bed, James gazed at his empty tumbler with mournful eyes.

Collecting Bennett's glass, James gestured at the cabinet. "I hope there are more where these came from."

Chapter Sixteen

Cheddar Cheese Grits

When James opened one eye, allowing the other to stay mercifully closed against the bright light infiltrating the room, he sensed that he'd overslept. No snores rose from Bennett's bed, nor was the morning stillness broken by the rush of water through the bathroom pipes. An unnatural quiet permeated the room.

As James fumbled for his glasses, a sharp pain came to life inside his skull and he froze mid-reach. Resting his head back on the pillow, he took stock of his physical state. His head hurt, his limbs felt like lead, his mouth was gritty as sand, and his tongue felt three sizes too large. He desperately wanted water but sensed that walking to the bathroom, turning on the tap, and tilting his mouth under the stream was more than his body could handle.

Easing on his glasses so as not to provoke the hangover dragon that was currently sticking its needle-sharp claws into his brain, James saw the litter of small bottles on his nightstand.

"One, two, three, four, five . . ." he counted. "No wonder I feel like a zombie." He also noticed a yellow stickie note affixed to the clock face. James peeled it off, noting that the time was seven after nine.

> *Sunshine:*
> *When you finally get up, come down for breakfast. I already picked up Gillian, and we're all meeting on the back porch.*
> *There's coffee and the best bowl of cheese grits you've ever tasted. I expect your head might hurt a bit, but there's nothing for it but to eat a big pile of eggs followed by an even bigger pile of grits.*
> *— Bennett*

"I don't know about food." James stumbled into the bathroom. After swallowing three ibuprofen, he took a long shower. Doused in a fog of warm water and silence, his headache began to subside. The thought of Gillian being back at the inn, seated at a table with her friends, lightened James's heart tremendously.

"Maybe my friends will be so glad to have her back that they won't get upset about Murphy's book," James said to his reflection as he toweled off the misted mirror. He shaved quickly, wanting to escape the image he saw in the glass. Unlike the small mirror in his bathroom at home, which focused mainly on the head and shoulder region, this one was large enough to capture the entire upper half of James's body.

Before him were the results of a summer   spent falling off the diet wagon.

"You've returned, I see." James morosely poked the loose flesh of his round belly. He pivoted sideways, blowing out his stomach so that it became even larger than before. He then sucked in his breath, causing the flesh to tighten and the fat to seem like it had miraculously evaporated. Finally exhaling, James rubbed his paunch one more time before pulling a polo shirt over his head, relieved to partially disguise the evidence of his weight gain under the loose shirt.

By the time he arrived on the back porch, several charming sights met his eyes at once. Directly to his left was the food: fluffy scrambled eggs in a warming tray; crisp bacon stacked into neat rows in the neighboring tray; and, adjacent to the bacon, a ceramic baking dish containing golden-tinged grits. Next in line was a bowl of plump strawberries and a platter holding what remained of an apricot and cream cheese coffee cake.

James glanced to his right. Francesca was cleaning leaves from the pool in a loose floral sundress. The early sunlight created a halo around her hair and her skin seemed to be effused with an ethereal glow. After every third or fourth scoop of her net, she'd dip one of her bare feet into the pool and wiggle her toes in pleasure.

James paid little attention to Francesca's beauty, however, for straight ahead of him, seated between Lindy and Bennett, was the most wonderful vision of all. There was Gillian, dressed in one of her wild, rainbow-striped T-shirts, an armload of tinkling bangles, and a necklace of plastic purple beads. Her hair was its customary riot of orange curls, and she'd reddened her fair cheeks with rogue and applied smudges of lavender shadow to her eyelids. When she looked at James, she smiled with the inner warmth he'd truly missed seeing these past few days.

With that smile, James knew that Gillian was her old self again. There was no doubt that she'd been wounded by painful memories—coming face-to-face with the man who'd ruined her chance at happiness with her young husband had caused her fresh grief—but James believed that what had happened in Hudsonville would not permanently alter her. She was Gillian. Spunky, spacey, and spiritual. And she was treasured by those gathered around her.

"I heard that you might be feeling a bit *off-center* today," Gillian said after James had hugged and kissed her hello. "Ginger tea can restore your body's balance after your corporeal vessel's been flooded with alcohol." She puffed up a cloud of orange hair. "I certainly could have used some of that tea after drinking Felicity's wine the other night."

"Have tea if you want, James, but you have to try some of these grits first." Lucy pointed at the small mound on her plate. "Even if you're not a grits guy, these will warm your body from the inside out."

"I have enough blubber around my waist to keep me warm," James said wryly. "Still, I need breakfast if I'm going to make it through another day of Hog Fest. I don't think I'd make a very good full-time food judge, Lucy. I'm getting a bit burned out on all this gluttony."

"Too true. I feel like all the pores on my face are clogged by fry oil!" Lindy moaned. "Oh, and don't worry about the pie-eating contest, Gillian." She gave their friend a tender look. "I think you've been through enough this weekend without having to watch grown men wreaking havoc on perfectly good blueberry pies."

"Hey, it won't be all guys diving into those pies." Bennett waggled his finger at Lindy. "You're forgetting about Virginia's own champion eater, the Black Widow. Why, on July fourth, 2005, she ate thirty-seven hot dogs in twelve minutes. And she's a tiny little thing." He held out his arms in a small circle and then pointed at Francesca. "Makes the beauty queen cleaning the pool look like a sumo wrestler."

"Can you imagine being a buffet-type restaurant owner in the Black Widow's hometown?" James quipped. "Every time she came to visit your establishment you'd know you were about to lose money. If she can eat thirty-seven hot dogs, imagine what she could do to a breakfast buffet."

Gillian giggled. "I'm *not* skipping out on the judging. I've missed so much time with you already, and I'm fully prepared to witness a *spectacular* display of binge eating. In fact, it might do me some good." She gestured at the greedy heap of bacon on James's plate. "I think my time of reflection has prepared me to be more open regarding the food tastes and preferences of my fellow human beings."

"So no more speeches on animal treatment?" Bennett was stunned. "What on earth would you talk about instead?"

"I'll always be an advocate for all animals!" Gillian glanced at Bennett with a flash of anger in her eyes until she realized that he was trying to provoke her. She smiled. "I'm so grateful that you've all welcomed me back with open arms. I did keep a secret from you, my closest companions, and I apologize from the very core of my being. I just wanted to leave the past in the past, but I was a fool to think I could bury those memories."

"It was your secret to keep," Lucy said softly. "There's nothing to forgive."

"Other than me and Gillian, has anyone else at this table been married?" James asked to lighten the mood.

"No ex-wives in my closet." After Bennett refilled his empty coffee cup, he pointed at the grits on James's plate. "Scoop them down your throat, and you'll be good as new."

James loaded his spoon with a mouthful of grits and lifted it to his nose, wondering how a gelatinous glob of grains could put an end to the remnants of his hangover. He inhaled the pleasant scent of baked cheese. As his lips closed around the spoon felt the familiar and comforting creaminess of the starch..

"They're so light and fluffy," he said after swallowing his first mouthful. Lucy was right, the grits were suffused with warmth, and the cozy feeling they created had nothing to do with temperature. In addition to the salty flavors of sharp cheddar and butter, there were hints of Worcestershire and hot sauce.

"Delicious!" he proclaimed to Eleanor when she appeared to check on the food. "You're an excellent cook, Mrs. Fiennes. I'd say that I'm going to waste away when I go back home to Quincy's Gap, but my father's girlfriend is an accomplished food guru such as yourself, so there's no chance of that."

Eleanor looked at James with interest. "A girlfriend? Do you think your father will get remarried?"

"Yes, and I'd be happy if he did," James said. "Milla's a wonderful woman, and I'd love for her to join our family."

Gazing at Francesca, Eleanor nodded in satisfaction. "Francesca idolized her father, but he's been gone for more than ten years now. I'd like to move on, but I worry about how she'll take it. If I wait too long, however, I'm afraid the man I love will give up on me."

"If you're talking about your feelings for R. C. Richter, your daughter already knows," Lucy said gently. "And I don't think she minds one bit."

"Really?" Eleanor flushed and clasped her thin hands over her small chest. "Oh, that's *such* a nice thing to hear! He's asked me to be his wife many times, but I keep putting him off."

Gillian rose to refill her mug with more hot water and a fresh bag of Mandarin orange tea. "It seems like you and Francesca are both ready to enter a new phase of life." Gillian lowered her voice. "Lindy tells me that your daughter's greatest hope is to become a teacher. What a noble and important profession. Think of the lives she can touch, of all the young girls she can influence! You must be very proud?" Gillian emphasized her last point by turning it into a question.

Flummoxed, Eleanor darted glances between Gillian and her daughter. Finally, her eyes lingered on Francesca's beautiful face. "I should be proud, shouldn't I? Her becoming Miss Virginia was always my dream. My dream, not hers. When I was younger, my family didn't have enough money for me to compete, but I wanted that crown so badly that I used to cry about it at night. All this time, I've been pushing and pushing Francesca to win that pageant. She's always done everything I asked of her until this summer. She's a good girl—a good person—and I didn't realize how lucky I was to be her friend until I acted so *unlike* a friend."

"Sounds like you've seen the light," Bennett said.

"I have." Eleanor dumped the pile of dishes she'd been stacking back onto the buffet table. "Thank you for talking to her about teaching," she said to Lindy. "I count myself a very lucky woman because R.C. invited you to Hog Fest. You'll go down in my guest book as some of Fox Hall's most memorable visitors. Now, if you'll excuse me, I'm going to invite my daughter to come inside and tear up her pageant entry."

The supper club members watched expectantly as Eleanor marched to the deep end of the pool. Francesca stood in the middle of the diving board, catching leaves and twigs in her net as she stared dreamily into the water. Though they were too far away to hear Eleanor's words, they were able to see Francesca's mouth break into a wide smile. Tossing the leaf-laden net onto the ground, she flung her arms around her mother and the two embraced for several moments.

"This is going to be a *splendid* day," Gillian declared and took a dainty sip of tea.

• • •

Since the blueberry pie-eating competition was scheduled for high noon, the supper club members took care of business first. They packed their bags, checked out of the inn, and drove to the sheriff's department to provide statements about their encounter with Mitch Walker. According to Deputy Harding, who stood on the front steps of the sheriff's building, both Mitch and Hailey were missing, and Bob Barker was beside himself with worry. Three deputies from the neighboring county had been enlisted to help search for the pair, but they'd found nothing to indicate where they'd gone.

"I'd rather not go inside," Gillian told her friends as they marched toward the front door. "I'll wait on this bench."

Harding sat next to her with a satisfied grunt. He then proceeded to strike a match using the bottom of his shoe, lit his cigarette, and took a grateful drag.

"I heard you found some hidden treasure last night," Gillian said, and the rest of the supper club members lingered to hear his answer.

"We sure did," the deputy answered. "A whole mess of tainted pot. Someone planned to make a bunch of fry sticks and sell them for a big pile of money."

"Fry sticks?" Gillian asked. "Is that some kind of unhealthy food?"

Harding chuckled. "No, ma'am. It's a joint, but not one made with run-of-the-mill weed. The marijuana we found in Jimmy Lang's cooker was dipped in formaldehyde. That kind of pot costs lots more per ounce." He cast a sideways glance at Gillian and, seeing the lack of comprehension on her face, held his thumb and index finger an inch apart. "An ounce is about this much."

Gillian frowned. "That's not much product. Is marijuana that expensive?"

"It's the formaldehyde. It gives you visions," Harding explained. "The kids really like it. And by kids, I mean high school and college students."

"They could achieve a genuine high by employing some meditation and breathing techniques." Gillian shook her head in dismay. "This special pot sounds dangerous."

Harding nodded. "It is, ma'am. It's like smoking five of these things." He eyed his cigarette with distaste before taking another drag. "The worst part is that the kids who smoke this laced stuff tend to overdo it. We've had several college kids hospitalized over the past year because of these fry sticks. Still, they see it as the *in* drug, and because they're given so much pocket money by their oblivious parents, they can afford to buy it."

Gillian was silent for a moment as she stared into the middle distance. "He really was a bad man," she whispered. "Jimmy Lang. He was tainted, just like the drugs. I was prepared to forgive him, but now that you're telling me he planned to sell drugs to teenagers, I can't. He spent his whole life ruining the lives of others."

"We have no hard proof that Mr. Lang was a dealer," Harding said. "And when we questioned Mr. Walker earlier yesterday, he claimed to have never known Mr. Lang beyond bumping into him at festivals. But now that Mr. Walker has disappeared, I'm feeling more and more like he's our guy." He sat ramrod-straight on the bench, his shoulders taut with tension. "We have to find him and get the truth out of him. He was lying to us yesterday, I'm sure of it. Just as I was certain that you were telling us the truth."

"You know, I strongly believe in the power of the inner voice." Gillian turned her palms to the sky. "It's the world's way of speaking to us. You seem to have heightened instincts, Deputy. How do you know all of these details about these laced drugs?"

"Used to live in DC. I moved here to get away from that stuff." He shrugged. "Guess you can never really run from the ugly things in life." He shifted his weight on the bench, looking suddenly uncomfortable.

Gillian took Harding's free hand. "You can't run, but you can make the most of where you are now."

Harding nodded in agreement. "I expect you'd know all about that, ma'am. I truly admire how you've handled yourself over the last two days. You're quite a lady." He threw his cigarette onto the ground. "And a mighty pretty one, too, if you don't mind my saying so."

"Oh, I don't mind." Gillian blushed. "I don't mind at all."

• • •

The R. C. Richter who handed a stack of signed waivers to the judges to review was a different man than the one who'd appeared in front of yesterday's crowd looking haggard and defeated. This R.C. had a spring to his step, and he smiled as he issued directions to a scruffy teenager wheeling a wagon filled with pies to a line of tables covered in white plastic cloths.

Chairs had been arranged in an orderly row behind the tables. At each place was a bottle of water and a white T-shirt with cobalt lettering that read *I Turned Blue at Hog Fest.*

After James finished inspecting his group of waivers, which had all been signed and dated according to R.C.'s requirements, he noticed a group of teenage boys unloading more pies from the back of a white van. Mrs. Phelps, the baker, hovered nervously nearby, clucking at the boys and pleading with them to be careful. The young men maneuvered carts of pies to a small tent alongside the row of tables and James frowned over their untidy appearance. Their hair was long and unkempt, their pants were baggy, and their soiled shirts were riddled with holes.

"Why are you frowning, James?" Lucy asked. "Don't you like blueberry pie?"

"I like all kinds of pie except rhubarb." He smiled self-effacingly.

"I was just being an old fart—wondering why those boys spend good money to look like they're homeless."

"Yeah, I know. That grunge style just won't go away." Lucy tugged at his arm. "But cheer up. Mrs. Phelps has brought all the judges a slice of pie, still warm from the oven. We get to eat while R.C. goes over the rules."

"He must enjoy what he does," James said. "The man's mighty chipper today."

"That's because Eleanor told him that she'd marry him. She stopped by the festival while we were with the sheriff. I overheard R.C. telling Mrs. Phelps all about it."

"So everything is looking up for him," James said. "Except for the fact that illegal drugs were recovered on festival grounds, the girlfriend of the man murdered here Friday night has gone missing, and a torch-wielding thief is on the loose, things are just peachy for the man"

"Not *peach*," Mrs. Phelps trilled as she appeared in front of a small card table and thrust napkins into the judges' hands. "Locally grown blueberries. The best in the state. Eat up, now."

James drove his fork through the perfectly browned crust of the pie and watched as indigo blueberries oozed from beneath the tines.

"This contest is going to be messy." He examined his plate in amusement.

"People love that part. This event's the best free advertising a baker can get!" Mrs. Phelps chirped gaily.

"Where do you get all of your extra help?" James asked, suddenly spotting a young man who could easily be the brother of the leather-jacket-wearing teen who'd been haunting his library on Friday nights.

"The boys? Oh, they come out of the woodwork right before Hog Fest," she replied. "It's the same every year. They're not the world's *best* workers, and I have to pay them right after we're done selling pies. After that, they scatter like the four winds until next year."

"That boy over there. Is he from Hudsonville?" James pointed at the Martin Trotman look-alike.

"Only one of them lives in town, but they all know each other." Her brows creased as she struggled to recall the young man's name. "What is it? Oh, I remember! It's Trotman! Donny Trotman."

James tried not to allow the surprise to show in his face. Martin's last name was also Trotman. "No offense, Mrs. Phelps, but why are they so eager to work during Hog Fest? Why is this particular time so important to them?"

She shrugged, still waiting for James to taste her pie. "They tell me it's their annual score, whatever that means. I figure they must be sweet on some of the vendor girls who travel here every year. Who knows?" She swatted at his shoulder with the edge of her apron. "But they're better eaters than you, honey! They'd eat night and day if they had the chance."

"It's called the munchies," James muttered and took a bite of pie. The sugary blueberries popped in his mouth as he crunched on bits of buttery crust. "Mmmm," he mumbled through closed lips. "Sublime."

Smiling, Mrs. Phelps resumed her role of overseer as the motley group of young men unhurriedly went about their tasks.

While James focused on his pie and wished that he had a cold glass of milk to cut the sweetness of his baked treat, the contestants for the pie-eating competition began taking their seats at the plastic-covered table. After donning the official T-shirts, the contestants exchanged nervous small talk.

"That's a *fine* piece of pie," Bennett declared as he pushed his blueberry-stained paper plate away. He smiled at James, displaying a row of purple teeth.

"You'd better brush those not-so-pearly whites before you see your sheriff again," James teased as Bennett frantically ran his tongue over his upper teeth.

"Yours aren't exactly white either." Bennett checked his watch. "Uh-oh. Time to act official. Come on, man. All we have to do is make sure the contestants don't use their hands to eat their pie and place a new one in front of them when their dish is empty. Easy."

James took up his station in front of a pair of newlyweds who were so busy kissing that R.C. had to blow the start whistle twice to get their attention. Their demonstration of affection caused them to be several bites behind the remaining eighteen contestants once they finally planted their faces into the center of their pies.

The contestants looked like pigs at the trough, burying their mouths and noses into the deep blue filling and scooping up the crust with their front teeth. At first, James found their slurping and squelching noises comical, but as the first round of pies were consumed and he had to slide two fresh pies beneath the stained and crumb-covered faces of the contestants before him, he began to feel slightly repulsed.

By the time the newlyweds had started on their third pie, half the contestants had dropped out. James noticed several older men cleaning their faces with moist wipes with one hand as they held their bloated stomachs with the other. At the very end of the table, where Lindy was officiating, a man in his early thirties dashed away from the table and bent over the closest garbage can, his entire torso heaving as he threw up the two pies he'd consumed.

"You're *so* disqualified!" one of Mrs. Phelps's helpers jeered at the man. Lindy scowled at the boy and placed a gentle hand on the sick man's back. After he'd emptied his stomach, she handed him several napkins and a tall glass of water. Encouraged by her kindness, the man smiled and waved at the crowd. He then wobbled off to an empty seat, his skin still a bit green beneath the faint stain of blueberry.

Following this incident, James had the unfortunate task of disqualifying the new bride for using her fingers to shovel a particularly slippery bite of pie into her mouth. Frustrated by his own inability to completely empty his pie dish, her husband followed suit a few minutes later, and the lovebirds sat and watched the remaining contestants slowly dig into their fourth slice of pie.

Seeing as he no longer had an official responsibility, James decided to find out more about the "score" the young men had mentioned to Mrs. Phelps. Hoping to appear as though he were merely in search of shade, James sauntered casually to the side of the disheveled young man named Donny Trotman.

"You guys unloaded lots of pies," James said pleasantly to the boy. "And in this heat. That can't be easy work." He wiped his brow with a napkin to emphasize the point.

"Man, I hope she sells the rest of them, so we don't have to put any back in the van," the boy said. "I'm sick of pies."

James glanced at him. "You look just like a kid I know from Quincy's Gap. His name's Martin."

Donny frowned, clearly offended over being called a kid.

"Martin's my first cousin. How do *you* know him?" He scrutinized James's creased khakis, spotless glasses, and leather loafers in disdain.

"Let's just say he and I share the same hobby," James said cryptically. And then as subtly as possible, James pinched his thumb and index finger together and mimed an inhalation.

"Dude. Rock on!" Even Donny's exclamations were tinged with lethargy.

"Know where a guy can score some around here?" James muttered out of the side of his mouth.

Donny held out his hand. "I can tell you, but you gotta make it worth my while."

Struggling not to show his dislike for Donny, James pulled out his wallet, extracted a twenty, and placed it on a palm stained with blueberries, flour, and dirt. Thinking that he might have consumed a pie created by Donny's filthy hands, James fought to control the bile rising in his belly.

"Did you bake any of those?" he asked, gesturing at the dozens of pies for sale.

"Hell, no. I don't wear an apron, man." Donny spit on the ground as a sign of his masculinity. "Listen. If you want to get hooked up, meet me at six at the bleachers where all the big shows are. During the closing ceremony, we can get what we came here for."

"Do you always use the same . . . contact?" James hoped that his choice of words sounded legitimate. When Donny's face clouded over with annoyance, he knew that he'd made the wrong choice.

"*Contact?*" The boy scowled. "What are you, like, a cop? Piss off, man." Donny clomped away.

Suddenly, the crowd's cheers swelled and James saw that R.C. was holding the victor's hand high in the air as he proclaimed a twig of a girl the winner of the pie-eating contest.

"Where did you put over eight pounds of pie?" R.C. held his cordless microphone below her blue chin.

"I've been stretching my stomach over at the Golden Corral," the young woman announced. "I'm a hostess there."

"But your stomach is flat as a board!" R.C. declared.

"Two babies have grown in there already, so I know it can

stretch," she said with a charming smile. "And my kids will benefit from this prize money and the gift certificate to the bakery, too. Easiest money I've ever made! I love pie!"

"Congratulations to all of our contestants! Don't forget to purchase your own scrumptious blueberry pie, and don't leave before the drawing for a brand-new recreational vehicle, which will occur at this evening's closing ceremony!" R.C. called to the crowd. "Sponsored by Richter's RV Sales & Rentals!"

As R.C. continued with a few other announcements, James grabbed Lucy by the arm and pulled her behind the bakery van.

"I may have part of this puzzle figured out, Lucy." He dabbed at his sweating temples with a fresh napkin. "These kids came to Hog Fest to buy the laced pot. They've gotten it here before and keep coming back for more. They buy as much as they can afford, and then, I think they resell some of it. In fact, this stuff may have gotten into *my* library through the hands of a rising high school senior named Martin Trotman, though I have no way to prove it."

Lucy digested this information. "And these kids think the deal's still on? Even though Jimmy's dead?"

James shrugged. "I don't know who their contact is. Maybe Jimmy didn't do the actual selling. You know, I could call the Fitzgerald twins and have them look up which festivals Jimmy and Mitch Walker attended at the same time. If they were partners in this nasty business, a pattern should emerge—something tangible you can show to the sheriff."

"Why me?" Lucy was taken aback. "*You're* the one figuring this out, James."

He touched her arm. "Any credibility you can get will only help advance your career. If you assist in a drug bust in Hudsonville that makes a ripple effect felt in our own county, you'll be irreplaceable."

Lucy leaned over and kissed James on the cheek. "You're the greatest, James. You always put other people before yourself. It just makes me want to wrap my arms around you in front of this whole crowd."

James was both relieved and disappointed when Gillian bounded over, trailing Deputy Harding in her wake.

"They found Hailey! She spent some time walking by the river, and, like me, she ended up meeting Felicity and the two exchanged stories. Hailey begged for forgiveness for Jimmy's behavior and Felicity gave it to her. Afterward, Hailey decided to go on with the competition. She rented her own RV and bought a cheap grill from Walmart. I guess she wanted to enter the final contest with no distractions. If she wins, she still has a chance at being named champion—all on her own!"

"Oh, I hadn't realized that she'd won in other categories," James said.

"Yeah, man. *All* of the ones we didn't judge," Bennett said.

"What about Bob?" Lindy asked crossly. "He's been worried sick about her."

"Bob is with her. Hailey's a frightened dove right now." Gillian flapped her hands as though they were wings. "She just needs to find a place to roost before she's ready to fly again."

Bennett rolled his eyes. "You're as loony as ever, woman! Still, I can see why Hailey might not be in a hurry to attach herself to another man. Shoot, her last one wasn't exactly the kind to bring home to mama."

"Deputy Harding tells me that Bob and Hailey are talking through Hailey's concerns about the future of their relationship," Gillian said. "I'm certain that Bob is willing to treat Hailey as his equal!" She beamed at Harding. "That was very thoughtful of you to give them some space to sort things out, Deputy."

Harding looked flustered. "We'll need to redouble our efforts to track down Mr. Walker. And by we"—he eyed the supper club members sternly—"I mean the sheriff's department."

James elbowed Lucy in the side. "Go on, tell him."

"Tell me what?" Harding's gaze sharpened.

"If you haven't found Mitch Walker by the closing ceremony," Lucy announced importantly, "I have it on good authority that he plans to be there tonight."

Chapter Seventeen

Chilled Watermelon Wedge

While Lucy conferred privately with Deputy Harding, James made himself comfortable in the shade of a large maple tree and called the Fitzgerald twins' home number.

Francis and Scott lived in a converted garage owned by an elderly widow. At first, the arrangement had come with the stipulation that the boys would help Mrs. Lamb with her yard work, but before long, the brothers had not only taken over the landscaping chores, but chopped wood and completed repairs around her house as well. In return, she cooked them hearty suppers. Over time, they'd become a family.

James glanced at his watch. It was a few minutes to two. The large midday meal typically served after church service would be over, so it was likely the twins were outside, trimming Mrs. Lamb's bushes or mowing her lawn. James listened as the phone rang and rang. When Scott's voice announced that he and Francis were unavailable, James hung up without leaving a message. He called Mrs. Lamb next.

"Hello?" a raspy voice answered. James could hear the whine of a motor in the background.

"Mrs. Lamb!" James shouted. "This is James Henry. I'm looking for Scott or Francis. It's important."

"Who is this?" she asked suspiciously.

"James Henry. From the library! It's important that I speak to Scott or Francis!" he shouted. "Are they there?"

"Oh, Jackson's boy? I haven't seen that handsome devil in a mighty long time." She issued a licentious cackle. "Stop hollerin' at me, child! I may be old as the hills, but I've still got two good ears attached to my head! Francis is on the mower, but Scott is just finishin' up the weedin'. He'll be in directly for some tea."

There was a clunk as if Mrs. Lamb had set the receiver on a hard surface.

"Hello?" James called into empty space. He waited, listening to a series of rattles and clanks in the background. After three full minutes, a door opened and closed, and there was a mumbled exchange in the background. James was pretty sure the male voice belonged to Scott, so why wasn't he picking up the phone?

"Scott!" James yelled into his cell phone. "*Scott!*"

"Hello?" Scott sounded surprised.

James blew out his breath in annoyance. "Didn't Mrs. Lamb tell you I was on the phone?"

"No, Professor. Sorry." He added with a whisper, "Her memory is like a sieve these days."

"I'd say," James muttered. "Listen, Scott. I could use some long-distance help." James gave a brief account of Jimmy's death, the discovery of the laced marijuana, and his suspicions about Mitch Walker.

"You should write a book about everything that's happened to you since you moved back to Quincy's Gap," Scott exclaimed. "You lead the most exciting life of any librarian in this country."

Naturally, Scott's words brought to mind Murphy's book deal. James struggled to control his anger. "Can you find out if Jimmy and Mitch have crossed paths at one of these festivals and call me right away if anything turns up? It's fairly urgent."

"Absolutely, Professor. These lightning-fast fingers are at your disposal. I'll go fire up the laptop right now."

After ending the call, James leaned against the tree trunk and wondered what to do about Murphy. He felt incredibly betrayed. Not only had she written about him and his friends, but she'd also sold the book without breathing a word to him about it. He thought of all of the evenings he'd left her apartment so that she could write. And there she'd been, adding colorful fabrications to characters and events based on *his* life. Her book was going to be published and he'd never read so much as a sentence. How would she portray him? How would she describe him physically? Would she reveal his secrets or the intimate details he'd shared with her?

Imagining his thoughts and actions put forth for all to read, and for all to judge, James balled his hands into fists. With the rough bark pressing against his back, he sat as still as a stone, realizing that it had been a long time since he'd felt such white-hot fury toward another person.

His cell phone, which was settled in a patch of scraggly grass growing between two tree roots, began to buzz. Because it was set on vibrate and was resting on uneven ground, it looked like a black beetle bouncing against a curve of root. James scooped it up.

"Professor. Your theory is dead on," Scott said. "Mitch Walker and the Marrow Men have been at nearly every festival or cook-off event that Jimmy Lang and the Pitmasters have attended over the last three years. They've been to fifteen events in total, so there's no way that Mitch guy can claim not to know Jimmy."

"Maybe so. But he can claim to know nothing about the drugs." James ran his hands through his sweaty hair. "Time's running out, Scott. I have to find a way to link these two as drug traffickers or the local sheriff won't have enough evidence to hold Mitch—if they ever find him."

"I thought you said there might be a drug deal tonight."

"That's a big maybe. The drugs have been seized, and though the kids who want to buy them don't know that, Mitch certainly does. If he shows, it'll be to tell the kids where to meet him in future." James paused. "The next festival's in North Carolina in two weeks, so he might just tell them to go there to complete the deal, though it's a pretty big chance to take."

Scott hesitated. "That sounds risky. I wouldn't take that chance."

"But Mitch lost a heap of money when the authorities seized his stash. He might be desperate to make it up," James said. "Also, I think Jimmy's been dealing solo this past year and may have cut Mitch out of his half of the earnings. Jimmy bought a big camper and seems to have hidden chunks of cash somewhere in that RV."

"But if Jimmy and Mitch were partners, and Jimmy had the drugs in his cooker, what was Mitch's role?" Scott asked. "How did he earn his share?"

James contemplated this for a moment. He then sat up with a jerk, his tailbone pressing against a sharp root. "What if Mitch's cooker is outfitted with a false chamber, too? Maybe *that's* why he's hiding. Maybe he still wants to sell his share and then get out of here. I'll have to ask the deputies if they checked his grill."

"That's a thought. I have another wrench to throw at you, Professor." Scott had a smile in his voice.

James grunted. "What's that?"

"If the pot's laced with formaldehyde, where's it coming from? You can't buy that stuff at CVS."

James stared at the grass in front of him. "I have no idea."

"Listen, Professor. Francis and I will see what we can dig up on this guy. But if you have only a few hours until everyone goes home, you'd better find out as much as you can about this Mitch Walker."

"Thanks, Scott. I knew I could count on you and Francis."

"And Professor, be careful. It sounds like this man has lots to lose. You know what they say about cornered animals . . ."

"They're twice as dangerous," James said before ending the call.

Later, the rest of the supper club members found James beneath his tree, still deep in thought. He had a paper napkin on his leg and had written some notes on it using a pen borrowed from Mrs. Phelps. Lucy waited until he'd finished writing before kneeling next to him, the sun highlighting her caramel-colored hair as it streamed through the canopy of maple leaves.

"One of the deputies from Russell County is going undercover. He's barely twenty-two, and if he sports some false tattoos, wears a baseball cap, and carries a skateboard, they're hoping he can get close enough to the other kids to see what happens at the closing ceremony.

"This is scary and exciting at the same time." Lindy shivered with anticipation. "And I thought we'd be spending most of the weekend focused on food."

"I think we've nailed the food part." Bennett patted his thick waist.

Gillian clasped her hands together. "Oh, I *do* hope these young people will get the help they need. Addiction robs the body of precious spiritual energy and the ability to remain balanced."

Bennett arched his eyebrows at Gillian before turning to James. "What are you doing over here anyway? Writing poetry?"

James pointed at the napkin. "I've been thinking about Mitch's cooker."

Lucy's eyes widened as she instantly caught on to James's line of thinking. "You think *he* might have been transporting drugs as well?"

"Oh, that would be terrible!" Gillian screeched. "We need to stop those drugs from getting into the hands of any more children. Because that's what they are. Children."

Bennett gestured at James. "Get up, big boy. We have to get over to the Marrow Men's cook site. And Lucy, if we find anything significant there, I'm going to hog all the credit. If I don't get Sheriff Jones to go to dinner with me before we leave Hudsonville, then I won't be able to concentrate on trivia ever again."

"The credit's all yours," Lucy replied. "But the sheriff is a pretty sharp lady. I bet she's already had her deputies check the other cookers. If not, you can call her yourself and announce your brilliant discovery."

Once again, the group set off for the cooking area. James felt like he'd walked the same path a dozen times already and was looking forward to bidding farewell to the crowds, the sticky heat, and the ever-present smell of fried food.

As soon as the supper club members approached the Marrow Men's cluster of grills, they quickly became aware that it was going to be difficult to glean information from the barbecue cooks.

Three men bustled around two large grills. Neither cooker was as big as Jimmy's commercial-sized grill and the Marrow Men seemed to have reached a crucial moment in their preparation. James found it challenging to pay attention to their equipment once he noticed that the pieces of meat the Marrow Men were placing on the grill racks came from a Ziploc bag inside a cooler. The chunks had a pink hue resembling lamb, but James didn't think he recognized the raw meat at all.

Deputy Neely, who stood behind one of the Marrow Men, was also fascinated by the unidentified hunks of meat. He put his hands on his hips and asked, "None of you have seen Mitch all day?"

The man retrieving the meat from the cooler frowned. "Look, we told you that we haven't seen him. And he didn't travel with his own grill. He always used ours. He told us that he had a boring office job pushing papers, and that's all he ever said about his work. We're grilling buddies, which means we hang out a few times a year and try to win some contests." He gestured at his companions. "We like beer, women, and meat. We don't talk about much else. That's the whole point of getting together—to have fun and forget about our lives for a bit."

Neely scrutinized the remaining three Marrow Men, but they met his gaze unblinkingly. After a few uncomfortable seconds, two of them resumed brushing sauce over the meat on the grill while the third slid pieces of the cubed meat onto bamboo skewers.

"Is that lamb or veal?" Neely asked, unable to quell his curiosity.

"It's goat," one of the men answered curtly and then noticed James and his friends staring. "You want to ask us questions, too?"

Gillian took a few steps backward, obviously uninterested in getting a closer look at the Marrow Men's preparations.

"We just wanted to see what folks were cooking for the Anything Butt category," James said innocently. "I've never had goat before. How will you prepare it?"

"Using mesquite wood chips, for starters," the Marrow Man replied. "Then, we season the meat with salt, pepper, and garlic. We're going to use a curry yogurt sauce to give it a bit of an Indian flavor. It's real good. Lots of folks turn up their noses at goat, but it's a nice meat if you don't overcook it."

"Is anyone else cooking goat?" Lucy eyed the Marrow Men's cooler.

"Don't think so," the man said as he deftly turned the skewers. "One of the teams is using venison, and I think the Tenderizers went with scallops. The Adam's Ribbers are going with rabbit, and Jimmy's girl claims to be cooking coon, but I think that's just big talk to draw attention to herself, just like her old man used to do."

James and his friends exchanged looks of disgust.

"Did Hailey and Mitch know each other?" James couldn't stop himself from asking.

"Not that I knew. Never saw them talk to each other. Now, can you give us some breathin' room?" The Marrow Man threw irritated looks at Neely and the supper club members. "We're trying to win a contest here."

"Sorry," Lindy quickly said. "Good luck to you and your team."

As they moved away from the fragrant smell of the roasting goat, Bennett said, "You're not going to like me saying this, Gillian, but I'm feeling peckish all of a sudden."

"Oh, Bennett." She rolled her eyes. "I cannot believe your appetite can be so active in this setting."

"Well, I need a snack, and that's that," Bennett said. "It doesn't have to be meat, but nothing will be open in town on a Sunday, so we're stuck with fair food."

"I can't take anything fried, stuck on a stick, or covered in powdered sugar!" Lucy declared.

"I saw a place by the community center selling chilled watermelon wedges," Lindy said. "Since it's so hot again, it might be nice to have something cold and sweet."

Everyone agreed on a snack of watermelon slices, and Lindy led her friends through the milling crowds to a small stand with a red, white, and green-striped awning. After paying for two thick slices of watermelon and collected a handful of napkins, the five friends decided to sit on the grass away from the crowds of festivalgoers.

"The sheriff's department isn't exactly inept," James said and then bit off the tip of his first piece of watermelon. "They're definitely on top of this situation."

"No one thought they were inept," Lucy said defensively. "We just don't *know* what they've investigated, and they don't want to share information with me anymore. I think the discovery of the drugs changed things. Now, they have a murder and the sale of illegal drugs on their hands, and very little time to solve both cases."

"Have the Fitzgerald twins gotten back to you yet?" Bennett asked James.

"Shoot!" James cried, reaching for his phone. "I forgot to turn the ringer back on. They could have called, and I wouldn't have known."

The black text on James's screen indicated that he had one new message waiting. He selected the speaker option, placed the phone on the ground, and beckoned for his friends to scoot closer. He pressed a button and Francis's energetic voice burst from the phone.

"Professor? Scott and I think we discovered something that you might find pretty interesting. We researched Mitch Walker of San Antonio, Texas. There were a couple of them, but we were able to narrow down the field by cross-referencing the info we learned about Mitch from a bunch of barbecue festival websites. Still, there's not much on cyberspace about this guy. It's not like he has his own website or blog."

There was a pause, and James rolled his eyes and said, "Those two have a flair for the dramatic."

Francis finally continued. "We think Jimmy was partnered with Mitch Walker in regards to the laced marijuana. You see, Mitch works for Sunset Gardens in San Antonio. That's a mortuary. Mitch was listed on their website's staff page as an assistant mortician. Do you know what that means, Professor? If Mitch works at a funeral home, he has access to formaldehyde."

"He's your bad guy number two!" Scott shouted with exuberance. "Now, all you have to do is figure out where they bought the pot. Unless Jimmy had a giant greenhouse or a big piece of land, they bought it somewhere cheap, like Mexico."

"How do you know Mexico has cheap pot?" Francis asked in the background and Scott responded to his brother, completely forgetting that he was leaving a message. "I researched it, bro. I went to a bunch of government sites and checked out filed newspaper stories and recent DEA busts . . . oh, sorry, Professor. That's all we have on Mitch. Call us if you need more info. We're ready and waiting to—" At that point, the voice-mail time allotment expired and Scott was cut off.

Lucy stared at the phone. "I think Mitch is Jimmy's partner *and* his killer," she said, and James could practically hear the gears turning in her mind. "James, when you saw the two of them arguing that first night, it must have been over the drugs."

"I agree," James said. "Jimmy has gone to several festivals without Mitch this year. He was able to buy that big RV and squirrel away extra cash. I think he's been stiffing Mitch, and Mitch decided to get his revenge by poisoning Jimmy with the propane. He planned to take all of the drugs for himself, but we interrupted him."

"If there *is* cash inside the camper, he couldn't search for it the night he killed Jimmy, because Gillian was sitting on the camper steps. Gillian, your being there also kept Mitch from getting into the cooker," Lucy continued. "Who else but a partner in crime would know the drugs were hidden in that secret compartment?"

"Well, if the drugs *did* come from Mexico," Lindy began before pausing to remove a watermelon seed from the tip of her tongue, "that's probably where Mitch is by now."

Gillian shook her head. "No. I don't think he'd leave. I think he's too angry."

"That's crazy!" Bennett practically dropped his fruit. "The law is after that pasty-skinned fool. Why would he still be here?"

"He has too much to lose," Lucy said, her gaze distant. "I have a strong hunch that Gillian's right, though I'm not sure what Mitch is planning."

"But the drugs have been seized," James countered. "What does he stand to gain by hanging around?" He rubbed his finger on the smooth green rind in his hand. "I doubt he'd risk prison just to tell a bunch of kids to meet him in North Carolina in a few weeks."

"For enough money, he just might," said Bennett.

The group fell silent. They finished eating their watermelon and tried to clean their sticky hands with their napkins, but bits of paper clung stubbornly to their fingertips. Lindy sifted through her bag and came out with a package of wet wipes.

Accepting a towelette, Bennett grinned. "I guess there's something to be said for overpacking."

"It's called being prepared," Lindy snapped. She immediately shook her head. "Sorry, Bennett, I didn't mean to bite your head off. I just don't like the way things are ending up. We've always stumbled upon the answers in time, but I'm worried that the bad guy is going to get away. We have only hours left."

Lucy stood, collected all the garbage, and walked off to a nearby garbage can. When she returned, she didn't sit back down. Instead, she paced around her circle of friends as though about to start a game of duck, duck, goose. "We need more evidence linking Jimmy and Mitch to the drugs." She stopped and looked at James. "Do you think there's anything to the Fitzgeralds' idea about Mexico? San Antonio isn't that far from there."

James shrugged. "Those boys are pretty smart, but even if the pot came from south of the border, we can't ask Hailey if Jimmy liked to take international road trips. She's in the middle of the Anything Butt judging."

"I doubt Big Jimmy would have told her anyway," Bennett added. "She seemed to be in the dark about his sideline business."

"Wait a minute!" James slapped himself on the forehead. "Murphy left me a bunch of papers, and one of them had the name and home phone number of Jimmy's boss. Maybe he could tell us more about what Jimmy did with his free time."

"Why would this guy be forthcoming to a total stranger?" Lindy was dubious.

James put his hand out and patted the ground next to him.

Perplexed, Lucy sat down. "Because he thinks he's going to be in Murphy's next book, and if I pretend to be her assistant, he'll tell me anything I want to know."

"She's writing a book?" Gillian was impressed. "What kind of book?"

James looked at Bennett in appeal. His friend held out his hands and said, "It's all you, man. Better get it over with."

"She's written a thriller. Or maybe two, I don't know." James shifted nervously. "The thing is, they're loosely based on, um, they're about . . ." He trailed off, his mouth going dry. He swallowed hard and spluttered, "Murphy's books are based on us."

• • •

James wanted to call Jimmy's boss immediately, but his phone battery had run low, and the reception on Lucy's was less than ideal. Therefore, James asked the receptionist at the community center for the use of an office and permission to make a long-distance phone call. After getting the okay from R.C. via walkie-talkie, the woman showed them into a small office and told them to make themselves comfortable.

As James sat in the swivel chair behind the tidy wooden desk, he noticed that only Bennett would make eye contact with him. All three of his female friends were still grappling with the news that their lives were about to become works of fiction. So far, their initial reaction was one of mistrust. This came as no surprise considering Murphy hadn't always painted them in the rosiest of colors in her past articles.

James dialed the Texas number, and when a man with a deep voice answered the phone, he asked, "Is this Mr. Leggett?"

"Depends who's callin'," the man replied cagily.

"I'm Murphy Alistair's assistant. I'm calling because Ms. Alistair requires a bit more information for her book. I apologize for phoning you at home, and on a Sunday, but the chapter she's writing about Jimmy Lang . . . and you, of course, is *very* important." James spoke quickly, trying to ignore the looks he was currently receiving from his friends. Their glances contained enough acid to burn holes right through his body.

"Well, sure thing. Anything to help that nice writer lady."

"I'm going to put you on speaker, Mr. Leggett. That way I can take notes for Ms. Alistair," James lied glibly. "What we're trying to figure out today is what Jimmy liked to do in his free time. For example, Ms. Alistair wants to know about his friends. Do you know if Jimmy had a friend in San Antonio?"

"Yep. Some fella he met at a fair a few years back." Mr. Leggett gave a dry laugh. "At first, I thought Jimmy was sweet on some gal down in San Anton', because he drove there quite a bit, but then he told me he was startin' a side business with some fella there. Don't know what they was up to, but Jimmy must've been doin' fine with it. He bought that big trailer with the money he made. That camper thang's so big my whole family could fit in there, and there's nine of us Leggetts."

"How do you know that Jimmy's new business paid for that? Hailey told me that Jimmy's aunt left him an inheritance."

"Pffah!" Mr. Leggett guffawed. "What aunt? Jimmy's been a ward of the state his whole life. He ain't got no family, and none of his foster families left him a pile of money. They ain't got none themselves."

"He could have taken out a loan," James persisted, hoping to elicit more information from Jimmy's boss.

His ploy worked. "Look, I *know* the fella who sold Jimmy his camper. He said Jimmy walked in with a grocery sack full of cash and drove that camper off the lot an hour later, neat as you please. Jimmy told *me* that he wasn't gonna work for me no more after his trip to Virginia, so it's a good thang I put an ad in the paper. I got me a new boy startin' Monday. Can drive the tow truck and help me with these confounded computers. Not a bad deal."

James felt a momentary pang of sympathy for the late Jimmy Lang. He had no family to speak of, his girlfriend had a new man, and his boss had a replacement driver ready and waiting to take over Jimmy's job.

Would anyone miss Jimmy? To be so easily forgotten, except by those trying to solve the mystery of one's murder, doesn't make a pleasant epitaph, James thought morosely.

"You still there?" Mr. Leggett asked.

"Yes, sir. I was just gathering my thoughts." James glanced

briefly at Lucy, but she was intently studying her fingernails. Finally, she looked up and whispered, "Mexico."

"Back to Jimmy's hobbies and such, did he travel anywhere besides to cook-offs?" James asked. "How about out of the country?"

"If you count Mexico as bein' another country, then yeah," Jimmy's boss answered. "Sometimes, you can't tell the difference between Texas and Mexico, but Jimmy went there. Always brought a bottle of Patron tequila back for me. I'm gonna miss those freebies."

"Did he happen to drive his cooker down with him?" James winced, knowing what an odd question he'd asked.

"Funny you should mention that, but he did. I figured he was givin' the Mexicans a few lessons in exchange for booze." Mr. Leggett chuckled.

"He liked tequila that much?" James shared in the joke.

"Jimmy liked to drink everything, eat everything, smoke everything, and talk to every cute girl he saw. He talked big. He lived big. That's why he and Texas were such a good fit."

James asked, "And Hailey? Did she live big, too?"

"Nah. She's a churchgoer and Jimmy's shadow. Ain't got nothin' of her own, that girl. She's gonna be lost without Big Jim," Mr. Leggett said.

Noting the frowns on Lindy's and Lucy's faces, James replied, "Oh, I wouldn't be too sure about that, Mr. Leggett. I have to type up these notes now. Thank you for your time."

"Hey!" Jimmy's boss quickly shouted before James could hang up. "You think this book's gonna be in Walmart?"

James took the phone off speaker mode. "I don't know, sir, but I'm sure Ms. Alistair will mail you an autographed copy or two."

"Hot dog! I'm gonna be famous!" Mr. Leggett hollered in farewell.

James replaced the receiver and remained silent. Mr. Leggett's reaction to Murphy's publishing success was quite the opposite of James's friends.

"You might not have been lying to the man, James," Lucy said acidly. "Murphy is probably busy as a little beaver gathering material for a book on the Hog Fest Murder."

Gillian touched Lucy's hand. "Let's focus on a woman who needs our help. Think of Hailey now."

Lindy nodded. "You're right. If Hailey found Jimmy's stash of cash, Mitch may go after her."

"She won't miss the announcement of the Hog Fest Barbecue Champion," Bennett chimed in. "She's bound to be at the closing ceremony."

James checked his watch. "We have two hours until then. Let's track her down and stay by her side. That way, nothing can happen to her."

In full agreement, the group trotted off to the camper Hailey had rented. The door was ajar, so James pulled it all the way open and called Hailey's name. After stepping inside, he immediately backed out.

"I'm having some serious déjà vu. Hailey's camper has been trashed." He jerked his head toward the door. "Gillian, I'm afraid you were right. Mitch Walker is still here. And he's seriously angry."

Chapter Eighteen

Cold Green Tea

As the rest of the supper club members debated over whether to report the state of Hailey's trailer to the sheriff, James decided to call to the Fitzgerald brothers again. He'd plugged his phone into a wall outlet at the community center and, while it was nowhere near fully charged, he had enough juice for a short call.

Francis answered on the second ring. "Do you need us to do more research, Professor?"

"Not exactly. I want to know the full name of the ringleader of that teen group coming to our library on Fridays. I know his first name's Martin, but I need to know his surname."

Francis murmured something to Scott. "Just wanted to confirm with Scott, it's Trotman. Martin Trotman."

"Gotcha!" James smiled. "I don't know what the outcome of the Hog Fest mystery will be, but I can tell you right now that we're going to solve the Shenandoah County Library mystery this Friday night."

"Really? Cool." Francis whispered something to Scott. "In that case, can we let Mrs. Waxman have the night off? Scott and I want to be there when it all goes down."

"Absolutely. I can't think of anyone I'd rather have by my side when we put a stop to their funny business."

"Are you going to tell us what their business is?" Francis asked.

"When I get back," James promised. "I'm not trying to hold out, but catching them in the act will take some planning, and I don't want to go into it until we can meet in person. However, I was wondering if you guys have one of those little cameras that you can mount in some unobtrusive location and watch the feed on a computer screen?"

"We do, actually. We tried to talk Mrs. Lamb into letting us set up a security system for her, but she said if anyone breaks in she'll crack them over the head with a frying pan, so we just use the camera as a web cam now. It's a piece of cake to hook up."

"Bring all that stuff to work tomorrow, will you? I have a special assignment for you and Scott. Technical stuff."

"Awesome! Sounds like a Special Ops mission. You can count on us, Professor."

James gazed at the blinking symbol indicating his phone's dwindling battery life and stuffed the gadget into his pocket. It would have to remain in sleep mode until he hooked it up to the car charger in the Bronco.

As James watched his friends talk, he noticed the bulges in Bennett's back pockets. James assumed his friend was carrying his wallet and his mini recorder.

"I'm not even going to ask why you're checking out my bum," Bennett said, noticing where James was looking. He jerked his thumb toward Hailey's camper. "We're off to visit Bob Barker — see if he and his fiancée are killing time before the announcement of the Hog Fest champion. If she's not with him, I'm going to call that fine, fine Sheriff Jones."

Bob Barker's camper was only minutes away. The door was propped open, and the contractor was inside, fussing with his hair. Bob told the supper club members to come in while he finished grooming.

"Almost time to find out the champ of 'cue." Bob grinned as he shaped his hair. "Doesn't matter to me, though. I've got my Hailey, and she's the *real* prize. If you folks are lookin' for her, she's primpin' for the closing ceremony. Did y'all know she won the Anything Butt category? She's got a shot at winnin' the whole shebang!"

"She won? With barbecued raccoon?" Lindy was shocked.

Bob laughed. "The rumors that circulate during cook-offs! You must've been talkin' to one of those Marrow Men. They're steamed up that a woman might nab that Heartland Foods contract."

Noting the look of pride on Bob's face, James assumed that he and Hailey had reached an understanding about equality in their relationship. "What was her entry?" he asked.

"Believe it or not, she made barbecued Spam," Bob said while rinsing his hand in the small sink behind him. "Some of the competitors argued that it was an illegal entry, but Mr. Richter said it was a-okay for the Anything Butt category." He dried his hands on a checkered dishcloth and then folded it neatly and placed it on the tiny countertop. "We came in second with my salmon specialty.

Don't know what those Marrow Men were thinkin', makin' goat with yogurt sauce. Came out way too runny."

Lucy stepped forward. "Are you sure Hailey's back at her camper? The one she rented?"

Bob nodded. "Absolutely sure. She'd never go back into the old one. She said she took what she needed from inside and gave the cops the keys. It's locked up. No one can get in except for Johnny Law. Why are you asking?"

"We just came from Hailey's RV, and she's not there," Lucy began to explain when Gillian interjected.

"Someone's been in her camper, and they were obviously looking for something." Gillian pushed Lucy out of the way and grasped Bob's shoulders. "Focus on my face, Bob, and take a deep breath. Her camper was ransacked, Bob. There's no sign of Hailey."

Stunned, Bob shook Gillian off. "Not again! Look, will someone tell me what's going on here? If you're not Jimmy's killer" — he pointed at Gillian — "and I'm not, and Hailey's not, then who is? Mitch? Is he after my girl now?" His face was tight with anger. *"Tell me!* Has he got her? What the *hell* is happening?"

"Hailey may be in danger," Lucy said in a calm, flat voice. "She might be in possession of money that Mitch Walker believes belongs to him. Mitch was Jimmy's partner in this drug business, but it appears that Jimmy kept more than his share of the profits."

"Good Lord! I've got to find her!" Bob tried to elbow James and Bennett aside. "He can have the cash. He can have whatever he wants as long as Hailey doesn't get hurt."

Gillian grabbed Bob's arm. "Wait! We need to stop and think about where she could be. There is too much ground to cover to just run off in all directions. Please, take a moment and concentrate."

Bob cracked his knuckles one by one in agitation but followed Gillian's advice.

"Bennett, you need to call the sheriff and wait for her at Hailey's rented RV," Lucy commanded in her deputy voice. "One of us needs to be at the closing ceremony in case Mitch shows up there. We know which kids to keep an eye on far better than the deputies do. There will be plenty of police, but anything can happen."

"I'll go," Lindy volunteered. "No one can read a high schooler like I can."

"Why would Mitch be at the ceremony?" Bob looked confused. "Isn't everybody huntin' him?"

James nodded. "Yes, but he may try to pass a brief message to his buyers."

"Okay, you guys get going." Lucy continued to deliver orders. She pushed her cell phone into Bennett's hand, and he and Lindy left Bob's camper.

Gillian, who'd dropped into the camper's passenger seat, closed her eyes and began to hum quietly. Bob, James, and Lucy exchanged perplexed glances.

"What's that lady doin'?" Bob demanded. "We should get moving!"

Lucy held up a finger. "Just give her a minute. Sometimes she comes up with the craziest ideas that end up making perfect sense."

They were quiet for several seconds, listening to the rhythmic sounds of Gillian's humming. Suddenly, she opened her eyes and swiveled around in the seat. "The Spam!"

"What?" the other three said in unison.

"Felicity had some in her tent. She said it's a convenient way for her to get protein when she's on the road." Gillian rose from her seat. "She told me she knows a dozen different ways of cooking it. Don't you see?" Her face was aglow with excitement. "Hailey was with Felicity yesterday. She and Felicity talked, and then, Hailey went out to rent her own RV from R.C.'s company. Felicity must have told Hailey how to barbecue Spam."

"So you think Hailey's seeking refuge with Felicity right now?" James asked.

"Yes." Gillian closed her eyes again. "Felicity has *such* a nurturing spirit. Someone like Hailey would be drawn to her, especially when searching for a safe harbor."

"Lead the way, Gillian," Lucy said. "I think you're on to something."

James thought of the agility with which Mitch Walker had handled the welding torch. "Shouldn't we take a weapon of some sort?"

Lucy shrugged. "The method Mitch used to kill Jimmy was pretty cowardly, so I don't think he's carrying a gun. Besides, there are four of us. I think we can take him, James."

Feeling a tad emasculated by Lucy's confidence, James was

relieved to note that Bob had armed himself with a grilling fork. "It's real sharp," he whispered to James as they jumped out of the camper and turned toward the river.

By the time they reached Felicity's tent, an announcement echoed through the loudspeakers in the distance. It was time for the festivalgoers to prepare for the final event of Hog Fest. The closing ceremony would begin in thirty minutes.

Felicity's tent was unoccupied and very tidy. It looked as though Felicity had packed most of her belongings and stowed them in her old Suburban. All four of her dogs were locked in their cages and were barking with such animation that Lucy gave them her full attention.

"These guys aren't just greeting us," she said. "They're upset." She squatted next to Vicar's pen and tried to soothe him with gentle coos, but he wouldn't cease his frantic barking.

"What's wrong, Vicar?" Lucy asked the collie while Bob rolled his eyes in disbelief. "Where's your mama?" At the word *mama*, Vicar's barking became frenzied and he repeatedly pawed at the door to his cage. Lucy ducked inside Felicity's tent and reemerged with a gauzy lavender scarf. Forcing the scarf through the bars of the cage, Lucy pressed it against Vicar's nose.

"Show me Mama!" she commanded and began to undo the cage lock.

"What are you doing?" Bob asked in alarm.

Ignoring him, Lucy swung back the door and repeated, "Show me Mama!"

Vicar seemed to understand. He immediately dashed from his cage and darted into the nearby woods, but he reappeared again a few seconds later, tail wagging and tongue lolling as he waited for the humans to catch up.

"He's probably on the scent of some possum," Bob said caustically. "We're wastin' time!"

"Don't come along, then. I'm following Vicar!" Lucy snapped as she raced after the dog.

Gillian pushed James in the back. "Go after her! I'll get help. I sense a threatening presence in those woods."

James took off after Lucy and Vicar, but found it challenging to keep up with the pair. Even Bob, who was in better shape than

James, dropped behind as he tried to decide whether to continue following Lucy and Vicar or search elsewhere on his own. Darting a glance over his shoulder, as though uncertain if Hailey was in the more populated areas or somewhere in the shadowy woods, Bob plunged ahead of James, shouting at Lucy to wait.

The blood in James's body pumped rapidly as he trotted around narrow loblolly pines and ducked under dead tree limbs and thin, whiplike branches. Needles and twigs crunched beneath his feet, which grew heavier as the pursuit progressed. Soon, the two humans and the tireless dog were completely gone from view.

Defeated by their stamina and speed, James leaned against an ancient oak and struggled to catch his breath. He bent over at the waist, panting like one of Felicity's canines, and tried to listen for Vicar's bark, but he was unable to hear a thing over the sounds of his own labored breathing.

James tried not to think about how much he'd like a drink of water, but they'd veered away from the stream several minutes ago. He sensed they were at least a mile away from the outskirts of the campground. There was no one around, and he had no idea where he was.

Plodding forward again, James thought he heard the sound of barking along with a woman's shout. He tried to pick up his pace, but the underbrush had grown noticeably denser, and his face and bare arms were already criss-crossed with dozens of scrapes and small cuts.

Here, deeper in the forest, the pine needles were so tightly woven that they blocked most of the late afternoon sun. James felt like night was already descending and that time was playing tricks with him as he barreled ahead into an even thicker copse of trees. Picking his way over a fallen trunk marred with a wide, black scar that only lightning could have produced, James heard a woman's cry coming from a group of trees off to his left.

Within seconds, he was able to see several figures in a small clearing. He slowed, deciding that stealth might be more effective than charging into the midst of a potentially volatile situation.

Peering between two pines, James was able to catch a glimpse of Hailey and Felicity. The two women had been forced to a sitting position with their backs pressed against a tree. Someone had wrapped duct tape around their torsos and the trunk. The tape also covered their mouths. There were little flashes of silver each time one of the women moved her head.

And then, James saw Lucy and Bob on one side of the clearing. Mitch Walker hovered by his captives.

"Is that the same tape you used to cover up Jimmy's vents?" Lucy's voice shook with anger.

"I just meant to teach him a lesson," Mitch said in a detached tone. "For screwing me over. No one's going to miss that fat bastard. I don't see why you're poking your nose into this mess. It's none of your concern."

"You have bigger problems than me. After all, it'll be tough running your illegal business alone. How are you going to get the pot from Mexico now?"

James wondered if Lucy was stalling in hopes of receiving help from an unexpected source. Was she waiting for him to come to the rescue? Daring to take in the full scene, James moved away from the shelter of the tree. He was dismayed to see the glint of metal in Mitch's right hand. He held on to a large, shiny carving knife, the kind used in horror films.

It was then that James noticed Vicar's limp body on the ground. Fighting back the impulse to scream with his rage over the sight of Felicity's loyal companion, James clenched his fists into tight balls and vowed to bring Mitch down.

The sound of Mitch's high laughter startled James and he ducked behind the trunk again. "I was the one with the contacts in Mexico," Mitch said, pointing at Hailey. "And now that I have my little nest egg back, thanks to *her*, I can get out of here. And I'd like to do that right now, so both of you need to cozy up to that tree and sit like Hailey and her doggie friend. If you do what I say, no one will get hurt."

"You're not going to be able to run, Mitch," Lucy said without budging. "The sheriff knows everything—about the drugs, Jimmy's murder, the extra cash. If you didn't mean to kill Jimmy, then you'll face a reduced sentence. But if you hurt someone else, it's going to mean years and years of prison time. I don't think you'll fare so well in prison, Mitch. You're too skinny to fend off the bigger guys."

"Shut up!" Mitch shouted. "And get down against that tree! If I have to tell you again, I'm going to put my blade into someone's neck! Got it?"

Both Felicity and Hailey issued muffled yelps and writhed against their bonds. James took the chance to begin an agonizingly slow tread around the perimeter of the clearing toward the place where Mitch planned to secure Lucy and Bob to tree trunks.

"How much cash did you get, Mitch?" Lucy taunted him even as she slid to the ground, her back against the scratchy surface of a pine. "A few thousand?"

Mitch gestured at the pink knapsack near his feet. "About ten grand. That's enough to buy a new identity, which is all I need to be back in business. Unlike Jimmy, I didn't spend all my profits on some fancy camper. I have money stashed in a safe place. After I collect it, I'll be just fine."

"Why did you partner with Jimmy at all?" Lucy asked. "If you had the connections in Mexico and the formaldehyde, why did you need him?"

"You met Jimmy," Mitch said emotionlessly and put the knife between his legs, so he could pry up the edge of the duct tape. "He had a way with people. Knew how to talk to them. He could sell our stuff for top dollar to all kinds of folks, though most of our customers are dumb kids." Mitch snorted derisively, and James stopped two trees away, afraid that Mitch would hear him. It was already miraculous that he'd been able to get this close. The thick layer of pine needles had been his saving grace.

"Me? I'm not a big talker," Mitch continued, and James heard the sound of tape ripping. "But to keep the money rollin' in, I'll learn to be one." He edged closer to Lucy and, despite the risk of being seen, James peered around the trunk to see when to make his move. He knew that he had to distract Mitch before Lucy and Bob were rendered immobile, or all would be lost.

"One last question," Lucy began, but Mitch shook his head.

"No. I've had enough of your blabber, girlie." He slapped a strip of tape over Lucy's mouth with one hand while keeping the point of the knife pressed against her neck. Bob shifted his weight on the other side of the tree.

"Don't be a hero, Bobby," Mitch growled as he prepared a strip for Bob's mouth. "You move an inch and I'll sink this into her jugular." Lucy issued an involuntary whimper and Bob froze. "All you've gotta do is be still and then I'll be gone," Mitch snarled. "Is that so hard to understand?"

Mitch pressed a piece of tape over Bob's mouth. Then, holding the knife close to Lucy's throat again, he stuck the end of the tape on her chest and prepared to wind it around her body until he reached Bob's chest. James waited. He could feel the pulse at his neck thumping in a fear-induced frenzy as every one of his muscles tensed in preparation to leap forward. He had to time his move perfectly or Lucy could get hurt.

It was necessary for Mitch to remove the knife blade from Lucy's neck and move it to Bob's as he wound the tape across Bob's torso. James allowed Mitch to complete his half circle around Bob's body, but as he passed behind the tree and the knife was momentarily suspended in the air, James burst into action.

He shot out from behind his cover and took two giant strides, leaves and sticks crackling under his feet. Mitch began to turn toward the sound. His eyes met James's and he raised the knife. Ignoring the blade, James leapt forward, his arms outstretched. It was his plan to barrel into Mitch's left side, avoiding the knife and pushing the other man off balance. But Mitch was too quick. Pivoting his body, Mitch lifted the knife arm higher, poised to strike his attacker as soon as James was in range.

Time seemed to stop. The small handful of seconds it took for the two men to react to each other was just enough of a window for Bob to reach behind his right hip and grasp the handle of the meat fork. Tucked into his shorts, the weapon had been hidden from view.

With an upward thrust of his muscular arm, Bob plunged the twin tines into Mitch's right side. Mitch's shoulder instantly crumpled. He dropped the carving knife at the same moment James collided with his left side. Both men grunted and fell.

James rolled on his hip and quickly got to his feet, bracing for retaliation, but Mitch was still struggling to get to his knees. Doubled over, he held the wooden handle of the fork embedded in the flesh between two ribs and stared at the bruised and bloodied tissue surrounding the area where the fork tines had disappeared into his side.

"Don't pull it out," James said urgently. "You'll bleed even more."

Mitch didn't respond, but his hands slid down his stomach and dropped to the ground. He began to cough, his eyes widening in surprise when he saw that his spittle was red. He stared fixedly at the spattered leaves as a thin line of blood trickled down his chin and stained the collar of his shirt.

As Mitch fought for breath, Bob ripped the tape from his mouth, grabbed the carving knife, and raced to free Hailey and Felicity. At the same time, Lucy rushed to James's side.

"Are you hurt?" She put her hands on his cheeks, her eyes wild.

"No," James assured her. "Are you okay?"

"Yes," she whispered, darting a glance at Mitch. "We have to get help."

Nodding, James pulled off his shirt, wadded it into a loose circle, and pressed it around the fork in Mitch's side. "He's having trouble breathing. I'll stay with him. You guys go."

James heard Felicity wail as she knelt over Vicar's prone form. "My baby!" she cried.

"He's going to be all right," Lucy told her. "Mitch knocked him out, but he's going to be fine. I promise! I gave my cell phone to Bennett. You guys need to run back to the festival and get help." Lucy pointed at Felicity. "Call the sheriff first. Request paramedics and an emergency vet. Hurry!" she shouted. "Follow the river and go!"

"I know the way back," Felicity said. She cast a miserable glance at Vicar. "I'll send help."

"You aren't coming?" Bob asked as he stooped to retrieve Hailey's pink knapsack. Hailey held on to his free arm and buried her face in his shoulder, weeping silently.

"No. Hurry!" Lucy turned away from the two women as they briskly jogged away. Bob and Hailey followed at a slower pace. Bob spoke gently to Hailey, urging her forward and promising her that all her troubles were over.

"I could have handled this alone," James scolded Lucy as he listened to Mitch's raspy breathing.

Lucy smiled. "I have no doubt about that. The way you shot out from behind that tree . . ." She inclined her head toward the pine.

"You looked so fierce! I knew, no matter what happened, that you were out there. I knew you wouldn't let anything happen to these innocent people."

"Or to you," James softly whispered.

They sat in silence, alternating between watching Mitch and checking on Vicar. He was breathing steadily and Lucy stroked his fur in hopes of bringing him around.

As she tended the dog, she glanced at James and said, "I miss you, James. I miss us."

That's exactly what I feel, James thought, but before he could explain how betrayed he felt by Murphy's book or confess how skittish he felt about trusting his heart again, Deputy Harding appeared in the clearing.

Without speaking to James or Lucy, he turned back to Gillian and grinned. "Thank you, Ms. O'Malley. Your instincts are as sharp as a spear. Now, it's best you walk back to that fallen tree trunk. There's no need for you to view this scene, ma'am."

As soon as Gillian moved away, Harding turned back to Mitch. The deputy's grin evaporated like morning mist, and he didn't bother with courtesies. Harding knelt beside Mitch and said, "If you'd step away, Mr. Henry, we'll take over now."

Lucy was about to protest, but when Harding assured her that both paramedics and the best veterinarian in the county were minutes away, she relented.

"Is Mitch dead?" Gillian asked her seat on the stump.

"No," Lucy said. "Sounds like he has a busted lung. It's up to the medical folks now."

Handing each of her friends a glass bottle of green tea from her hemp purse, Gillian sighed. "I'm glad he has a chance to live. There's been enough death at this festival."

James and Lucy joined her on the fallen tree and drank deeply from their tea bottles. "James Henry, I am very proud to be your friend," Gillian said after a brief silence. Her eyes shone with tears. "You saved the day."

"It was mostly Bob's doing," James said. He then listened as Harding received a burst of information over his radio. "Without thinking things through, we worked together to help one another."

Gillian sighed in contentment. "That's *exactly* how we should live *every* moment of our lives. Perhaps this festival was meant to serve as a reminder of that lesson." She smiled as Harding came toward her, wiped the tears from her cheeks, and fluffed her hair. "And to learn some new ones."

Chapter Nineteen

High-Protein Smoothie

On Monday morning, James was once again seated at a table opposite Deputy Harding. The rest of the supper club members had already finished signing what they hoped would be their last statements for the Hudsonville County Sheriff's Department. As James reviewed his statement, Harding reminded him that he might be called to testify in court, especially if Mitch Walker failed to confess.

"How's he doing?" James asked the deputy after adding his signature to the typewritten statement.

Harding shrugged. "He'll be fit enough to answer a mess of questions in a day or two."

Sheriff Jones waited for James and Harding in the hallway. "I know you're anxious to return to Quincy's Gap, but after speaking with Ms. Hanover about her dietary goals, Deputy Neely was inspired to make protein smoothies for everyone. Your friends are already enjoying their refreshments. I hope you'll join us."

The conference room in the sheriff's department was packed. Not only were Lindy, Bennett, Lucy, and Gillian gathered around the table, but Bob Barker, Hailey, and Felicity were there as well. Men and women from the department mingled with the civilians, sipping smoothies or bringing refills from the kitchen.

As soon as James entered the crowded room, Lucy put a cup in his hands.

"It's a berry smoothie," she explained. "Deputy Neely is interested in trying the protein diet I've been following." She frowned. "Not that I stuck to it over the last few days, but I'm going back to it, starting today."

James took a hesitant sip of thick pink liquid. It tasted like creamy sherbet. "This is too tasty to be healthy. What's in it?"

"Fresh blueberries, bananas, strawberries, raspberry-flavored frozen yogurt, whey protein, and natural fruit juice," Lucy said. "Even though Eleanor let us stay an extra night at Fox Hall, I knew we were going to have an early start today, so I thought it would be wise to consume a good source of energy."

James dropped into a seat next to Gillian, who was sliding a raffle ticket across the table to Felicity. "This is for you, my dear."

Felicity looked surprised. "What is it?"

Lindy swooped over from where she was arranging a tray of smoothies and grabbed the ticket. "Gillian! *You* have the winning ticket?" She waved the stub in her right hand. "This is for a brand-new RV from R.C.'s company! That's so cool!"

Gillian shook her head. "It's my *partner's* new camper." She gazed fondly at Felicity. "You're going to need this when you take the Yuppie Puppy obedience classes on the road. I've already been in touch with two other grooming facilities, and they'd like you to run training classes for their clients as well. I can't have one of my employees sleeping in a tent. How would that make me look?" She fluffed her hair and shot a flirtatious look at Harding. "Not that I don't adore nights spent beneath the moon, with the air brushing my naked skin, but you need to regain your professional footing. This is a start on that journey."

Felicity stared at the raffle ticket, which Lindy had placed reverently in the dog trainer's hand. "Gillian. This is much too generous. Knowing that Vicar and the rest of you are okay is all I need."

"You and I were meant to meet this weekend," Gillian told Felicity, her voice trembling with emotion. "Because of your kind heart, you sheltered two lost and frightened women. Your destiny came full circle when you aided the girlfriend of the man who tried to ruin you. You are worthy of success and happiness." She dabbed at her moist eyes with a tissue. "Besides, I can't wait to see the Yuppie Puppy's logo painted on that camper. There's nothing more thrilling than a new entrepreneurial venture. And R.C. already knows that you possess the winning ticket."

"Thank you, Gillian," Felicity whispered gratefully. "I'm eager to move to Quincy's Gap. From what you've told me, it must be a charming town."

"You got that right!" Bennett declared. "And we have the best diner in the valley," he added. "Dolly's. We're talking *real* homemade cooking. Dolly's serves a meat loaf so tender that you want to cry, with a side of mashed potatoes so smooth you'd think they were mixed with cream from heaven, and a pile of butter beans that pop in your mouth with a shout of hallelujah! If you like that kind of grub, you'll be glad you moved."

Sheriff Jones strode over to Bennett's side. "Did you say Dolly's Diner?"

"Yes, ma'am, I did."

"I ate there a few years ago when I was passing through Quincy's Gap, and I can still remember the homemade pecan pie I had for dessert." The lovely lawwoman rolled her eyes at the memory. "What I wouldn't give to have Dolly's coffee and pie."

"Well, when all this mess is straightened out, I'd love to have you as my guest for pie and coffee." Bennett shot her a nervous glance. "And maybe some dinner before dessert?"

Allowing herself a small smile, the sheriff nodded. "I'd enjoy that, Mr. Marshall."

"There's one condition, though," Bennett added coyly.

The sheriff looked intrigued. "A condition? What might that be?"

"I might need you to quiz me on some trivia during our date. See, I'm taking the test to be a contestant on *Jeopardy!* and I only have two weeks left to prepare. Every waking moment must be filled with facts and statistics." He cleared his throat. "Is that a complete turnoff, Ms. Jones?"

Her smile grew larger. "Oh, quite the opposite, Mr. Marshall. Quite the opposite." After trailing a finger down his arm, the sheriff left the room.

Bennett sank into the nearest chair. "I do believe that woman just set me on fire."

Giggling, Lindy handed him another smoothie. "That's *exactly* how I feel every time I see Luis." She checked her watch. "I can't wait to get back home and tell him about our adventures!"

At that moment, two gentlemen dressed in light gray suits entered the room. They shook hands with the deputies and made their way toward Hailey, who was leaning against one of the back walls as Bob shared his barbecued salmon grilling techniques with Harding.

Instinctively, James and his friends grew silent. With the exception of Gillian, who hadn't been on Fox Hall's back porch the day the rest of them had met Jimmy Lang, the supper club members all recognized the businessmen as the representatives for Heartland

Foods. Even though they'd been wearing polo shirts and khakis during lunch that day, the small heart pins attached to their suits identified them. They'd worn those same pins on their shirt collars while dining at Fox Hall.

"Ms. Lang?" the first man asked as he approached Hailey.

"My name's Hailey Mellon. Jimmy and I weren't married."

The man stuck out his hand. "My name's Dan Bicknell, and I'm here to congratulate you on winning the title of Hog Fest Barbecue Champion."

Hailey, who was modestly dressed for the first time since James had met her, smiled at the two men. "You must've nearly fell over when you realized that y'all were gonna have to offer that contract to a woman."

"And a lovely woman at that," the second man said, trying to sound as though he hadn't been floored by the announcement that the winner was female.

"Just don't look her over too closely," Bob pretended to protest. "This is my future wife you're talkin' to here."

James noticed that Hailey was wearing her engagement ring. In fact, she raised her left hand and proudly wiggled the piece of jewelry so that the light caused it to twinkle like dozens of tiny mirrors.

The two men from Heartland Foods exchanged relieved looks. "Ms. Mellon? This might seem like an unusual question, but will you be taking your husband's name when you get married?"

Hailey shrugged. "Hadn't thought about it, but since I've never had a man offer his name to me before, I think I will become Mrs. Bob Barker." She smiled adoringly at Bob. "I've never had a man do all the things you've done for me, darlin'."

Mr. Bicknell grinned at the pair. "Seeing as you two are going to be starting a new life together, how do you feel about being the *joint* faces of Heartland Foods barbecue line?"

"Kind of like the First Couple of Barbecue," the second added quickly, his eyes shining with excitement. "I can almost see the labels on our sauces and rubs. Both of you, wearing denim overalls and standing in front of a cooker with a slab of glistening ribs grilling over a low flame."

Hailey grabbed Bob's hand. "I'd love it. We're gonna do everythin' as a team from now on. And I'm not going back to Texas—not ever—so you can reach me at Bob's place."

"Don't you have things in Texas that you want to fetch?" Bob asked Hailey.

"Nope. The apartment lease runs out this month, and all I care about is my gran's quilt and my photo albums. The landlady will send them to me if I let her sell all our junk. She's a good soul."

Bob shrugged and then licked his lips greedily. "What about Jimmy's new RV?"

Hailey waved him off. "I already got rid of that. Now, I know you liked that big fancy camper, Bob, but it gives me the creeps. Jimmy *died* in there, remember?" She stroked her fiancé's shoulder. "We got a world of riches, baby. We got the cash prize from the contest, this here contract, and each other. We've got everythin' I've ever dreamed of."

Confused by the exchange between Hailey and Bob, Mr. Bicknell turned to Harding. "We have a flight to catch, Deputy. Do you think we could speak to these folks in private before we go? We'd like to review the contracts in person. The wording can be mighty complicated," he added. "Do you have a room we could use?"

"Sure thing. Follow me, everyone."

As Hailey passed by James, she hugged him and whispered an emotional thank-you. "Bob couldn't have saved me without your help. You're the hero who backed up my hero." She pressed something into James's hand. "A sweet, orange-haired birdie told me you might spread some good with this. I sure hope so. Bless you, James Henry."

Hailey then proceeded to hug, kiss, and bless the rest of the supper club members. After Bob shook everyone's hands and promised to invite them all to the wedding, he followed Mr. Bicknell and his partner from the room.

James finished the last of his smoothie and dropped his cup in the trash. He unfolded the thin pink piece of paper crumpled in his left hand. It was the title to Jimmy's trailer, which had been registered in both Jimmy and Hailey's name. Hailey had signed it over to the Shenandoah County Public Library. On the line identifying the sale price, Hailey had carefully penned "charitable donation."

Speechless, James gaped at Gillian. "How did you . . . ?"

Gillian smiled. "Hailey didn't want anything to do with Jimmy's camper. She was looking for a quick and easy solution to get rid of it, and the idea to donate it to the library just blossomed in my mind. If you find someone who does custom work on recreational vehicles, such as Richter's RV Sales & Rentals, then you could transform the camper into something much more beneficial."

"Like a bookmobile," James breathed, overwhelmed by his sudden good fortune. "Yes! I could apply the donations earmarked for a new vehicle toward making the necessary alterations. We'll only have to rely on Wendell's old school bus until R.C. can work some magic on our new bookmobile."

"Precisely." Gillian sighed in contentment. "You see, James. There are no coincidences. We were all meant to meet these particular people and to come away changed by our interaction with them. Everything that happened here was predestined." She gestured theatrically at the ceiling. "It was all written in the stars."

James looked back at the title in his hands. "Maybe wishing on those twinkling balls of gas really does pay off." He touched his friend on the arm. "Thank you, Gillian. Hundreds of patrons will benefit because of you. You saved our bookmobile program. It's practically the heart and soul of our library."

Gillian shook her head. "No, James. *You're* the heart and soul of that library. And all of Quincy's Gap knows it."

Embarrassed, James tucked the title into his pocket. His vision was filled with the upcoming transformation of Jimmy's luxurious RV into the most cutting-edge bookmobile in all of western Virginia. Checking his watch, he interrupted Bennett's conversation with Deputy Neely about the upcoming Virginia Tech football season by saying, "It's time to hit the road. I'm ready to go home."

• • •

The Fitzgerald twins knew their boss wouldn't make it into work until lunchtime, and they had trouble going about their tasks with their usual fervor because they were both so curious about what had happened in Hudsonville. When James had phoned earlier that morning to say they'd have to open the library, he'd sounded elated.

However, their boss had claimed that he was in too much of a hurry to explain the source of his good news, or provide more details about his plan to catch Martin Trotman engaging in illicit activities within the hallowed stacks of the Shenandoah County Library.

Francis was the first to spot James's old white Bronco pulling into the parking lot.

"He's here!" he told his brother in an excited whisper.

James breezed in, clutching a Polaroid in one hand and the battered briefcase from his days as a professor at William & Mary in the other.

"Gentlemen." He was beaming. "Gather around."

"What's the photo, Professor?" Scott pointed at the Polaroid. James showed them the image of an enormous recreational vehicle. "This is Hailey, our new bookmobile."

"Whoa!" Francis leaned over the photo until his heavy glasses slid down his nose. "How did you manage this, Professor?"

"It was donated to our library," James said. "I'll tell you the whole story later. Right now, let's get down to brass tacks and figure out how we're going to coerce our teenage criminal into confession. Show me your surveillance gadgets."

Scott rubbed his hands together and elbowed his brother at the same time. "Bro, don't we have the coolest job?"

• • •

Many hours later, after James turned off the lights and locked the library's front door, he slid into his Bronco and headed for Main Street.

"You must be as tired as I am, old girl," he said, affectionately rubbing the worn leather of the steering wheel. "But we have one more thing to do before we go home."

As James climbed the stairs to Murphy's second-floor apartment, he felt a growing sadness over the realization that he was probably ascending her steps for the last time. He thought about how many summer evenings he had practically bounded up the stairs, taking them two at a time in his eagerness to see his girlfriend. Today, he trudged up each one. Even his knock was tinged with regret.

Murphy opened the door slowly, a halfhearted smile of greeting on her face. "I thought I might see you tonight," she said in a heavy voice. "At least you came to tell me in person. I hate being dumped over the phone." She gestured for him to come inside. "Would you like some wine?"

"No, thank you." James looked at the familiar living room. He had always felt comfortable in Murphy's home. He liked her sense of orderliness and how she had decorated each room in neutral tones. Her beiges and creamy coffee colors were highlighted with bright splashes of the primary hues in the pillows, table runner, and the still-life paintings she bought from local artists.

Glancing around, James suddenly became aware that he didn't want to go back to living in his boyhood bedroom. He'd like a place of his own where he could listen to music without hearing his father's blistering commentary on every song, where he could choose what show to watch on television, and where he could entertain his friends without clearing it with Jackson first.

Murphy had disappeared during James's musing. She now returned from the doorway of her spare bedroom, which also served as a home office, with a shopping bag in one hand and a rectangular box in the other. She dropped the bag by her feet and held the box out to him, as though it was a valuable offering.

"This is the book. The first one, that is," she added sheepishly. "You can read it if you like."

James kept his hands down at his sides. "It's too late for that, Murphy."

Murphy placed the box on a table, tears pooling in her eyes. "I'm sorry. I guess I wanted it all. The paper, the book, and you. But it didn't work out."

"It could have." James felt anger stirring but fought to quell it. This was not the time to assign blame. They'd moved beyond that point. "You should have trusted me, Murphy. We never stood a chance once you told me about the book. You should have explained what you were doing before you signed a contract."

"Really?" Murphy was dubious. "Are you telling me that you would have supported my work, knowing that I was writing about you and your friends?"

James shrugged. "I don't know. Maybe I would have read some of it and protested about certain things. Maybe I would have begged you not to submit the manuscript for publication. I don't know what I would have done, but we'll never know, because you didn't trust me. Without trust, there's no point in being together."

Murphy reluctantly nodded. "I know." She picked up the shopping bag and handed it to him. "This is some of your stuff. I almost stole your *Best Country Duets* CD," she teased morosely.

Digging the CD out of the bag, James placed it on the coffee table. "It's yours."

"So . . . are you going to talk to me anymore?" Murphy asked after a brief hesitation. "I don't want you to say the *we can be friends* line, but are we going to be civil?"

"Of course. We're Southerners, remember?" James joked. He then gave her a tender kiss on the cheek. "No hard feelings, Murphy. I still want you to succeed. I don't know how I'm going to feel about the book when it's released, but I'll deal with that when the time comes. That's the best I can offer you."

"Fair enough." Murphy squeezed his hand and walked him to the door. Part of him longed to wipe away the twin tears racing down her chin, but he let them fall undisturbed. "Good night, James Henry," Murphy whispered and closed her door.

James sat in his Bronco for a moment, grieving the loss of the happiness he'd felt with Murphy Alistair. He stared up at her building, at her bedroom window, and at the sheer white curtains that billowed in the breeze like a pair of tethered ghosts. When the light came on in the room, James started his engine and drove away.

Chapter Twenty

Celebratory Tiramisu

That Friday afternoon, James and the Fitzgerald brothers tried to appear as if the evening shift at the Shenandoah County Library was business as usual. Scott and Francis had shown incredible skill in outfitting the men's restroom with a tiny camera. Scott was now manning the action on his laptop while Francis shelved books. The twins had played rock, paper, scissors to determine who'd be on surveillance duty and who'd be replacing stray books. Francis, whose paper was cut by Scott's scissors twice in a row, was a very gracious loser.

The regular crowd of high school seniors had returned. Nerdy Harris and Martin's short-skirted female assistant were there, along with half a dozen college kids James had never seen before. Not only that, but some twentysomethings were also milling about the magazine section.

Harris had stationed himself at one of the computers in the Technology Corner and was trying to be as inconspicuous as possible. James watched Francis walk over to the young man and calmly whisper to him. Harris's eyes snapped open in alarm, and he gathered his things and got to his feet, briefly shaking Francis's hand on his way to the exit. When Francis turned to James and issued a contrite shrug, James gave him a thumbs-up to let him know that he heartily approved of giving Harris a chance at a clean slate. After all, James and the Fitzgerald brothers all knew what it was like to be a bookish and shy high school boy desperate to be accepted by the popular crowd.

Sometimes we act really dumb to fit in, James thought. He wasn't looking to punish the wayward teens, but he wanted them to learn a lesson they'd never forget so that they'd stop using dangerous drugs.

It didn't take long for the noise level inside the library to rise to the point where the older patrons began to cast inquisitive looks in James's direction. Mrs. Waxman, who refused to take the evening off and miss all the excitement, made a cursory sweep through the magazine section, frowning and shushing as she moved. The teens momentarily quieted, but resumed their raucous banter with renewed vigor the moment the elderly librarian returned to the information desk.

Finally, when James feared that Martin was truly going to spend the evening absorbed in the September issue of *Bon Appetit*, the young man whispered in the ear of the giggling blonde seated beside him and sauntered off to the lobby. This was the point where James would know whether his guess about Martin's destination was correct. The young man could linger in the lobby, but James predicted that he'd enter the men's restroom instead. Nodding briefly to Francis, James pretended to focus on the computer at the circulation desk, but all he did was scroll the library's home page while his heart thumped loudly in his chest. Seconds later, one of the college students also left the magazine area. Fidgeting with impatience, James looked up the weekend's forecast and saw that some much-needed rain was on its way.

At last, Scott emerged from the break room and slipped behind the circulation desk. "I saw the deal, Professor. Martin handed another kid a snack-sized plastic bag, and the kid paid him. Martin pocketed the money and made a mark on a piece of paper. Looks like he has several people waiting to buy from him tonight."

"Could you tell what was in the bag?" James whispered.

Scott shook his head. "Not exactly. The film quality's too grainy. I couldn't even see how much money Martin got."

"My beloved library is being ill-used." James scowled. "And that young man could become very sick if those drugs are laced like the stuff Donny Trotman hoped to buy from Jimmy Lang. Alert Francis and Mrs. Waxman."

Scott walked purposely toward Francis and handed him a book to be reshelved. The book was *Old Yeller*, and it was a signal that part two of the plan was taking place. Francis then handed Mrs. Waxman a copy of *Spot Goes to School* to be returned to the children's section. Mrs. Waxman issued a satisfied smile and bustled off. As he watched his devoted employees, James dialed Lucy's cell phone number. She answered immediately and promised to be there within minutes.

It was at that moment that James saw the college student who'd been Martin's first customer return to the magazine section. He elbowed one of his buddies, took the magazine from his hands, and dropped into the chair his friend had vacated. He looked quite pleased with himself.

"Hurry, Lucy," James muttered as Martin's second customer headed for the bathroom.

Scott lingered for a few minutes at the Tech Corner before disappearing into the break room again. James abandoned the circulation desk and dashed into his office, just in time to see Lucy's sheriff's cruiser pull into the parking lot. Something about the sight of her in uniform, opening the rear door so that all three of her monstrously large German shepherds could exit the car, flooded James with relief. Lucy said she knew exactly how to handle the situation at the library, and James had complete faith in her.

Lucy led her dogs straight into the library and met James at the circulation desk. While they exchanged casual small talk, James did his best not to stare at the cluster of students in the magazine section. He could only imagine what they thought about the presence of a local deputy and her enormous canines.

"These guys have been out on patrol and are super thirsty," Lucy said, gesturing at Bono, Benatar, and Bon Jovi. "Do you have a bowl I can use for water?"

"Sure thing," James gave his scripted answer. "In the break room. I'll show you."

"Thanks," Lucy said and turned away, the dogs trailing her with bright, eager eyes and open mouths. All three seemed to be smiling in anticipation, their pink tongues hanging over rows of pointy teeth.

Lucy walked right up to the laptop on the table and was just in time to witness the exchange between Martin and his second customer. Unfortunately, one of the dogs decided to bark and, as James, Lucy, and Scott watched, the two young men suddenly looked at each another in apprehension. Martin retreated into a stall while his friend gestured for him to hurry. Then, they both left the bathroom, coming to an abrupt halt before the black muzzles of three snarling hounds.

"Hello, gentlemen." Lucy allowed her dogs a few additional inches of leash.

The college student looked terrified, but Martin did his best to maintain an expression of disinterest.

"Do you smell something?" Lucy asked her dogs and narrowed her eyes at the two boys. "You wouldn't be carrying anything my K-9 officers would be interested in, would you?"

The college student paled but remained silent.

"Like a bone?" Martin scoffed.

Lucy gave the dogs even more slack. The college student inched backward. "No, no, no," he whimpered, his eyes never leaving the three sets of flashing white teeth aimed directly at his crotch.

"A bone? Let's see if that's true." Lucy released one of the dogs completely from its tether. "Seek, Bono, seek."

The shepherd with the blackest coat made a beeline for the college student. The dog had barely sniffed up and down the legs of his pants when the young man shrieked like a little girl assaulted by a spider. He then plunged his hands into the front pocket of his hooded sweatshirt and tossed the plastic bag he'd purchased from Martin onto the floor. "Take it! Just get that dog away from me! *Get him away!*"

Lucy took a step forward and grabbed Bono by the collar. She made no move to scoop up the bag. "Go sit with your friends," she ordered the college student. "Tell them no one is free to leave."

As the frightened young man scuttled back into the library, Martin shoved his hands into the pockets of his leather jacket. "You can search me, lady. I'm clean."

Ignoring him, Lucy opened the restroom door and gestured for Martin to follow her inside. She held her finger out to James, indicating that he should remain in the lobby.

James immediately returned to the break room so that he could watch Lucy, but Scott's computer screen was filled with snow.

"What happened?" he asked anxiously.

"Ms. Hanover told Martin to pull the camera out of the ceiling," Scott replied, his voice soft with surprise. "What's she doing in there?"

"I can't even imagine," James answered and returned to the lobby.

He didn't have long to wait, for Lucy reemerged from the bathroom a few minutes later just as Deputy Glenn strode into the library. "The goods are under the ceiling tile above the second toilet," she told him. "Martin's inside. He'll show you." Donning his sternest expression, Glenn brushed by Lucy and stormed into the bathroom. Soon after, he led Martin out. The teen was handcuffed and on the brink of tears. His head was bowed, and his movements were so reluctant that Glenn practically had to drag him to the front door.

"What did you say to Martin in there?" James asked Lucy once Glenn and his captive were outside.

"First, I told him to rip down the camera." Lucy smirked. "Then, I pointed out that there were no witnesses and that my dogs were very, very hungry. That did the trick. Martin was quick to confess that he's been selling pot and fake IDs all summer, and that his cousin Donny was his supplier. He also claimed that there isn't much real pot left in those bags because Donny was unable to provide him with a fresh supply. Apparently, Martin's mixed the leftover marijuana with tea leaves, cigarette tobacco, and his own Ritalin." She shook her head. "What an idiot! Good thing we got the stuff before anyone actually smoked it. They could have gotten really sick."

"Indeed," James murmured in agreement.

Lucy stroked her dogs. "Listen, I'm going to speak to the rest of the kids, but at the end of my little lecture, I plan to let them go. We have nothing on them, except for the two who paid Martin, and we can only question them if Martin gives us their names." She turned to Scott and put a hand on his shoulder. "You did a fine job with this setup, Scott. You and your brother are mighty talented. You tell Francis I said so, will you?"

Scott's cheeks flushed with pleasure. As he watched Lucy enter the main room of the library, he cast a sideways glance at his boss. "She's so cool, Professor."

James watched Lucy march toward the magazine section. "I've always thought so."

• • •

Just before the library closed for the evening, an unusual thing happened. Jackson Henry called his son at work for the first time since James had become the head librarian.

"Can you stay away from the house a bit longer tonight?" Jackson asked in as nice a tone as he could muster.

"Sure, Pop," James replied. He was about to hang up when curiosity got the better of him. "How come?"

"Just find something to do!" Jackson roared and disconnected the call.

Wondering what had made his father so agitated, James called Bennett and asked if he'd like to be quizzed.

"Only if we can do it over some cold beers," Bennett answered. "Jade is coming up for dinner tomorrow, and I'm having trouble concentrating on European history when all I want to do is dream about her sitting across the table from me."

"Don't worry," James said. "I'll stop for a six-pack on my way over."

• • •

James spent the next two hours asking Bennett a barrage of questions using a trivia website Bennett routinely turned to for his *Jeopardy!* practice. After finishing his beer and completing the website's segment on migrating birds, James decided to make his way home before he was tempted into having another beer.

Later, as he drove through the quiet streets of Quincy's Gap, James rolled down the window and stuck his arm into the cool, summer night air. There was the scent of change in the breeze that blew inside the Bronco and circulated around James's face. He detected the expectant aroma of one season gaining momentum while another faded. The very thought of autumn inspired James. When the Sunday paper arrived, he'd begin his search for a small house to rent. Someplace close to work, but with a yard where he could plant a small garden. Perhaps, he'd plant an apple tree or adopt a pet.

James was so busy conjuring images of his future home that he almost walked right past the painting propped on the kitchen table. However, he stopped short as he realized that the two candle tapers burning were the only source of light in the room, and that the dinner dishes were still piled in the sink.

James immediately recognized that the painting was one of his father's works. Like the other paintings Jackson had completed over the summer, this piece also featured a pair of hands. On the left side, was a woman's hand. It was petite and soft, and there was a dusting of flour over the first and second knuckles. James recognized the gold charm bracelet Milla always wore dangling from the wrist. The hand reached out, as though to take something offered by the second hand.

The hand on the right side of the painting was turned palm upward. In the center of the palm, which had a multitude of lines etched in the skin—the marks of a long life and of hands that had held many objects and worked with many tools—was a wedding band. At the bottom of the canvas where Jackson normally signed his name were the words *Will You?*

Jackson had asked Milla to marry him using this painting.

James put his hand over his heart, overwhelmed at the tenderness expressed in the painting. As he sat down at the kitchen table, staring at his father's finest work, he noticed that a piece of cake, a clean fork, a folded napkin, and a small note had been left on the table for him to find.

> *Dear James,*
> *There's leftover barbecued brisket in the fridge if you're hungry. I do believe I could hold my own in any BBQ contest with this recipe. I think your father proposed just so I'd cook this meal for him again! I also saved a piece of tiramisu for you. Seems it turned into an engagement cake because I said "yes" when your daddy asked if I'd marry him. My heart is filled with delight over the thought of joining this family. And you are part of that delight. See you in the morning, my dear.*
> *Love,*
> *Milla*

Even though James wasn't hungry, he took several bites of the dessert in honor of his father's engagement to the kind and lovely Milla. He nibbled the sweet, creamy cake and stared at the painting. Then, after blowing out the candles, he went back outside. Jackson and Milla deserved privacy on a night such as this, so James returned to the Bronco and retrieved his cell phone, wondering which of his friends to call in hopes of crashing at their place until morning.

He pressed one of his speed-dial numbers, expecting to hear Bennett pick up, but Lucy answered his call instead.

"Hello, James," she said. She sounded surprised, but pleasantly so.

"I'm sorry to call so late," he said, suddenly realizing that he'd hit the wrong digit. "But I need a favor."

"Anything for you, James," Lucy replied without hesitation. "But you already know that, don't you? It'll always be you."

Recipes

Inn at Fox Hall's Warm Chicken Salad

3 cups cooked chicken, cubed
1 cup green seedless grapes, halved
1 cup sliced celery (optional)
1 cup mayonnaise
½ cup toasted slivered almonds
2 tablespoons lemon juice
2 tablespoons onion, finely chopped
½ teaspoon salt
½ cup grated Parmesan cheese
½ cup bread crumbs

Preheat the oven to 325 degrees and lightly grease a 2-quart baking dish. In a large bowl, mix all of the ingredients except for the grated cheese and the bread crumbs. Spoon mixture into the baking dish. Mix the cheese and bread crumbs together and sprinkle them over the chicken mixture. Bake in the preheated oven until warm and the cheese is melted, approximately 20 minutes. Serve on croissants or toasted buns.

Inn at Fox Hall's Checkerboard Cucumber Cream Cheese and Chive Sandwiches

20 slices cucumber, peeled and sliced very thinly
pinch of salt
1 (3-ounce) package cream cheese, softened
½ teaspoon dried chives (or fresh, if available)
10 slices crustless white bread (tea-sized)
10 slices crustless rye bread (tea-sized)

Sprinkle the cucumbers with salt and set them in a colander to drain for at least 1 hour. Stir the cream cheese and chives in a small bowl. For each sandwich, spread 1 slice of rye bread with the cream cheese mixture, layer 1 slice of white bread with 2 cucumber slices, then combine it with the rye bread slice, cream cheese side down. Cut in half to form two triangles.

Adam's Ribbers' Spicy Barbecue Sauce

An all-purpose sauce for use on ribs and steak, chicken, fish, and grilled vegetables.

1 tablespoon minced garlic
1 large onion, chopped
1½ tablespoons olive oil
1¼ cups commercial chili sauce
⅓ cup tomato paste
¼ cup Worcestershire sauce
¼ cup red wine vinegar
1½ teaspoons hot sauce (Thelma uses Tabasco)
1 tablespoon oregano
½ teaspoon crushed red pepper
1 tablespoon lemon juice
¼ cup honey

Sauté the garlic and onion in olive oil for 5 minutes or until tender. Stir in the remaining ingredients and bring to a boil over medium-high heat. Reduce heat to low and simmer for 30 minutes. Remove from heat and brush on food while grilling. For an even spicier sauce, add more crushed red pepper.

Inn at Fox Hall's Cheese Grits

6 cups water

1½ cups quick-cooking grits

¾ cup margarine or butter

1 pound extra-sharp cheddar cheese, grated

2 teaspoons seasoning salt

1 tablespoon Worcestershire sauce

½ teaspoon Tabasco sauce (more or less to taste)

3 eggs, well beaten

paprika for garnish (optional)

Preheat oven to 350 degrees. Lightly grease a 9 x 13-inch baking dish. In a medium saucepan, bring the water to a boil. Stir in the grits. Reduce heat to low. Cover and cook 5 to 6 minutes, stirring occasionally. Mix in the butter or margarine, cheese, seasoning salt, Worcestershire sauce, and Tabasco sauce. Continue cooking for 5 minutes, or until the cheese is melted. Remove from heat, cool slightly, and fold in the eggs. Pour into the prepared baking dish. Bake 1 hour in the preheated oven, or until the top is lightly browned.

Milla's Amazing Oven-Barbecued Brisket

1 (3- to 4-pound) beef brisket
1 teaspoon garlic powder
1 teaspoon onion salt
1 teaspoon celery salt
¼ cup apple juice
2 tablespoons Worcestershire sauce
½ teaspoon liquid smoke
Dry rub (Milla uses Emeril's Original Essence spice or Napa Valley Spicy American Barbecue Rub, but use any kind you like)
½ cup store-bought barbecue sauce (Milla uses KC Masterpiece—Original)

Trim the fat from the brisket. Mix the garlic powder, onion salt, celery salt, apple juice, Worcestershire sauce, and liquid smoke in a small bowl. Using a flavor/marinade injector, inject the liquid mixture into the brisket (at an angle works best). You won't use it all, so discard the rest. Sprinkle the rub generously on the meat and pat it into the surface. Brush on the barbecue sauce (Milla just spreads it around with her fingers) and wrap the meat in heavy-duty aluminum foil. Place it in a roasting pan and chill for 8 hours. Bake in a preheated 300-degree oven for 5 hours or until a meat thermometer reads 190 degrees. Let stand for 5 to 10 minutes and then cut the brisket on a slant (against the grain) into thin slices. Serve with a small bowl of warmed barbecue sauce on the side.

About the Author

New York Times bestselling author Ellery Adams grew up on a beach near the Long Island Sound. Having spent her adult life in a series of landlocked towns, she cherishes her memories of open water, violent storms, and the smell of the sea. She now writes full-time from her home in North Carolina, which she shares with her husband, two trolls, and three keyboard-hogging felines. Adams loves coffee, champagne, kickboxing, 1,000-piece jigsaw puzzles, Pinterest, and black jelly beans.

Her traditionally published series include the Secret, Book, and Scone Society Mysteries; the Book Retreat Mysteries; the Books by the Bay Mysteries; and the Charmed Pie Shoppe Mysteries.

Her indie series include the Supper Club Mysteries, the Hope Street Church Mysteries, and the Antiques & Collectibles Mysteries.